CAPTAIN INGRAM'S INHERITANCE

Captain Ingram's Inheritance

Carola Dunn

THORNDIKE
CHIVERS

This Large Print edition is published by Thorndike Press, Waterville, Maine, USA and by AudioGO Ltd, Bath, England.

Thorndike Press, a part of Gale, Cengage Learning.

Copyright © 1994 by Carola Dunn.

The moral right of the author has been asserted.

The Rothschild Trilogy #3.

Previously published as "The Captain's Inheritance."

LIBRARY OF CONGRESS CATALOGING-IN-PUBLICATION DATA

Dunn, Carola.
  Captain Ingram's inheritance / by Carola Dunn. — Large print ed.
    p. cm. — (The Rothschild trilogy; #3) (Thorndike Press large print gentle romance)
    ISBN-13: 978-1-4104-2867-7
    ISBN-10: 1-4104-2867-2
    1. Large type books I. Title.
PR6054.U537C35 2010
823'.914—dc22   2010033030

BRITISH LIBRARY CATALOGUING-IN-PUBLICATION DATA AVAILABLE

Published in 2010 in the U.S. by arrangement with Carola Dunn.
Published in 2011 in the U.K. by arrangement with the author.

U.K. Hardcover: 978 1 408 49120 1 (Chivers Large Print)
U.K. Softcover: 978 1 408 49121 8 (Camden Large Print)

Printed in the United States of America
1 2 3 4 5 6 7 14 13 12 11 10

CAPTAIN INGRAM'S
INHERITANCE

CHAPTER 1

"Come in, quick, and close the door." Dropping her book, Lady Constantia straightened the faded blue Paisley shawl draped over her high-necked nightshift. It was more for propriety than warmth, for the coolness of the night air was pleasant after the heat of the day. "If Mama discovers you in my dressing-room, you will be ejected and I shall be reproached for unseemly behaviour, and I do so want to talk to you, Felix. You have been away nearly a year!"

"I might manage to come home more often if Mama and Father were not so quick to find cause for reproach." Her brother moved a vase of sweetpeas and perched on the corner of the dressing table opposite her chaise longue. Tall, broad-shouldered, with golden hair a few shades darker than her own ringlets, he was a handsome figure in his black evening coat and dove-coloured inexpressibles.

Constantia regarded him with affectionate sympathy. "I suppose Papa raked you over the coals again about working for Mr Rothschild?"

"He did."

"I guessed that must come next when Mama sent me out of the room as soon as you announced that he had rewarded you for an extraordinary service."

"Father will persist in calling him a Jew-moneylender, when he is a highly respected banker and on the friendliest terms with Wellington. He provided all the funds to pay the army and subsidize the allies, you know. The Duke told me he holds Nathan Rothschild as responsible for beating Boney as he is himself. I'm proud to have acted as liaison between them, and I've enjoyed it, too."

"Paris, Vienna, Brussels — all the gayest cities of Europe. I daresay you have enjoyed yourself! But tell me about your reward."

"I'll buy you a silk dressing gown," he said, regarding her shawl with disfavour, "and how would you like a cashmere one for winter?"

"Did Mr Rothschild give you so much money? What did you do to earn it?"

"This is strictly in confidence, Con. Even the parents don't know this bit."

"I shan't breathe a word."

"The moment I learned of the victory at Waterloo, I dashed back to London and informed Mr Rothschild, long before Wellington's messenger arrived. We went straight to Downing Street to notify the Prime Minister, but he and Castlereagh and Bathurst refused to believe us."

She smiled at his indignation. "Disbelieved Lord Roworth, son and heir of the Earl of Westwood? How very undiscerning of them."

"Was it not?" he said with a grin. "But as a result, Mr Rothschild made a great deal of money on the Exchange. The percentage he had promised me came to a very pretty sum. Father will be able to pay off the last of the mortgage, and to make me an allowance suited to my station."

"Heavens, a pretty sum indeed!"

"And you and Vickie shall have your Seasons in Town."

"No!" Her heart sank.

"No? When I went up to the schoolroom just now to tell Vickie my news, she informed me that she will be seventeen next month and ready to put up her hair. While I believe her more than capable of trying to mislead me, her governess was present."

"Vickie will certainly enjoy a Season, but

I am too old to make my come-out," Constantia protested.

"To be sure. I'm nine-and-twenty, so you are two-and-twenty, a veritable ape-leader. And an antidote, besides, which is why that callow puppy of a curate never took his languishing gaze off you throughout dinner."

"Oh dear, I simply don't know what to do about Mr Jones."

"Let him languish!"

"Miss Bannister advises me to avoid tête-à-têtes and strolls in the garden, and never to ask after his health, since he is a dreadful hypochondriac and would take it as an expression of interest."

"Sound advice, but forget the wretched fellow." Felix was not to be diverted. "You will enjoy London, Con, the balls and the theatre and concerts, and you will meet gentlemen more proper than a country curate to be your husband."

She didn't want to disappoint him. How was she to tell him that she did not expect ever to marry? He'd demand an explanation, and to her brother, of all people, she could never confide her secret.

He was looking at her questioningly. He must never guess. She had to find a reason for not going to London, for not seeking a husband, that would satisfy him.

"Felix, I don't want to go. I have had offers from eligible gentlemen, you know, even here in the country. Mama has invited friends with suitable sons or nephews. Two or three times I was quite in disgrace for refusing splendid matches, but I could not bring myself to marry a man I did not respect, only for the sake of the family." And that was true, too.

He frowned. "You did not care for any of them?"

"How could I, when they all seemed to believe they were doing me a favour by offering for my hand? Oh, they lavished praise upon my face — and stared at my dowdy gowns with horrified dismay. Mama said I must not regard it, that a daughter of the Earl of Westwood, even portionless, is a fit bride for the highest ranking peer in the land."

"So she is, and you, my dear, are a prize beyond compare."

She shook her head at him, knowing herself to be his favourite sister, though Augusta, long since wed, was closer in age. Gussie had always been priggish, whereas Constantia had followed her adored brother into many a scrape.

"You are partial, Felix. I believe you are

stunned by the transformation into a decorous young lady of the tomboy who was used —"

"Gammon! I'm glad you were strong enough, diffident as you are, to hold out against the coxcombs who did not properly appreciate you. But now you'll have a dowry, everything will be quite different."

"I don't want to be appreciated for my dowry. I don't want to go," she insisted.

"Even if you had my wife to chaperon you instead of Mama?"

"Your wife!" Constantia sat up straight, forgetting her troubles. "Felix, are you going to marry? Tell me all about her at once!"

"She's known as the Goddess to her admirers, of whom she has many, alas." Felix explained that he had not yet asked for Lady Sophia Gerrold's hand as he had not seen her since his financial situation had changed.

As he described Lady Sophia's fair, graceful beauty, cool dignity, and fastidious sense of propriety, Constantia's heart sank once more. He did not sound as if he were wildly in love. She was afraid that their parents' disapproval of his work for Mr Rothschild had hurt him more than she realized, and he had chosen a bride more to please them than himself. Lord and Lady Westwood could not possibly find fault with Lady Sophia Gerrold, daughter of the Marquis of Daventry, as a daughter-in-law.

"She sounds very like Mama," she murmured, and sought for something complimentary to say. "I expect she will make a superb countess one day. Who are her other beaux?" She wished she could believe that anyone courted by her handsome brother might choose to wed another.

"Mostly officers, with the advantage of showy uniforms. However, some may have met their end at Waterloo. Believe me, that's not how I would wish to overcome my rivals."

"Those poor soldiers! I wish I could do something to help them. Did you . . . . did you lose many friends?"

Sombrely he named several killed and others wounded, members of Wellington's staff some of whom he had known for years. "And Frank Ingram was blown up by one of his own shells and dashed near kicked the bucket," he added.

"Ingram? I remember you mentioned in one of your all too rare letters that you were sharing lodgings with a young couple called Ingram."

"Brother and sister, twins, not a couple. He's an artillery officer, as was their father.

Miss Ingram has followed the drum all her life." He spoke with far more enthusiasm than Lady Sophia had aroused in him. "She's an admirable person, Connie. Though she has been through the greatest hardships, she keeps a sense of humour, and she is always kind and hospitable. She and Frank adopted the daughter of a fellow officer who was killed in Spain, an adorable little girl. Fanny could not care for her better if she were her own child."

"I should like to meet Miss Ingram."

"Impossible, I fear. They have no connections and don't move in the first circles. Indeed, when I brought them to England, Fanny was quite overcome by the grandeur of Miriam and Isaac's establishment, and the Cohens live in a simple, unpretentious way, you know. That's where I've been since Waterloo, as a matter of fact. I went back to Brussels to fetch them, and then I thought I'd best stay at Nettledene until Fanny felt at home there."

Constantia was startled and intrigued. "You brought the Ingrams to England?"

"Frank needed Miriam's care. I've told you how she saved my shoulder in France with her medical skill."

"Yes, of course." She envied Miriam Cohen the opportunity of nursing a wounded soldier back to health. "And I have wanted to meet Mr and Mrs Cohen this age."

"You're a dear, Con." He crossed to the chaise longue and gave her a hug. "I'd like nothing better than to make them known to you, but it can't be done. Mama would flay me alive with her tongue if I introduced my friends to you."

He bade her goodnight and took himself off, leaving her with a great deal of food for thought.

It was all too true that Felix's friends would never be welcome at Westwood. Though the Cohens lived like country gentry, Miriam's father was a wealthy merchant, a Cit, and they were Jewish. Felix had met them when he worked for the Treasury. After travelling across France with them, smuggling gold to Wellington in the Peninsula, he had returned a different person, no longer an arrogant boy sulkily resentful of his lot in life. Constantia had long wished to make the acquaintance of the people who had wrought such a change.

Before that change, he'd never have considered befriending the Ingrams, an obscure artillery officer with no connexions in Society, and his sister who had grown up in the army's train.

Yet he spoke of Miss Fanny Ingram with

eager admiration. He had returned to Brussels to fetch them to England rather than speed to the bosom of his family with his splendid news — or to Lady Sophia with a proposal of marriage. Constantia was suddenly horridly afraid that her brother was going to marry the wrong woman, just to regain their parents' esteem.

Though she had summoned up the resolution to reject the suitors proposed by her mother, Constantia was diffident by nature and had not been brought up to trust her own judgement. She decided the best way to make Felix see his own mind clearly was to encourage him to talk about Fanny Ingram.

The next morning, she put her plan into effect. Having donned her favourite rose-sprigged morning gown, with the little ruff at the high neck, she went down to the sunny breakfast parlour. Felix was already embarked upon a plateful of kidneys and bacon.

He looked up with a grin. "It's my belief the superiority of the British Army is due to the Englishman's proper appreciation of breakfast. How I suffered in Paris and Vienna with nothing but coffee and a *tartine* to begin the day!"

"But not in Brussels?" She helped herself

16

at the sideboard to a thin slice of ham, a muffin, and a dish of raspberries, and sat down opposite him.

"Miss Ingram taught Henriette, the cook-maid at our lodgings, to provide a decent meal."

"Miss Ingram sounds like a most practical person."

"She has had to be. Foraging for every scrap of food in the Spanish mountains must have been arduous, to say the least, though she makes an amusing tale of it."

"Tell me."

As Felix talked, prompted by occasional questions, Constantia found her interest in Miss Ingram's brother growing. He had followed his father into the Horse Artillery as soon as he was old enough. The elder Ingram had been killed in battle while Frank was still a mere ensign, but he had cheerfully shouldered responsibility for his mother and twin sister.

Their mother had died on the retreat to Corunna.

"So they had only each other left?" Constantia asked. "They must have come home to England after Corunna. Had they no family here at all?"

"None on their father's side. It seems their mother was the daughter of a nobleman, but she was cast off when she ran away with an artilleryman. Frank and Fanny know nothing of her family, not even a name, and if they did they have too much pride to go a-begging."

"It sounds like a mystery out of one of Vickie's favourite Gothic novels. But if they do, after all, have noble connexions, surely they cannot be unacceptable to Mama and Papa."

"Unidentified connexions. They are very much aware that such an empty claim would be received with incredulity and contempt. I learned of it quite by accident. They are modest people, Con, not given to fruitless boasting. Fanny doesn't aspire to enter Society, only to take care of her brother and bring up Anita as best she can."

Constantia found herself envying Fanny for having a straightforward goal in life. All she herself had to aim at was to be a good aunt. She did hope Felix wouldn't marry Lady Sophia and have lots of cool, haughty daughters just like Mama.

"You said Anita is a charming child," she said. "How old is she?"

"Three and a half. Her mother was a Spanish lady. She died in childbirth and the father was killed very soon after."

"Then she must regard Miss Ingram as

her mama."

"Yes, and Frank as her father, of course, though she calls them aunt and uncle. She adores both of them. I flatter myself I have wormed my way into her affections, too." He laughed. "She used to call me Tío — that's Spanish for uncle — Tío Felix my lord, but she has dropped the 'my lord.' "

"I do so wish I might meet them all!"

"So do I, m'dear, but it's simply not possible. Do you still have that sluggish old mare? Will you ride with me later?"

Though he had changed the subject, Constantia was satisfied that Miss Ingram was very much on his mind. "I'd love to go riding," she said, "if you are willing to dawdle along at Skylark's pace."

In a flurry of white muslin, Vickie burst into the breakfast room, her long, flaxen hair flying. "Felix," she cried, "let us ride together this morning."

"You're just too late. Connie's going with me."

"Drat! It's too bad you and I have to share poor Skylark, Connie, or we could all go."

"Weather permitting, I'll take you tomorrow," Felix promised. "And I shall look around for another mount. I'll have to check with Father, but I believe you need not share any longer."

"Prince of brothers!" Vickie swooped on him and kissed his cheek, then stared across the table at her sister's breakfast. "You have raspberries. We didn't get raspberries for breakfast in the schoolroom." She dashed to the sideboard, helped herself to a heaped bowlful, and sat down beside Constantia.

"Fruit for breakfast is bad for little girls," Felix teased. "You will break out in spots all over."

"Pooh, I'm not a little girl. I . . . Oh! Good morning, Papa." She jumped up and curtsied, and Felix rose to his feet, as Lord Westwood entered the room.

Though the earl's hair was grizzled, his face lined, he bore a strong resemblance to his heir, tall and broad-shouldered, with a still-handsome patrician countenance. His haughty air had not been crushed by a decade of struggling to stay one step ahead of the bailiffs. Nor was it softened, Constantia noted, by the end of the struggle.

He responded courteously to his children's greetings, then turned his stern gaze on the youngest. "You are not at your lessons this morning, Victoria?"

"Miss Bannister let me come down to see Felix, Papa, since he has been away so long. I must go back now." She made a hurried escape, taking with her the bowl of raspberries. Constantia caught Felix's eye and smothered a smile.

"Miss Bannister appears to be less successful in inculcating a sense of propriety in Victoria than she was in your case, Constantia," said Lord Westwood austerely, moving to the sideboard.

A maroon-liveried footman came in with fresh coffee. When he left, and the earl was seated at the table, Felix said, "Sir, will it be possible to purchase another horse for my sisters? Victoria will doubtless learn a more ladylike style of riding from Connie than she can from a groom."

"Doubtless. Yes, by all means look about for a suitable mount. Now that the burden of the mortgage repayments is lifted, the income from the estate will be sufficient to support a proper style. I have not allowed the farms to deteriorate during our difficulties."

"Of course not, sir."

"I fear perhaps I did not make myself plain last night, Felix. I would not have you suppose that, because I cannot approve the means, I am ungrateful for your most valuable assistance to the family."

Looking thoroughly uncomfortable, Felix muttered something Constantia failed to catch. She felt quite uncomfortable herself, and she was about to make her excuses and depart when her father continued.

"If you should be so happy as to win the hand of the distinguished young lady upon whom your affections are fixed — I daresay you have mentioned her to your sister?" He bestowed an indulgent smile on Constantia. "She is in your confidence, I know. If, as I say, you wed Lady Sophia Gerrold, the family fortunes will be more than restored and you will earn the wholehearted esteem of your mother and myself."

"Thank you, sir."

Felix's obvious gratification vexed Constantia. Under the sun of their parents' outspoken approval of Lady Sophia, Miss Fanny Ingram's chances melted like snow. She reminded herself that she had never met either young lady. Perhaps Felix was inarticulate on the subject of Lady Sophia's amiable characteristics because he was so much in love.

But in that case, why was he so eager to talk about Miss Ingram?

Her breakfast finished, Constantia changed into her old grey riding habit and went down to the stable yard. She and Felix rode up the steep track behind the mansion, up into the Mendip Hills. At the top, they stopped to look back over the green

Somerset plain, to the isolated prominence of Glastonbury Tor with its tower, and beyond into the hazy distance.

Felix told Constantia how Fanny had crossed the Spanish mountains on mule-back, and how terrified he had been seeing her mounted on a huge troop horse at a Review in Brussels.

"I was all ready to rake her escort over the coals for endangering her," he said ruefully. "Then I discovered that she was quite capable of handling the brute, and that Frank was among her escort."

An image of Captain Frank Ingram was building in Constantia's fancy. She envisioned him tall, strong, and handsome on a powerful charger, smart in his regimentals, a valiant soldier yet gentle and loving to his sister and the child. Like the knights of King Arthur's Round Table, he was both bold and chivalrous. How different from the fashionably languid gentlemen she had rejected!

When they returned to the stables, the earl's steward was just leaving to ride around the farms, and Felix turned around to go with him. The train of her habit over her arm, Constantia went into the house.

Crossing the spacious vestibule, with its Corinthian columns framing each doorway and Classical statues posed in niches, she felt the usual twinge of regret. The Tudor Great Hall — the panelling carved with fruit and flowers and mythical beasts, the min- strels' gallery, the hammerbeam roof — had vanished along with a fortune in the earl's passion for modernization.

As she started up the magnificent marble staircase, balustered in gilt wrought-iron, her mother's abigail appeared at the top.

"Lady Constantia, her ladyship wishes to see you in her sitting-room, if you please." The last phrase was undoubtedly added to the countess's command by the tactful maid.

"Oh dear, I cannot go in riding dress," Constantia said in dismay, "and with my hair all blown about. I shall come as soon as I have changed. Pray send Joan to me at once."

Her own maid soon had her fit to be seen by her ladyship and she hurried to Lady Westwood's apartments. She met Vickie on the threshold. Exchanging a curious and apprehensive glance, they entered together. Their mother's private sitting-room retained its formal elegance despite the slight fading of green-striped satin. As a child, Constantia had often been summoned here to receive rebukes for falling into mischief, but Felix had always been chastised more severely for leading her into scrapes than she for following.

More recently, her rejection of several perfectly acceptable suitors had led to lengthy lectures on obedience and obstinacy. In her quiet way, she had held firm.

Lady Westwood was seated at her cherry-wood bureau, writing letters. She turned when her daughters entered and motioned them to a pair of spindly-legged chairs. The countess's hauteur was no more reduced by straitened circumstances than her husband's. Beneath pale-blond hair with no hint of grey, her smooth, calm face was untouched by any mark of anxiety, passion, or sorrow, by smile or frown. Constantia sometimes wondered whether her mother had ever succumbed to any emotion stronger than displeasure.

Displeasure was not now in evidence. In fact, Lady Westwood appeared coolly complacent.

"You have heard, no doubt, of your brother's good fortune. It is your good fortune that, unlike many young men, his concern is for his family, not for a life of idle pleasure. I trust you will express to him your appreciation of his generosity."

"Yes, Mama," they chorussed.

"Constantia, I shall take you to London

in the autumn for the Little Season. Victoria, you shall be presented in the spring. That is time enough, I believe, for you to amend your carriage and conduct so that I shall not be put out of countenance by your lack of decorum."

Vickie opened her mouth to protest, and closed it again. Though she blithely disregarded her mother's prohibition on reading romances, with that cold gaze upon her she did not quite dare to argue "Yes, Mama," she said meekly.

"I shall speak to your governess. You may leave us now, Victoria."

Curtsying, Vickie departed with the energetic gait the countess so deplored. Constantia wished she could follow. Her hands, clasped in her lap, tightened as she steeled herself to object to Lady Westwood's plans.

"I daresay Felix has spoken to you of his hopes of marriage, Constantia?"

"Yes, Mama."

"I venture to disclose to you that your father and I have been deeply concerned by Felix's propensity for forming an undesirable acquaintance. In the position he insisted on taking up, against all advice, no doubt a certain amount of social contact with persons of no consequence was inevitable. However, your brother has an unfor-

26

tunate tendency to regard some such persons as friends. We even feared that he might so disgrace his name as to choose a bride of low condition, thus injuring your hopes of contracting an eligible alliance."

She paused, but Constantia had nothing to say. No words of hers would convince her mother either that she did not hope for a husband, or that Felix was perfectly capable of choosing his own estimable friends.

"However, in fact his choice has fallen on an excellent *parti,* Lady Sophia Gerrold, daughter of the Marquis of Daventry. Such a match cannot fail to enhance your chances, and Victoria's also, of course."

Constantia was driven to demur. "I understood that nothing was yet settled!"

"True, but now that financial difficulties are no longer in the way, it can only be a matter of his making formal application for her hand. Surely you do not suppose that the heir to the Earl of Westwood might be judged unworthy of any female to whom he paid suit?"

"No, Mama." Alas! If Felix proposed he'd be accepted by any female with eyes in her head.

"Nonetheless, as you say, the matter is not settled, so you will not speak of it. I merely wished to advise you that you are likely to have the pleasure of the company of your prospective sister-in-law when we go up to Town."

"Mama, I don't wish to go to Town in the autumn!" Constantia cried.

Lady Westwood stared at this unseemly display of emotion. "You prefer to wait to accompany your sister in the spring? To bring out two girls at once is generally considered unwise, as one is certain to overshadow the other. It would hardly be fair to Victoria. Of course, you are too old to be formally presented to the Ton."

"Much too old, Mama."

"You have lost a great deal of time, owing entirely to your own obstinacy. No, you cannot afford to delay. We shall go to London for the Little Season."

Taking silence for consent, she dismissed her daughter.

Constantia imagined refusing, and having to live with her mother's constant reproaches. How much easier to submit! After all, it was not London she feared, not the balls and theatres and concerts Felix had described, which sounded delightful. Perhaps she'd find Lady Sophia good-natured and charming. Perhaps, in the bustle of Town life, she'd even be able to slip away with Felix for a few hours and meet his friends.

But in Mama's eyes, the sole reason for going to London was to acquire a husband. The compulsion to conform might be more than Constantia could withstand. Felix would support her if she explained, but he must never learn the truth.

If Felix ever discovered why she refused to marry, he'd blame himself. She had never held him responsible for the childhood accident, for the hateful scar, but their parents did and he had accepted the guilt. Seven years older than his little sister, he should have known better than to help her climb the towering cedar.

When she fell, when the broken branch tore her tender skin and blood poured forth from the jagged wound, he had been devastated. Yet by now the accident was tucked away in a hidden corner of his memory. He did not know — only her abigail knew — that the white, puckered scar still slashed across her chest, an ugly furrow from the hollow of her right shoulder to the swell of her left breast.

The décolleté London fashions were not for her. And even if she managed to persuade her mother to let her wear high-necked, concealing gowns to balls and soirées, sooner or later the moment of truth must come. On her wedding night, if not before, her lover would see the dreadful disfigurement and turn from her in revulsion.

CHAPTER 2

How could anyone be so muttonheaded as to prefer that ice maiden, Lady Sophia, to his sister? Frank wondered. Not that he had ever met her ladyship, but sharing quarters with Viscount Roworth he had taken an interest in the Goddess and picked up snippets of information. A cold, supercilious beauty was the general concensus — except among her besotted suitors.

And Roworth was one of those suitors, and Frank very much feared that Fanny had lost her heart to Roworth.

Lying back against his pillows, he watched her leave his chamber. Though slim and pretty in an altered evening gown of Miriam's, with her round face and brown curls she could not compete with Lady Sophia in looks any more than in rank or wealth. Damn Roworth if those were more important to him than a warm heart!

Bravely though she tried to hide it, she

had been blue-devilled since Roworth left Nettledene. Had Frank been wrong to agree to leave Brussels? Not that he had been in any case to argue, especially when Roworth, with that high-and-mighty air he put on sometimes, accused him of sacrificing Fanny's comfort to his own pride. No, he could not regret coming to the Cohens. Anita was happy, Fanny did not have to struggle for existence, and much as he had mistrusted the notion of a female physician, Miriam was working wonders.

The doctors had expected him to be crippled, yet he had walked about his chamber each afternoon for a week, feeble, unsteady, but on his own feet. He could move his arms freely, if painfully. Miriam's salves made him smell like a rose garden, the exercises she prescribed made him ache all over, but they worked. Beyond that he must not think.

She looked in on her way down to dinner, a strong-willed, handsome woman with richly red hair. "We shall have you downstairs tomorrow," she promised.

"I own I'll be glad to see something beyond these four walls. I know every nick in every beam, every rough spot in the plaster . . ."

Miriam laughed. "You shall have new

beams to study, or even go out on the terrace if it's fine. Try to eat well tonight to build up your strength."

Shortly after she left, a footman came in with his dinner on a tray. "His lordship's back, sir," the lad reported, helping him to sit upright. "Lord Roworth, that is."

"Lord Roworth!" What the devil was the man about, returning to torment Fanny again?

"Just come in this minute, quite unexpected, like. Treats Nettledene like his own home, he does," he added with pride.

Frank pondered the news as he picked at his roast beef, carved wafer-thin to tempt an invalid's uncertain appetite. Roworth must have come to report his success or failure at winning Lady Sophia's hand. Success would dash Fanny's hopes forever, but failure would keep them alive, in all probability to die a lingering death. Frank didn't know which to wish for. He felt helpless, unable to protect his sister.

Everything would be easier if only Roworth were not on the whole a deuced good fellow.

The footman returned to remove his tray, shaking his head when he saw how little had been eaten. Frank picked up a book of travellers' tales he had been reading and tried to forget his troubles.

A knock on his door, some time later, was a welcome distraction. "Come in," he called.

Lord Roworth stuck his head round the door. "Still awake, Ingram? I've brought you a brandy. With Miriam's permission, I hasten to say." He set two glasses on the bedside table and pulled up a chair.

Taking his glass, Frank warmed it between thin, white hands. "Am I to wish you happy?" he enquired cautiously.

"Not yet. I reached London at an awkward hour to call upon Lady Sophia so I decided to ride on and spend the night here. Now I'm here, I might as well stay a couple of days."

Nothing settled yet. Frank suppressed a groan. Sipping the brandy, he felt a glow of warmth pervade him.

"Armagnac," said Roworth. "Isaac takes my advice on his cellar."

"I haven't tasted anything like this since one of my men snabbled a couple of bottles after we crossed the Pyrenees." He grinned. "Naturally, I was forced to confiscate them to maintain order in the ranks."

"Naturally. Everyone knows Wellington don't stand for looting. Here's to your very good health."

The commonplace toast reminded Frank

34

of his debility. With an effort he responded, "And to yours, my lord." He drank again, more deeply than the quality of the brandy deserved.

"My lord? As I recall, Captain, you were wont to use my name."

"My humble apologies, Roworth." He tried to match the rallying tone. "I intended no insult, I promise you."

"Then I shan't sink to the infamy of calling out a sick man, though Miriam and Fanny both think you well on the road to recovery. What's wrong?"

"Wrong? What makes you think anything's wrong? They are right, I grow stronger every day."

"If you don't want to tell me, that's your privilege, but perhaps I can help."

The Armagnac loosened Frank's tongue. "No one can help, or Mrs Cohen would have. I expected too much of her skills. Look at me." He threw back the covers, pushed himself to the edge of the bed, and stood up, a trifle wobbly. Stripping off his nightshirt — altered at Miriam's suggestion to button down the front — he revealed a body seamed and knotted with countless scars, white and red and purple, from shoulders to thighs. "What woman will want me now?" he asked bitterly.

Roworth visibly steeled himself. "You appear to be . . . er . . . intact where it matters."

"Would that I were not," he said in despair, "for then I might not care. Or that at least some sign appeared on my face as a warning of what is below. Better, perhaps, that the blast had blown off my head instead of leaving me like this, a sight to send any female into hysterics."

"Did Fanny and Miriam run screaming at the sight?"

"They are not ordinary females. They saw only the hurt, not the hideousness." Shivering despite the warmth of the night, he reached for his nightshirt.

Roworth failed to deny that Fanny and Miriam were remarkable. His meager strength exhausted, Frank accepted his help to put his arms in the sleeves and return to bed. Lying back, he closed his eyes. "It's bloody humiliating being so weak," he said, aiming at wryness.

"Are you too weak to lift a glass? It would be a pity to waste the Armagnac."

"True. That much I think I can manage." He sat up and took the glass.

They chatted for a while longer, then, draining the last drop of his brandy, Roworth said, "I'd best let you sleep, or

36

Miriam will be after me." He hesitated. "The scars are bound to fade over time, you know. And one day you'll find a woman as exceptional as your sister, who loves you and doesn't give a damn."

"Then Lord help her, for I'm not likely ever to be in a position to marry. Roworth, thank you. You've been devilish good to us — don't think I don't appreciate it."

Both embarrassed, they clasped hands briefly and Roworth left.

At least he recognized that Fanny was special, Frank thought, his head muzzy from the unaccustomed drink. Roworth really was a good fellow. He'd be wasted on the Ice Goddess.

Look at the way he'd reacted to the grotesque horror of the scars: sympathetic, without being pitying. All the same, Frank wished he hadn't made an exhibition of himself. The brandy was to blame, that and an urgent need to voice his despair. He hadn't been able to tell Fanny or Miriam, nor even the sober, kindly, intellectual Isaac, of his dread that no woman would ever again respond to his desire.

Roworth was no saint. He'd had a mistress in Brussels. He understood and had done his best to reassure. A good fellow . . .

Frank dropped into a restless sleep, beset

with pretty faces that smiled and flirted —
and then snarled rejection with outraged
disgust.

The two days Roworth had said he was staying stretched to a week. Fanny was happy,
and Frank could not bring himself to suggest that she was living in a fool's paradise.

He was carried downstairs each afternoon,
now. Often his sister and the viscount were
absent, walking or riding, or taking Anita
and little Amos Cohen on an excursion.
She'd return rosy-cheeked and laughing.
How could he put a shadow in her eyes?

The shadow came soon enough. One
evening, as he was about to snuff his bedside
candle, she came into his chamber and,
though she smiled, he knew at once that the
blow had fallen.

"Felix is going to Town with Isaac tomorrow, to propose to Lady Sophia." Her voice
struggled to sound casual. "I'm not sure
when we shall see him again, but he repeated that we must call on him if we find
ourselves in difficulties."

"Never!"

She clutched his hand. "No, never. But he
has been a good friend to us," she said
pleadingly. He nodded, too full of her hurt
to find words. Stooping she kissed his

38

forehead. "Goodnight, my dear. Sleep well."

"Goodnight, Fanny." He touched her cheek in a rare, tender gesture. With a dry, strangled sob, she tore her hand from his clasp and hurried out.

He lay and swore silently all the foul oaths he could recall or invent. If it were not for his damnable weakness, he'd call Lord Roworth to account for this! Yet Roworth was not to blame. He had never made any secret of his intention to marry Lady Sophia.

Fanny was quiet the next day, but as always covered her unhappiness with a mask of cheerfulness. In the afternoon, Frank was carried downstairs and walked out to the terrace to recline on a chaise longue in the sun. Fanny and Miriam sat on a bench nearby, with Miriam's baby. Anita and Amos, black ringlets and red curls, played happily with sticks and stones on the steps down to the garden.

Fanny looked up as the sound of footsteps came from the house. Frank saw her smile a subdued greeting, then saw her expression change to incredulity, hope, apprehension. Before he turned his head, he knew that Isaac had brought Roworth home with him.

Then Miriam turned and at once demanded, "What is wrong?"

Isaac went to take her hand. "Your father, my love. He has suffered some kind of seizure."

"Oh, poor Papa." Her voice shook. "I must go at once. Can we leave this evening, Isaac?"

"Of course, if you can be ready. I'll send to the inn for fresh horses."

"Yes. There are a hundred things to be done before we can go."

Frank hardly listened. He was watching Roworth's face, and Roworth was watching Fanny. Frank had seen admiration in those blue eyes before, had seen shared amusement, concern, even warmth. Now he saw a sort of surprised joy, a passionate hope, that looked to him like love.

But Fanny's attention was on Miriam, and it was no time for declarations. Miriam handed the baby to Fanny and stood up.

"I'd be happy to take care of the children for you," Fanny offered, disentangling her hair from the baby's fist.

Miriam turned to her. "Thank you, Fanny dear, but I shall take them with me. I cannot tell how long I shall be gone." She glanced at Isaac, who nodded. "Fanny, Frank, we had not meant to speak so soon, but Isaac and I have decided we should very much like to adopt Anita."

"No!" cried Fanny instantly, horrified. "No, it is excessively generous of you, but I cannot give her up."

"It would make your lives much simpler," Isaac pointed out in his sober way, "and I believe she would be happy here. Take some time to consider and talk it over."

"I don't need to." Fanny cast a look of frantic appeal at Frank.

Isaac was right: their lives would be easier without Anita. Though Roworth was fond of the little girl, even if he truly loved Fanny, he might well balk at accepting a love-child into his family. If he did not his parents would, and Fanny had enough counts against her already. Rather than let Anita ruin his sister's hope of happiness, Frank might find himself trying to bring up the child single-handed.

Miriam and Isaac would give her a loving, stable home. Yet if Isaac had logic on his side, Fanny had sentiment on hers.

Frank glanced at Anita, so busy with her sticks and stones and the fallen rose-petals she had collected. As if feeling his gaze, she looked up, beamed, and waved to him, then returned to her game. So many honorary uncles had come and gone in her short life. He and Fanny were her family.

With a somewhat rueful grimace, Frank made up his mind. "It's not that we don't think she'd be happy, but her father was my friend and she's been part of our family pretty much since she was born. It wouldn't be right to hand her over, even to you, as if she were a foundling."

"Bravo!" Felix exclaimed, with such heartfelt relief that Frank knew his decision had not harmed Fanny's chances.

"We expected you to choose to keep her," said Miriam with approval. "Fanny, Hannah will go with us to London, but you are accustomed to taking care of Anita yourself. If you wish to have a truckle bed for her moved into your chamber, just tell Samuels."

"But we ought not to remain here when you are gone," Fanny protested. "I cannot believe it is proper to stay on in one's hosts' absence."

"My dear, pray do not be nonsensical. Where else should you go?"

"I don't know."

"It doesn't seem right." Frank had to agree, but more to the point, with the Cohens going Roworth had still less excuse to stay at Nettledene. He and Fanny must not be parted before all was settled between them. Frank was prepared to continue to insist on the unsuitability of remaining in the absence of their hosts until his lordship took the hint.

Fanny looked at him, at Anita, and back. "We have no real choice, Frank."

For a moment Frank feared she had sabotaged his plan, but in fact Roworth seized the opening.

"Yes, you do," he said nonchalantly. "I'll take you to Westwood."

The others were all stunned into silence. Frank, his aim achieved, hid a grin.

After a moment, Miriam said calmly, "An excellent solution. Now I really must go and make arrangements for our departure." She went into the house.

Following her, Isaac turned on the threshold and said, "If you don't mind waiting until tomorrow, I shall send back our carriage to take you to Somerset. It's more comfortable than anything you can hire around here."

Roworth thanked him, just as Fanny found her voice. "But your family!" she protested. "Lord and Lady Westwood —"

"I told Connie about you and she's eager to meet you," Roworth interrupted.

Noting the evasive answer, Frank assumed that the Earl and Countess of Westwood were unlikely to welcome the Ingrams. Too bad. He wasn't going to let qualms about their reception stand in Fanny's way.

Unfortunately, Fanny had also noticed Roworth's evasiveness. "And your parents?" she insisted.

"Any family in England should be proud to welcome a wounded hero of Waterloo."

"Quite a hero!" said Frank. "Blown up by his own shell." He grinned. "Come on, Fan, I'm sure Lord and Lady Westwood are too polite to throw us out on our respective ears. Let's take our chance to see how the nobility lives."

"Good, that's settled then," Roworth said quickly. "Frank, let me help you in. You'll want to be rested for tomorrow."

They escaped before Fanny could voice any further objections. As Roworth supported his shaky steps up the stairs, Frank had sudden doubts. Suppose he had misread Roworth's expression? In that case a visit to Westwood could only prolong Fanny's misery.

"Was your trip to London successful?" he said. "Am I to wish you happy?"

"Wish me . . . ? Oh, no, I'm not going to marry Lady Sophia."

So he was right, Frank thought, triumphant. At last Roworth had come to his senses and fallen in love with Fanny. She didn't know it yet. She was sure to come up with a dozen reasons not to go to Westwood but he'd dismiss every one.

He hoped Connie — Roworth's sister, he assumed — would prove a friend to Fanny. She sounded less toplofty than Lord and Lady Westwood. If she had half Roworth's looks, he'd enjoy making her acquaintance. An earl's daughter was so far beyond his reach, he need think no further than the pleasure of her beauty.

To Westwood they should go.

CHAPTER 3

"Pssst!"

Startled, Constantia looked round. Her brother lurked beneath the grand staircase, beckoning to her, finger to his lips.

Her mother and their lady guests proceeded towards the drawing-room, oblivious of her defection. Joining him, she whispered, "Felix! I wondered what all the commotion was about. Mama did not say and everyone was much too polite to ask what the butler was muttering to their hostess."

"I've brought guests." He raised his voice to normal as the door closed behind the last of the visiting ladies. "The Ingrams."

"Oh Felix, how delightful!" Her smile turned to an anxious frown. "You told me I should never meet them, yet you have brought them to Westwood? What will Mama and Papa say?"

"I hate to think," he admitted, "and Fanny is terrified. You wouldn't think someone who has been through innumerable battle campaigns would be afraid of a mere earl and countess. Connie, will you go up now and talk to her, try to put her at her ease? She is in the yellow chamber."

"Of course, but I must be in the drawing-room before the gentlemen come in or Mama will put me on bread and water."

"Figuratively, I trust. Don't worry, I'll go and keep 'em circulating the port for at least half an hour."

He headed for the dining-room, and she hurried up the stairs, her mind a-buzz with speculations. Why had Felix brought the Ingrams to Westwood?

She tapped on the door of the yellow chamber. After a moment the door opened and by the light from the passage she saw a slight young woman in a shabby brown travelling dress. Her face was tired, her dark eyes apprehensive.

"Miss Ingram, I am Constantia Roworth. My brother said . . ." Catching sight of a child sprawled fast asleep on a cot, black hair spread across the pillow, she stopped abruptly, then continued in a lowered voice, "My wretched brother did not say that the little girl is sharing your chamber! I beg your pardon. I hope she will not rouse."

"No, she is exhausted. Felix — Lord

Roworth would never speak so loudly as to wake her, but it would not dawn on a man to warn you." She smiled and their eyes met in a glance of understanding. "Will you not come in, Lady Constantia?"

She stood aside and Constantia entered the room. Decorated in primrose and white, it was rarely used and so retained its elegance, unfaded and unworn at least by lamp-light, unlike her own chamber.

Seating herself on a low, tapestry-work chair, she gazed with curiosity at Fanny Ingram, who dropped wearily onto the second chair. The first thing that struck her was that Miss Ingram was in her mid-twenties, not in the first flush of youth and by no means a beauty. She had supposed that Felix must have been attracted by her looks before he came to admire her character, but neither face nor figure was anything out of the ordinary. Perhaps she had too hastily jumped to the conclusion that his feelings went beyond friendship.

A hint of challenge in Miss Ingram's eyes made her realize she was staring. "Welcome to Westwood," she said quickly. "I am so glad you have come. I only wish Felix had given me a little notice so that I might have prepared properly for your arrival." She knew perfectly well why he had not: he didn't want to give their parents any opportunity to veto the visit in advance.

"Has he not explained? He had no chance to warn you. Mrs Cohen's father was taken suddenly ill and the Cohens departed at once for London."

"So you found yourselves with nowhere to stay."

"Oh no, you must not think that they asked us to leave Nettledene. They are quite the most hospitable people in the world. It was Lord Roworth who insisted on bringing us to Westwood and I could not persuade him that we ought not without an invitation from Lady Westwood. If he had not said that you. . . ." She faltered.

"That I would be happy to make your acquaintance? He was quite right. I have longed this age to meet the Cohens, and ever since he told me about his new friends, I have wished to meet you and your brother and the child."

"My brother!" said Miss Ingram with some asperity. "You may thank him that we are here. Against your brother I might have held out, but Frank supported him. He'd not have done so had he realized how tiring he would find the journey."

"Captain Ingram is not yet fully recovered?"

"By no means. He . . . he was very badly hurt. He would have died, I believe, if Lord Roworth had not helped me nurse him, and he might be crippled but for Miriam. I only hope he will continue to exercise properly without her to both urge him on and stop him from overtaxing his strength."

"Between us, Miss Ingram, we shall make sure he does what is necessary," said Constantia with fervour. So she was to have a chance to help the gallant captain, after all!

"If you mean to help, I daresay we shall." A merry, quizzical smile dimpled her cheeks, making her look suddenly younger and exceedingly pretty. "However, though he bowed — with reluctance! — to Miriam's authority, I believe you and I shall have to resort to coaxing. Remember that Frank is an officer and used to command."

"Indeed, I should not venture to give him orders, I promise you. Oh dear, I must go. Mama will be wondering why I am not in the drawing-room. I shall send my abigail to you, Miss Ingram. Just tell her if there is anything you need."

"You are kind, but it is not necessary. I am used to looking after myself."

"Joan will be glad to help you. Goodnight, Miss Ingram."

How different the Ingrams' life had been

from anything she could imagine, Constantia reflected as she hurried downstairs. Despite her family's impecunious circumstances, no one had ever suggested that she should manage without a personal maid. Reaching the hall, she directed a footman to send Joan to the yellow chamber.

To her relief, the gentlemen had not yet joined the ladies in the drawing-room. When they arrived, Felix contrived to snatch a brief tête-à-tête with Constantia.

"Did you see her?"

"Yes, and I like her prodigiously. We talked about her brother — you did not mention that he is still an invalid. I shall do all I can to help the poor, brave young man recover his strength," she said earnestly.

"You are a sweetheart, Con. That will give me more chance to have Fanny to myself."

"Oh, Felix, you are in love with her! I half suspected as much when you first told me about her. But what about Lady . . . ?"

She was obliged to defer her curiosity as one of the visitors approached with a request for music. When she looked up from the pianoforte a few minutes later, Felix had seized his chance to slip out of the room.

Constantia's first thought when she woke the next day was that today she would meet

Captain Ingram. She donned a cornflower-blue morning gown trimmed with white satin ribbons at the throat, the high waist, and the hem. Then she fetched Miss Ingram from her chamber and together they went down to the breakfast room. Felix was already there. He rose with a smiling greeting for each of them, but Constantia saw that he had eyes only for Fanny Ingram, who smiled back at him with a sparkle in her brown eyes.

"Lord Roworth," she said gaily, "how is it you never told me what jewels you have for sisters? Lady Victoria has taken Anita to the nursery for breakfast, while Lady Constantia lent me her abigail and would not let me come down alone."

"I was prepared to make my breakfast last until you appeared, Miss Ingram," he assured her.

"I did not know you would be here already," Constantia said, giving him a look that demanded last night's postponed explanations at no very distant time. "The customs of a strange house can be sadly confusing. Miss Ingram, come and help yourself from the sideboard. We are informal at breakfast."

"Informal? Do Lord and Lady Westwood not come down to breakfast?" she asked hopefully.

"In general Mama does not, but today they both will, because we have guests."

Miss Ingram promptly lost her appetite, but Felix filled a plate for her. He seated her and set about distracting her from her fears.

"I've told Connie how you taught Henriette to make a proper English breakfast."

"I always tried to give Frank a good breakfast, since one could never be sure what the day would bring. Poor Henriette! She was growing very fond of Hoskins when he had to return to the battery. Corporal Hoskins was my brother's batman, Lady Constantia, his personal servant. He helped me nurse Frank when he was first wounded. I wonder where he is now."

"He may have been discharged from the army by now," said Felix. "By the way, I don't believe I've told either of you that I gave Mr Rothschild my resignation."

Constantia clapped her hands. "Oh, splendid, Felix. Was he dismayed to lose you?"

He grinned. "Not precisely dismayed, though he was kind enough to say that he rates my abilities highly. He's an odd, dour chap, but I like him and I'll call on him whenever I'm in Town. I witnessed the most singular incident when last I saw him. He was writing in his ledger when the Duke of Oxshott burst unannounced into his private office and started berating him for some offense committed by the chief clerk.

" 'Take a chair,' says Rothschild, as cool as you please, writing on.

"Bellowing, 'Do you know who I am, sir?' the duke tosses his card on the desk and starts to recite his lineage in a voice fit for the battlefield.

"Rothschild glances at the card. 'Take two chairs,' he says."

Constantia and Fanny Ingram laughed. "A quick wit," said Miss Ingram with her merry smile.

"I was afraid the duke was going to have an apoplexy," Felix went on. "He was purple in the face, with popping eyes and his mouth opening and closing silently like some exotic fish. I left in a hurry before . . . Oh, good morning, sir." He jumped to his feet as Lord Westwood came in. "I'd like to present Miss Ingram."

The merriment vanished from her suddenly pale face.

"Miss Ingram." The earl nodded, no affability softening his aristocratic features.

Though Constantia had not really expected her father to offer a cordial welcome, she was mortified by his coldness. She admired Miss Ingram's composure as she responded.

"How do you do, my lord."

"Pray do not let me interrupt your meal, ma'am. I trust you have been made comfortable?" The polite enquiry was uttered in a tone of absolute indifference.

"Thank you, sir, very comfortable." She toyed with the remains of her breakfast while Lord Westwood helped himself at the sideboard.

Felix, his mouth tight, addressed his father. "I hope to make Miss Ingram's brother known to you later, sir, if he is well enough to come down. Their little ward, Anita, is in the nursery."

"Captain Ingram fought at Waterloo, Papa," Constantia put in boldly.

"Indeed. Which regiment, Miss Ingram?" The earl joined them at the table.

"The Artillery, sir."

His eyebrows rose and he cast a piercing glance at Felix. Constantia guessed that the Artillery was not a distinguished branch of the army. Felix had once wanted to join the Life Guards, she recalled. Captain Ingram's regiment must indicate his lack of noble connexions.

Her brother seemed unaffected by his father's censorious stare. "Frank Ingram was wounded at Quatre Bras, sir," he said calmly. "Shall I ring for fresh coffee?"

The butler and a footman were replenishing coffee, tea, and chocolate pots when Lady Westwood entered with her noble guests. Felix presented Miss Ingram, who was received with cool courtesy. In the confusion as the new arrivals were served and seated, he and Constantia abstracted her from the room.

"I must see Anita and Frank," she said as the breakfast room door closed behind them.

"I am looking forward prodigiously to making the captain's acquaintance," Constantia said eagerly.

"Not in his chamber," her brother warned as they started up the stairs. "You'll have to wait until he comes down."

Disappointed, she realized that in seeing herself as his devoted nurse she had ignored that problem. Mama would be quite justified in prohibiting her attendance at a gentleman's bedside. Then her spirits rose.

"I have a splendid notion. Felix, you know the little room that opens off the gallery? It is scarcely ever used. If we turn that into a bedchamber for Captain Ingram, he will not have to go up and down stairs, and he can exercise in the gallery or easily walk into the garden."

"That is a wonderful idea, Lady Constantia." Miss Ingram turned an appealing gaze on Felix. "Do you think it possible?"

"Consider it done."

Impatient to meet the captain, Constantia was ready to rush off and see to preparing the room but she felt it would be impolite not to go with them to the nursery. They found Anita exercising an aged rocking horse. She was a beautiful little girl, with a pale olive complexion, black ringlets and very dark eyes. Constantia was amused to see Vickie watching her with an almost maternally anxious eye.

"Look!" Anita cried. "I'm galloping. Look at me galloping, Aunt Fanny. Uncle Felix, 'member when you were my horse? This horse gallops."

"And I never even managed a trot," said Felix, shaking his head.

Constantia laughed, though she found it hard to imagine her dashing brother giving rides to a child. Vickie was frankly incredulous. "You let her ride on your back, Felix? An out-and-outer like you? You are a complete hand!"

"Lady Victoria!" The tall, grey-haired governess called her to order for her language. Miss Bannister was more than willing to take charge of Anita. "I am in hopes that caring for Miss Anita will impart to Lady Victoria a sense of responsibility, a quality in which she is sadly lacking," she confided.

Constantia was fond of her ex-preceptress and still asked her advice on occasion. She assured Miss Ingram that Anita would be safe in her care.

At last Miss Ingram was satisfied that the child was happy. She went to see the captain, while Felix and Constantia went downstairs together.

"Wish me luck," said Felix. "I am commanded to an interview with Father."

"He cannot turn a wounded hero out of doors," she assured him, and hurried to the housekeeper's room to order the room off the gallery made up as a bedchamber for the hero.

The rarely used sitting room was furnished as a writing and sewing room for visiting ladies. Constantia had a small bureau and a work-table carried out. She was arranging a bowl of roses on a chest of drawers, while footmen set up a truckle bed and maids dusted and polished, when Felix came in, looking grim. He drew her out into the gallery.

"It went just as I expected. The Ingrams

are obscure nobodies, who do not belong at Westwood. Such people are unfit to make my sisters' acquaintance. I pointed out that such people as Frank Ingram saved us all from Napoleon."

"Oh, well said, Felix!"

"And I told them that I mean to marry Fanny, if she will have me, with or without their approval. They are furious, of course, and almost equally angry that I changed my mind about Lady Sophia."

"So you did not propose to Lady Sophia? I am glad. I thought perhaps she had refused you."

"No." He smiled ruefully. "I came to my senses just in time to fail to come up to scratch. You do like Fanny, don't you, Con?"

"Very much. I shall be happy to have her for a sister. When you first described her and Lady Sophia to me, I thought at once that Miss Ingram sounded much more amiable."

"Amiable, adorable, but not eligible. I don't give a tinker's curse for eligibility! It's not as if she were a butcher's daughter, let alone an opera dancer."

"If they cannot change your mind, Mama and Papa will try to convince Miss Ingram that an artillery officer's daughter is as unfit as a butcher's daughter to join the family," she said, worried.

"They may well succeed. What am I to do next, Con?"

"I don't know. You will think of something, but keep her away from Mama and Papa until you do. Why not take her riding, for a start? Though I fear she will despise poor Skylark after mules and warhorses!"

"She'll be glad of a normal, if slothful, mount."

"If Captain Ingram is recovered from the journey enough to leave his bed, I shall keep him company while you are out," Constantia offered hopefully.

"He seemed to be in good spirits when I dropped in to see him before breakfast. I'll go and find out if he is ready to come down."

At last she was going to meet the brave captain. Everything must be arranged for his comfort. She looked around.

The gallery was a long room, draughty in the winter but pleasant in summer, with curtains of cream-and-gold brocade and a polished floor scattered with Turkey carpets. All along the west side, windows and french doors opened onto a flagged terrace and a formal Italian garden beyond, now suffering somewhat from a lack of outdoor servants. On the opposite wall hung the family portraits of three centuries, from Holbein to Reynolds and Gainsborough.

Constantia called a pair of footmen to move a sofa nearer to the french doors. Surely Captain Ingram would prefer a view of lobelia and scarlet geraniums straggling from stone urns, and slightly shaggy cypresses, to the massed haughty stares of her ancestors.

She collected several cushions and piled them on the sofa, then removed some and placed them on a chair near at hand. Would he be warm enough? Though the night's rain had passed, a brisk breeze chased clouds across the blue sky. She sent one footman running for a rug, and directed the other to set a small table beside the sofa. Hands clasped, she surveyed her preparations. A revivifying cup of tea? Or did soldiers despise anything weaker than ale? Wine? Brandy?

Would he want her company? Perhaps he'd prefer to be left in peace.

Why was she so unsure of herself, almost agitated? The captain was Fanny Ingram's brother, Felix's friend. She did not have to impress him. He was more likely to be grateful than critical.

She sat down on a chair facing the sofa, and willed herself to her usual serenity.

The servants finished their tasks. Constantia checked the small room and thanked them, and they departed. She was standing by a window, gazing out at the fast-drying flagstones, when she heard slow, halting steps approaching. She turned as Felix supported Captain Ingram into the gallery.

"Oh!" Her breath caught in her throat. How stupid she was! She knew he had been desperately ill, at death's door, yet her image of him had remained that of a strong, vigorous man.

He was pale, his thin face scored with lines of suffering. His threadbare uniform jacket, dark blue with scarlet facings, hung on his wasted body as on a scarecrow. Leaning on Felix's arm, his shoulders hunched against the pain, he was half a head shorter than Felix and looked ten years older.

No handsome, stalwart champion, yet his chin was resolute, his brown hair sprang in crisp curls from a broad brow. He smiled at her, a crooked, rueful grin that brought a warm light to his brown eyes and took a dozen years from his age.

"Forgive me for not making my bow, Lady Constantia, but I fear your brother would have to pick me up off the floor. I'm still a trifle unsteady on my pins."

And suddenly it did not matter that he

was not the romantic, story-book hero of her imaginings. He was Fanny's brother and Felix's friend. What, after all, could she have found to say to a hero?

She stepped forward with an answering smile. "A bow is a paltry gesture, sir, since gentlemen ceased to wear plumed hats to be flourished. Welcome to Westwood, Captain Ingram. Do come and sit down. Will you take tea, or do you consider it a wishy-washy beverage fit only for females?"

He laughed as he lowered himself with care onto the sofa, wincing. "By no means, ma'am. The first thing the British soldier does on stopping to bivouac is light a fire to boil water for tea."

"Truly?" She looked at him, doubtful. Her heart ached at the sight of that white, drawn face. "But tea is not very nourishing. Felix, what was it Nurse used to drink when she felt poorly?"

"Malt-and-milk, that is, half milk and half stout or porter, I believe. And she's still lively as a cricket at eighty-three."

"It sounds horrid. Though if it helps to restore your strength, Captain. . . ."

"I'll try it," said the captain valiantly. "I place myself entirely in your hands, Lady Constantia."

CHAPTER 4

Frank had rarely done anything so difficult in his life as to make a joke of his weakness to Lady Constantia. He had noted her momentary hesitation on first catching sight of him, and he knew that at all costs he must avoid her pity.

At least he had walked into the room. Two stout footmen had carried him down the stairs, seated on their linked hands, his arms about their shoulders, which left his shoulders aching. A humiliating necessity, and one he was glad Lady Constantia had not observed.

He had expected beauty of the handsome Lord Roworth's sister, but not perfection. Her hair was of a brighter gold than her brother's, her eyes a deeper blue — the summer skies of Spain to his England — set in a heart-shaped face. Her cheeks and tender mouth were touched with the delicate hue of the wild rose. When she smiled, her air of shy gravity vanished in a burst of sunshine.

As an insignificant half-pay officer and a semi-invalid, Frank was in no position to set up as a worshipper of the lovely daughter of an earl. The best he dared hope was to make a friend of her.

Nonetheless, he could not tear his gaze from her graceful slenderness as she turned away to ring for a servant. Luckily, Fanny came in at that moment, distracting Roworth, and by the time anyone looked at Frank again he was in full command of himself.

"I trust I have not kept you waiting, Felix."

Fanny was cheerful, her eyes sparkling. Her delight in the prospect of riding with Felix appeared no whit diminished by the shabbiness of her brown riding habit. Frank dismissed the guilt awakened by her un-happy report of her cold reception from the earl and countess. He had been right in insisting on coming to Westwood.

She turned to him. "I see Lady Constantia has made you comfortable, Frank."

"I'm in clover. Off you go and enjoy your ride."

"I shall keep the captain company, Miss Ingram," Lady Constantia promised.

Felix moved towards Fanny as if drawn by

a magnet. He offered his arm and she laid her hand on it, looking up at him with a joyful smile. Glancing at Lady Constantia, Frank saw that she was aware of the attraction between his sister and her brother. Her eyes met his and a message passed: she was content to have it so. Somehow she had found the strength to repudiate her parents' disdainful arrogance, the pride that counted most of the human race unworthy of respect and friendship.

"I am so glad you came to Westwood," she said softly.

Perhaps Felix heard her. As he and Fanny reached the door, he swung round with a frown. "You ought to have a chaperon, Connie."

"Not Mama!"

He grinned. "No, not Mama. I'll send for your abigail."

They departed, and a footman entered. Lady Constantia ordered tea, milk-and-stout, and plenty of biscuits and cakes. The servant, a lad by the name of Thomas, was too new to his position not to show his surprise at this curious repast, but he knew better than to question it. He went off, leaving them alone together.

Silence fell in the long gallery. Outside, a blackbird perched in an Italian cypress and sang his heart out.

The mention of a chaperon had disconcerted both Frank and Lady Constantia. She sat with downcast eyes, while he searched desperately for something to say. He was suddenly conscious of the need to mind his tongue. Fanny was used to a soldier's rough-and-ready speech — duly expurgated in the presence of respectable females — and Miriam Cohen had taken it in her stride. It would not do for the sensitive, delicate creature sitting opposite him. He thought back to the days before his mother died, when she had demanded gentlemanly manners of him.

"Your brother has . . ." he began, just as she said, "Your sister told me. . . ."

They looked at each other and laughed, she with a rosy blush. Her maid came in, a small, middle-aged woman in grey who curtsied and took a seat at a distance. She set about some needlework, but Frank noticed that she kept a watchful eye on her mistress.

Lady Constantia seemed once again tongue-tied, so Frank completed his sentence.

"Your brother has been a most generous friend to us."

"Felix is a dear, the kindest and best

brother in the world. Oh," she cried, flustered, "but I expect Miss Ingram says the same of you!"

"Not Fanny. I could not ask for a more devoted sister, but she is more apt to roast than to praise me."

"I have already observed that Miss Ingram has a lively sense of humour. You are twins, are you not, and you have always been together? You must be very close. Vickie is five years younger than I, and my other sister, Augusta, is five years older. She left home to be married eight years since."

Her wistfulness touched him. She was lonely, this daughter of privilege in her great mansion with servants running to do her bidding.

Two came in now, one with a laden tray, the other to set up a small pie-crust table between Frank's sofa and Lady Constantia's chair. He transferred from tray to table several plates of confections, a pewter tankard, and tea things including two elegant porcelain cups and saucers.

"In case your drink is nasty, you can have tea instead," Lady Constantia explained.

"Am I not to be bribed to drain every drop with promises of sweet things?" Frank teased.

A gleam in her eye, she retorted, "Miss

68

Ingram advised me to coax rather than command you. She said nothing of bribery."

"I am perfectly amenable to bribery," he assured her, delighted by her show of spirit.

"Splendid." She passed him the tankard, then heaped a small plate with Shrewsbury biscuits, almond cakes, and blackcurrant tarts, and set it close to him. "If ever I meet Mrs Cohen, I want to be able to tell her that at least her patient was well fed at West-wood."

"Roworth has told you about Mrs Cohen?" He sipped at his concoction. "Hmm, odd but by no means undrinkable."

"I hope you will like to live to be eighty-three, like Nurse. Yes, Felix told me about the Cohens when he came home from France after smuggling Mr Rothschild's gold to Spain."

"I was on the receiving end of that gold. Isaac brought it down from the Spanish mountains like manna from heaven, the day before the battle of Fuentes de Oñoro. Believe me, it put heart into the men to have it jingling in their pockets. Of course, Roworth didn't make it so far. He was stranded in the Pyrenees with a dislocated shoulder, being nursed by Mrs Cohen."

"He and Miss Ingram say that she has performed wonders in healing your . . . your injuries," Lady Constantia said hesitantly.

"She has, indeed." Refusing to think of the limits of Miriam's skills, he took a long draught from the tankard. "Aha, now I know why you and Fanny have been discussing my differing susceptibility to commands and coaxing! I am to be wheedled into performing Miriam's exercises."

She looked absurdly guilty. "Yes," she confessed, "but you must not tire yourself."

"You have an awkward task, Lady Constantia, to make sure that I take precisely the correct amount of exercise."

"Are you a difficult patient, Captain?"

"Madam, I am at your command."

His teasing gallantry set Constantia quite at her ease. "Then I decree that you shall rest here until after luncheon." She refilled his plate, which he had absentmindedly emptied as they talked. A tinge of colour in his cheeks encouraged her to hope he was not quite the invalid he had appeared on entering the gallery. "Miss Ingram said you found the journey from Kent exhausting, and coming downstairs tired you still more, did it not?"

"A little." He stiffly flexed his shoulders. "It will be a relief not to have to face the stairs again for the present. I have you to thank for that, I believe?"

"It is common sense; anyone might have thought of it." She pointed out the door to his new chamber, at the far end of the gallery. "You will be able to come and go as you please. The gallery is little used except just before dinner. After luncheon, we shall stroll on the terrace."

"Yes, ma'am." His eyes laughed at her.

"You said you are mine to command. But I was forgetting, walking is all very well but has not Mrs Cohen prescribed more particular exercises for you?"

"She has. I do them night and morning, as I find them easier in my nightshirt."

"Oh." Constantia's cheeks burned but she resolutely continued, "Then I shall have to trust you to perform them faithfully."

He grimaced. "I shall, I promise you, for I'm all too aware of the consequences of neglecting them."

She recalled his sister saying that he might be crippled but for Miriam's care. Could that dreadful fate yet be his if he failed to follow her orders?

"Uncle Frank! Uncle Frank!" Anita scampered into the gallery, followed at a slightly more sober pace by Vickie and with dignity by Miss Bannister. "I came to see you, 'cos I haven't seen you today." She gave him a smacking kiss, climbed up onto the sofa,

71

and settled snugly beside him.

"Hello, sweetheart." He dropped a kiss on the top of her head. Their obvious affection touched Constantia's heart.

"Are you awright today?"

"Not bad. Who are your new friends?"

"That's Aunt Vickie and that's Miss Ba-nis-ter. It's a hard name, but not so hard like Lady 'Stansha." She regarded Constantia thoughtfully, then transferred her gaze to the table. With a sideways peep at Constantia, she whispered loudly in the captain's ear, "May I have a bixit, please, Uncle Frank?"

Constantia passed the plate, noting that Captain Ingram had made very satisfactory inroads into the provisions. "You had best call me Aunt Connie, Anita," she said, and performed proper introductions of the others.

"We're going for a walk," Vickie explained, helping herself to a tart, "down to the stream, before it starts to rain again. So we can't stay now, but please, sir, will you tell me all about Waterloo sometime?"

"I regret to say, Lady Victoria, that I missed Waterloo."

"Oh yes, Felix said you were wounded at Quatre Bras. That was before, wasn't it? You can tell me about another of the Duke of

Wellington's victories that you fought in, instead."

Her governess intervened. "Lady Victoria, I hardly think it proper. . . ."

"Don't worry, ma'am," the captain said with a grin, "I'll leave out all the unsuitable bits."

Vickie made a moue. "The best bits, you mean. Come on, Anita, let's go while the sun's shining."

"There's fishes in the stream, Uncle Frank." The little girl slid down from the sofa and ran to take Vickie's hand. "I'll come and see you again soon."

They went out through the french door. Smiling, he watched Anita cross the terrace. At the top of the steps down to the garden she turned to wave, and he waved back, wincing as he raised his arm. She took Miss Bannister's hand and went off happily to see the fishes.

"Merry as a grig," said the captain. "With the unsettled life she's led, it's fortunate that she has a knack of making friends."

"She is an enchanting child," Constantia said, "but it is to your credit, and Miss Ingram's, that she is so confident in a novel situation."

"The credit is all Fanny's. She took charge when Anita's mother died and she wouldn't give her up for the world. It's not made a hard life any easier, but you'd never hear her complain."

His pride in his sister was endearing, and justified, as Constantia realized when he described the difficulties of life in the army's train. He said not a word of the hardship to a young, poorly-paid officer in supporting a sister and a child not his own. Instead, he was full of praise for the way first his mother, then Fanny, had made the most dilapidated quarters homelike for their menfolk.

Thomas came in to remove the tea-table, and later returned to announce that luncheon was served.

"Heavens, is it so late?" Constantia exclaimed. "I shall have to put in an appearance, Captain Ingram, since we have guests. You must order whatever you wish to be brought to you here. I shall come straight back to . . . Oh, bother, it looks like rain. You will have to exercise indoors today."

Calling Joan to go with her, she started towards the door, then stopped as Fanny entered, pale and agitated, still in her riding habit. Constantia guessed she was in a quake at the prospect of meeting the earl and countess again at luncheon. Where was Felix when his beloved needed his support?

"Shall I wait for you while you change your dress, Miss Ingram?" she offered. "Or would you prefer to take luncheon in here with your brother?"

"Oh no!" She sounded distraught. "Thank you, I am not hungry. Pray excuse me, I must speak with Frank."

"Of course." Constantia laid her hand on Fanny's arm. "If there is anything I can do. . . ."

Fanny's mouth quivered and she shook her head, her eyes bright with unshed tears. Had she quarrelled with Felix? Helpless, Constantia signalled to the footman to leave, and she and her maid followed him.

Frank stared at his sister in dismay. "Fanny, what is it?" he asked, holding out his hand to her.

With a visible effort, she regained her composure and gave him a smile, slightly wobbly, as she came to sit on the end of his sofa.

"You're not going to believe this. I can scarcely believe it myself. Did I ever tell you about the man who was asking questions about us, in Brussels, months ago?"

"No." He waited patiently for her to tell him in her own way, rather than risk throwing her into high fidgets again. He could not recall ever having seen her so overwrought.

"He wanted to know things like our dates of birth, and Mama's maiden name. It seems F-Felix has seen him several times since, and now he has caught up with us. Frank, you didn't know that Mama's father was a duke, did you?"

He gaped at her. "A duke? No, she'd never talk about her family, to me any more than to you. Our grandfather a duke? The devil!"

"The late Duke of Oxshott. His lawyer sent the man, Taggle, to look for us. Are you feeling strong?" She reached out and took his hand. "It seems the duke was at outs with all his relations, especially his heir, the present duke, but having banished Mama thirty years ago, he couldn't come to cuffs again with her. He left all his unentailed property to her, and so to us."

"And that's what this fellow wanted to tell us?" Frank laughed. "Roworth has been protecting us against him all this time?"

"If only we had known, you could have sold out before Quatre Bras."

Did that explain her distress? "Come now," he said, "you know better than that. I'd never have sold out just before the battle. Do you mean we'll inherit enough to live on?"

"We're going to be rich."

She spoke in such a dull tone that for a moment he didn't take it in. "Rich?" he said blankly. "Rich? How rich?"

"I didn't ask. F-Felix talked to him, and he said I am a very wealthy woman." For the second time her voice trembled on that name.

Frank frowned, for the moment ignoring her extraordinary, scarcely credible announcement. Something was wrong between her and Roworth. Nothing else could have thrown her into such a megrim. But she was not angry with him, or she'd have called him Lord Roworth, not Felix. So, thank heaven, he had done nothing that demanded retribution from her brother.

Feeling abominably weak and impotent, Frank quailed at the thought of delving into a complex tangle of female emotions. They'd have to sort matters out for themselves.

He reverted to her news. "So the Duke of Oxshott is our uncle?" he asked.

"Yes, Mama's brother. Quite by chance I heard a story about him just this morning, and I fear he is as much a curmudgeon as his father, besides being very full of his own importance."

"It sounds as if Mama was well shut of her family. Do we have to acknowledge them to receive the inheritance?"

77

"I daresay he won't acknowledge us," Fanny said dryly. "Not that I care a groat. But let us not tell anyone of the connexion, Frank. Lord and Lady Westwood will suppose that we are hoaxing, or if they believe us, that we are vulgar braggarts. In any case, I don't want their respect based on noble connexions or money if they will not grant it to me for myself."

"Lord, no. We won't mention the money, either, until we're quite sure there's no mistake. It all sounds like a Banbury tale. I must speak to this fellow Taggle. Ring for a servant, will you, Fanny."

Before she reached the bell, a pair of the maroon-clad footmen came in. They seemed to come in pairs, Frank reflected, and in amazing proliferation for a recently impoverished household. One set up the pie-crust table again, and unloaded from the other's tray a lavish selection of cold meat and fruit.

"Lady Constantia's orders," he announced, setting out two plates.

Frank discovered that he had an excellent appetite, despite the confections he had consumed not so long ago. Lady Constantia was certainly taking seriously her mandate to oversee his health.

"Thank you," he said. "Do you know if the man, Taggle, who came to Westwood this morning is still about?"

"He's taking a bite in the kitchen, sir, and says he won't stir till he's had a word wi' you."

"Good." He was going to ask for Taggle to be sent to him in twenty minutes, when he remembered that Lady Constantia expected him to stroll with her after luncheon. Presumably, since the man had been on their trail for months, he'd not object to a further brief delay. "Tell him I'll see him later this afternoon."

"Very good, sir." As rain was beginning to fall, the footmen quickly closed the open windows and departed.

"Come and eat, Fanny," Frank said. "I can't eat alone in the presence of a lady."

She sat down, buttered a roll, and nibbled on it. Then she shook her head. "I'm really not hungry. And, heavens! I quite forgot! I told Lord Westwood I'd see him as soon as I'd changed out of my riding dress, and here I am an hour later still wearing it. I only hope he has gone to luncheon and is not waiting for me."

She hurried off, leaving Frank thoughtfully munching on a chicken leg. Perhaps Roworth had not caused her unhappiness after all. The coming interview with the earl might well be enough to overset her, since his lordship had made it plain enough that he heartily despised his heir's guests. If Lord Westwood knew or guessed Roworth's love for Fanny, he'd do his best to nip the business in the bud.

Once again Frank bitterly regretted being unable to protect his sister.

The room was growing dark as the rain pelted down in earnest. Frank found he was not very hungry after all, but rather than risk disappointing Lady Constantia he ploughed through a solid meal.

Constantia, again accompanied by her abigail, returned to the gallery before the dishes were removed. She cast a calculating glance at the table and nodded, pleased. The captain had eaten well. She'd soon chase the pinched look from his face.

A second glance at the luncheon remains made her frown. "Miss Ingram ate only a few crumbs? Felix did not come in to luncheon at all." If they had had a tiff, perhaps the captain was aware of the cause and between them they could reconcile the pair.

Though he hesitated, as if tempted to respond to her implied question, a gentlemanly reticence about his sister's feelings prevailed. Or perhaps he held her parents to blame, and was not only too gentlemanly but too kind to say so.

"I have eaten enough for three," he said in a funning way.

She accepted his lead. "Then you had best wait a while before taking any exercise. What a pity it is raining! It is grown quite chilly. Are you warm enough?" Pulling her shawl closer about her shoulders, she handed him a carriage rug.

He draped it across his knees and leaned back against the cushions as she sat down opposite.

"I must not detain you," he said awkwardly.

Constantia flushed, afraid she was inconsiderately imposing her unwanted presence upon him. "Do you wish to rest upon your bed?" she asked, rising. "Or if you would like to read, I shall send for. . . ."

"No, no, I am delighted to have your company, but surely you have more important or interesting things to do than sitting with an invalid."

"Nothing! I have just been congratulating myself because Mama is too occupied with her guests to concern herself with my whereabouts. Oh, I beg your pardon, I did not mean. . . ."

"Come now, Lady Constantia." He shook his head at her in mock reproach. "You did

81

mean . . . but we shan't discuss that. Tell me how you usually pass your time."

"Not in anything interesting, or important, or even useful. I read a great deal, embroider, walk with Vickie and Miss Bannister, ride with a groom, visit the more consequential of our neighbours with Mama. She and I go over the household accounts every week with the housekeeper."

"That's a useful habit."

"I suppose so. I do visit poor and sick tenants with comforts, though Mama insists that I send in a footman and not set foot in their houses. I arrange flowers for the house. I am not permitted to pick them, but the gardeners have more work than they have time for, so often I do anyway," she said defiantly.

Captain Ingram laughed. "I am thoroughly disabused of any notion that you are a compliant female! Fanny is fond of flowers."

"Is she? Our gardens are in poor condition, alas, but I shall be happy to show her around."

"She'll enjoy that. She likes to read, too, though she never had much opportunity before we went to the Cohens'."

"Westwood has an excellent library. Unless she will prefer to borrow Vickie's Gothic romances?"

"She may. I doubt Mrs Cohen owns any."

"Vickie ought not. Pray don't give her away to my parents."

"Most unlikely. Do you not read them?"

"Sometimes," she confessed. "I daresay Miss Ingram has had no opportunity to learn to play upon the pianoforte?"

"None. Do you play?" Sitting up, he twisted stiffly to look around the room. "There is no instrument in here," he said, disappointed. "I should like to hear you play. I enjoy music though I've heard little enough besides military marches and soldiers' songs — most of them unfit for a lady's ears," he added with a grin.

Constantia properly ignored this last comment. "There is an old spinet in the school-room. I shall have it brought down later — if you truly wish it?"

"I do."

"You are not just being polite?"

"How can you think so, when I was so impolite as to bring a blush to your cheeks not a moment since?"

"You are a great tease, sir," she said with dignified severity. "Since your spirits are so high, I believe it is time for you to take your exercise."

"Your belief is my command, ma'am." He

pushed aside the rug and made an effort to rise. Constantia saw the mortification in his brown eyes as he said wryly, "I am a little stiff from sitting, I'm afraid. A footman. . . ."

"I am perfectly able to assist you." She hurried to his side. "I am stronger than I appear, as well as less compliant!"

As, with her aid, he painfully stood and straightened, she realized that he had only seemed short in contrast to her tall brother. In fact, he topped her by several inches. His hand on her arm, though thin, was square and well-kept, giving an impression of strength, and there was a faint, clean, herbal fragrance about him.

Leaning on her arm, he took several slow steps, then Joan arrived beside them.

"Let me help the gentleman, my lady," she said, stiff with disapproval.

He flashed the maid a smile that visibly thawed her. "Thank you, but I'll try how I can do without support."

Once the stiffness wore off, Captain Ingram's physical condition was much improved since the morning, Constantia was pleased to see. With occasional rests, they strolled up and down the gallery for half an hour. He commented on the portraits in their heavy gilt frames, and Constantia offered to show them to him one day when there was more light from the windows.

"And when you are a little more recovered," she said. "My ancestors are enough to cow the boldest."

"They are all ancestors?" he marvelled. "No doubt my . . . er, many noble families have such collections."

"I am sure they do." She wondered what he had been going to say.

Soon after, he declared that he was ready to retire to his chamber for a while, and he asked Constantia to ring for a footman.

"This time you cannot assist me," he said firmly.

The walking had obviously tired him, yet there was an inexplicable air of suppressed excitement about him. Puzzled, Constantia reluctantly went off to join her mother and the guests before her absence became so prolonged as to arouse interest.

She liked Captain Ingram, and had no desire to be banned from his company.

CHAPTER 5

Frank looked around his new chamber. On the chest-of-drawers stood a bowl of roses, surely Lady Constantia's work. She was a sweet-natured girl, and he was sorry for her. He had never expected to pity an earl's daughter for her circumscribed life.

He crossed to the chest and bent awkwardly to smell the pink and white blooms.

The low truckle was well furnished with a mountainous featherbed and a gay quilted counterpane. Frank was tempted to retreat to its depths but undressing seemed too much effort, though Miriam had had his shirts remade to button right down the front instead of just at the neck. It was out of the question to request aid of a strange footman who'd then go gossiping in the servants' hall about what he had seen. Felix's valet, Trevor, wouldn't condescend to gossip, but if he agreed to help it would be grudgingly, with a sour face.

Frank missed Hoskins and wondered what had become of the stalwart, faithful corporal. He had had to return to his unit when the Ingrams left Brussels. Without Felix's help, Frank could never have managed on that journey, too weak to dress and undress himself, too much recovered to let Fanny help.

Sprawling fully clothed on top of the bed, he grinned. The Westwoods would be devilish out of countenance if they ever discovered that their noble son had played bodyservant to a paltry artillery captain.

One who was about to metamorphose into the wealthy grandson of a duke!

Thomas entered and Frank sent him to fetch Taggle and to ask Fanny to join him. Fanny arrived first. Her eyes sparkled with anger, a vast improvement over her earlier apathetic misery, in her brother's view.

"What's put you on your high horse?" he asked, sitting up.

"Lord Westwood! He is the most odious, toplofty brute, looking down his nose at me as if I were a scullery maid caught pinching the silver."

"You didn't tell him about our windfall, I take it?"

"I wouldn't lower myself to cater to his crotchets."

"What did he say?"

"He tried to convince me I should find myself so uncomfortable among my betters at Westwood, that for my own sake I ought to leave. I told him I shall take his opinion into consideration."

Frank laughed. "I wager he had no answer for that. Ah, here's Taggle."

The lawyer's emissary was a small, bright-eyed man in a frieze coat and catskin waistcoat. "Well, I caught up wiv yer at last," he said with an exaggerated sigh. "I am addressing Capting and Miss Ingram, I s'pose?"

"You are," said Fanny, her mouth twitching. "Won't you sit down, Mr Taggle?" She took a seat on a Windsor chair.

He pulled up another. "Capting Francis and Miss Frances Ingram?" he persisted.

"That's right." Frank fixed him with a warning glare. Through a mix-up of the twin babies at their baptism, he had been christened after his mother. His middle name was not to be bandied about even before Fanny, who knew it but loyally kept the deep, dark secret.

Taggle winked. "Places and dates of birf?" he proceeded.

"Nilgapur, India," said Fanny, passing two sheets of parchment to him. "I found our baptismal certificates among Mama's papers. You must know that we are twins, surely. We were both born on the twelfth of May, 1790."

He perused the papers and nodded in satisfaction. "To Lieutenant Thomas Ingram, Royal Horse Artillery, and Frances Cy . . ." With a knowing grin at Frank, he tapped his nose. "Mum's the word, Capting. I weren't 'ired for me beauty so musta bin acos I'm a discreet sort o' cove. Lady Frances Ingram, née Kerridge, is what we'll say. Got yer ma's marriage lines, 'ave yer, miss?"

Fanny shook her head. Taggle tut-tutted. For a moment Frank feared that would be the end of the matter. Though deeply disappointed, he was glad they had told no one. He'd never really quite believed it anyway.

But the little man just said, "Now wou'ncha think a mort'd 'ang on to them lines like the very dickens? Specially a gentry mort. Never mind, eh. I seen the church register and all's bowman. I'm 'appy to announce as 'ow you two's the grandchildren o' the late Duke of Oxshott and heirs to all 'is unentailed property."

Frank and Fanny exchanged an awed glance, then Fanny asked, "That's everything that didn't legally have to go to the new duke?"

"Right, miss. Not but what 'e'da bin 'appy enough to leave you the ruddy lot, I reckon. You'd never guess what 'is grace called 'is rightful heir in 'is will. Right there on the legal dockiment, I seen it wi' me own eyes: nincompoop."

Frank laughed, but said soberly, "I daresay there wasn't much property unentailed."

"Oh, I wouldn't say that, Capting. The new Duke's not going to be 'appy I run you to earth, I'll tell you that. How d'you like two estates — small uns, mind — and a plum apiece? That's an 'undred thousand, miss."

"A hundred thousand?" Frank was utterly incredulous. He'd been thinking in terms of a few hundred a year, if they were lucky. Enough, perhaps, to quit the army and rent a cottage for the three of them if Fanny didn't marry Roworth. "A hundred thousand pounds each?"

Taggle shrugged, obviously pleased with the effect of his announcement. "Could be guineas, give or take a few. Mr Mackintyre, the lawyer, 'e'll give you the numbers. I got to get back to Lunnon, give 'im the news. 'E'll come down 'ere to see you, wiv papers to sign and that. Don't look for 'im for a week or ten days, though. Lawyers!" he grumbled. "Always on at you to 'urry but you don't see them doing nuffink in an 'urry." He stood up.

Fanny also rose, looking dazed. "All I can say, Mr Taggle, is thank you for persevering in your hunt."

"Bless your 'eart, miss, it's my pleasure. Get paid by the day, I do. Well, Capting, 'ere's 'oping a spot o' the ready and rhino'll put you on yer feet." He shook Frank's proffered hand with painful heartiness. "And that reminds me. Be fergetting me own 'ead next." Delving into an inside pocket, with the air of a magician he produced a roll of flimsies. " 'Ere's a bit to tide you over, like."

He tossed it on the bed. Frank counted the Bank of England notes while Fanny went out to the bureau in the gallery to write out the requested receipt. Mr Taggle departed with a cheery wave of the hand.

"Two hundred pounds!" Fanny exclaimed, dropping into the chair again. "Frank, with so much money we need not wait here for Mr Mackintyre."

"You want to leave? After defying Lord Westwood?"

"I defied him, but he was right," she said sadly. "We don't belong here. Perhaps we could go to one of the estates we have inherited."

"Hardly. We don't know where they are, nor who's in residence, nor even what sort of condition they're in." Frank looked about the cosy room. His gaze came to rest on the bowl of roses. Leave, when Lady Constantia was resolved to make him comfortable and restore him to health? "I hate to admit it, but I'm not sure I'm up to another journey so soon."

"We need not go far," she pleaded. "Wells is close, and Bath not too far, I believe, and both must have respectable hostelries."

"Travelling in a hired chaise," he said with exaggerated gloom. "Roworth has already sent the Cohens' carriage back to them. And think of Anita. She hated to leave Amos, and now you would tear her from her new friend."

"I know she is already fond of Lady Victoria, but. . . ."

"And what about Mr Mackintyre? He won't know where to find us." He rushed on before she worked out that they could easily warn Taggle of their departure and write to the lawyer once they were settled elsewhere. "No, we had best stay until Mackintyre arrives. I'm tired, Fanny."

"You're right," she said, all contrition. "You ought not to travel again so soon, and you would not be near so comfortable in an inn. Come, let me help you out of your coat so that you can rest properly."

Frank's guilt was momentary. His sister might find Westwood uncomfortable at present, but he remained convinced that she and Roworth loved each other. If she left they'd have no chance to patch up their differences.

And then there was Lady Constantia, he thought drowsily, drifting into sleep.

He woke to the drip-drip-drip of a steady downpour outside, and a faint sound of music. For several minutes he lay listening, until he recalled Taggle's visit. Or had the odd little man been a dream? No, there on the bedside table lay the roll of banknotes.

With a rush of energy, Frank sat up. He put the money in the drawer of the table, out of the way of the prying eyes of servants. Until the lawyer had confirmed Taggle's news, he wanted no talk of sudden wealth. No making of plans, either, he decided; no castles in Spain to come tumbling down if Mr Mackintyre failed to accept them as the late duke's grandchildren.

Cautiously he swung his legs over the edge of the bed and stood. The slight dizziness he had come to expect failed to materialize. Perhaps Lady Constantia's milk-and-stout restorative was already working its wonders!

Miriam was right, as usual: despite her efforts to tempt his appetite, at Nettledene he had not been eating enough for the needs of his battered body. Somehow Lady Constantia's gentle, diffident determination that he should eat was irresistible.

Crossing to the door, he opened it a crack to let in the sound of the spinet. She — it must be she — was playing a slow, dreamy air on the soft-toned instrument.

He went to the looking-glass to tie his cravat and brush his hair. It was longer than he had worn it in the army, but not too long for a fashionable gentleman. For the first time since Quatre Bras, he deliberately studied his face, by the gloomy light from the window. The sun-brown of his once active outdoor life had faded to a sickly pallor, and sharp cheekbones stood out above hollow cheeks. No wonder Lady Constantia had been hard pressed to hide her dismay on first seeing him, yet there was no mark on his face to hint at . . .

Forget it! he told himself sharply. This is at best a short interlude. Enjoy her company while you may.

As he put on his coat, he noticed that even that was suffused with the herbal smell of Miriam's unguents. At least he had persuaded her to change from the rose essence she'd originally used for the lotions and ointments he had to rub in twice daily, before his exercises. Sniffing, he hoped the odour was not offensive to a lady's delicate nostrils. Lady Constantia had not recoiled when she rushed to support him for that all too brief moment.

With one last glance at the mirror, he went out into the gallery. The spinet had been set up on a stand at the far end. Bowed over her music, Lady Constantia's head gleamed pure gold by the light of a branch of candles. Her slender hands plucked a plaintive melody from the ivory keys.

A sudden vision overwhelmed Frank: a winter's evening; himself seated by a cheerful fire, a child on his knee; Constantia's golden head bowed over her music. . . .

Savagely he cursed his imagination. Rich or poor, duke's grandson or insignificant soldier, he was not for her. She deserved a husband whose appearance would not drive her to hysterics on her wedding night. He must think of her as the sister she would become if Fanny married Roworth. What man could complain with two such sisters?

Looking up with a smile as the captain approached along the gallery, Constantia caught a fleeting melancholy on his face. The shadow vanished as he answered her smile. At once she was reassured that the bond of friendly sympathy between them was not a mere fancy on her part. So quickly formed, it had seemed too good to be true.

His pace slow but steady, he held himself with a military uprightness no debility could disguise. She started to play Handel's *See the conquering hero come*, and he laughed.

"I recognize that," he said. "Mama used to sing it whenever my father returned to whatever quarters we happened to call home at any moment. Play some more."

"The spinet is a little out of tune, I fear. Vickie uses it to practise on. I hope you will soon be able to come to the drawing-room to hear the pianoforte."

"Very soon. I feel the effect of your nurse's favourite remedy already."

"The milk-and-stout? Oh, splendid!"

Whether that peculiar concoction was responsible; or his willingness to oblige her by devouring the meals and snacks she pressed upon him; or the easy access to the gallery for exercise; or the sunshine that succeeded the rain and made possible strolls and idle lounging out on the terrace; whatever the cause, Captain Ingram's health improved visibly over the next two days. With delight, Constantia watched his wan face begin to fill out and take on colour, his steps grow firmer and swifter.

He still tired easily, breakfasted in bed and retired thither before dinner, but the moment came when she could no longer postpone presenting him to her parents. Their guests left, and the countess was becoming curious about the invalid who occupied so much of her daughter's time.

Felix ought to have performed the introductions, but Felix was always out riding, or fishing, or searching for a mount for his sisters or himself. Doubtless for that reason, the Westwoods had softened towards Fanny, her ladyship even going so far as to commend her neat stitches. Nonetheless, Constantia was apprehensive when her mother informed her that they intended to repair to the long gallery at noon to make the captain's acquaintance. She hurried to warn him.

"You must lie on the sofa," she urged, "with the rug over you."

Turning unexpectedly stubborn, he adamantly refused. "Lord no, not I. I'll face 'em on my own two feet."

Constantia bit her lip. "But —"

"I've stood up to Boney's *Grande Armée*." He touched her hand. "You wouldn't want a soldier to show the white feather in the

97

face of . . . er . . . hm. . . ."

"The enemy?"

"An adversary, let's say." He grinned and she had to smile. "I wager they'll not shoot me without a declaration of war."

The meeting passed off much better than she had dared to hope. Her parents were stiff but civil, the captain courteous and undaunted. The countess remarked upon his having been wounded in the service of his country, and hoped he was being made comfortable; the earl asked a question or two about fighting under the Duke of Wellington.

As, in obedience to her mother's signal, Constantia followed them from the room, she tried to guess the reason for their lack of antagonism. Captain Ingram had gentlemanly manners, though of a plain, soldierly kind. He was neither handsome nor possessed of a dangerously insinuating charm that might make their daughter forget herself. By their reckoning, having rejected several highly eligible suitors she was not likely to fall for a shabby invalid. After all, even Felix had come to his senses and was now paying as little attention to the captain's sister as any uneasy parent could possibly desire.

Lord and Lady Westwood probably failed

to notice that Felix went around with a set face, nor did they care that Fanny was utterly miserable. Constantia did. She could not sit by and let her brother ruin his own life and Fanny's.

As soon as she was able, she returned to the gallery. Captain Ingram was seated at the bureau, a pen in his hand, Anita on his knee. The little girl jumped down and ran to Constantia, took her hand and tugged her forward.

"I'm drawing a picsher for Amos, Aunt Connie. Come and see. Uncle Frank's going to send it to him, 'cos he's writing a letter to Aunt Miriam."

Writing to Miriam! Why should that send a stab of an emotion very like jealousy through Constantia's heart?

"Trying to write," the captain amended. "I don't have a way with words, I fear. I know Fanny's written to thank the Cohens for all they did for us, but I cannot any longer postpone writing on my own behalf. I don't suppose you'd be willing to advise me?"

"If you wish," she said shyly, pulling up a chair as Anita scrambled back onto his lap and picked up her pencil.

"You see, it mustn't be too formal, because Mrs Cohen is not at all a formal person, nor too casual, because we owe them a great deal, and I wouldn't wish to be disrespectful."

Constantia smiled. "A nice distinction, but I expect we can manage." She suggested several phrases and he wrote them down.

"Excellent. And now I must tell them about the angel of mercy who is so kindly ministering to my needs here."

"That you will have to work out for yourself!" she said, blushing. "Captain, I want to talk to you about your sister and my brother."

He sobered at once. "Yes, it's time something was done about that situation. Anita, love, that's a beautiful picture. Why don't you take it to show to Aunt Fanny?"

"And Aunt Vickie." She slipped down again and ran off, her paper clutched to her chest.

"She already feels quite at home in this great mansion," said the captain. "If she can't find Fanny she'll just ask the nearest maid or footman. I believe she thinks the footmen are some odd kind of soldier, because of their livery."

"All the servants adore her. Even our starchy butler has been seen to smile at her, which he never has for me." She hesitated, reluctant to voice so uncharitable a thought about her brother: "You don't think Felix and Fanny came to cuffs about her, do you? That he asked Fanny to marry him but refused to take on Anita? He seems so fond of the child!"

As if he guessed how the suspicion hurt her, he reached out and took her hand. A loud cough reminded them that Joan was not far off. The abigail spent a great deal of her time sewing in the long gallery these days. The captain dropped Constantia's hand like a stinging nettle plucked by mistake.

Or perhaps it was his hand that resembled a nettle. Certainly his touch left the oddest tingling sensation in her fingers.

She concentrated on what he was saying.

"It's always possible, of course, that Roworth don't choose to bring up Anita. If that's it, you mustn't think too hardly of him." He went on awkwardly, "I daresay I ought not to speak of such things to a delicately bred young lady, but Anita is a love-child."

Shocked, but conscious of his serious scrutiny, Constantia swallowed a gasp and took a deep breath instead. "You mean, her mother and father were not married?" she asked, her voice a trifle unsteady.

"Such things happen in war-time." He

smiled wryly. "Indeed, as you visit your father's tenants, you must be aware that they happen in the most peaceful settings. Anita's mother was a refugee from the French, a Spanish lady, a Catholic, and her father was an English soldier. They loved each other, but circumstances at that time, in that place, made marriage impossible."

"And then they both died." Tears rose to Constantia's eyes. She blinked them away. "The poor child! Or, no, she is not to be pitied, for she has you."

His eyes were warm. "I knew you would understand. I trust you not to spread the story. I'd not have told you but that I didn't want you to judge your brother too harshly if he rejected Anita. However, I doubt that's the case. Have I mentioned that the Cohens wished to adopt her? When Fanny and I declined their offer, Roworth cried out 'Bravo,' and it's my belief that was after he'd realized he loves Fanny." Now he was uncertain. "He does, doesn't he? It's not my imagination?"

"He has told me he loves her and wants to marry her."

"That's more than Fanny's told me, though I don't doubt for a moment that she loves him."

"The trouble is, perhaps he has changed

his mind, as he did over Lady Sophia."

The captain considered this. "In my opinion, he courted Lady Sophia for her suitability, not because he liked her."

"In other words, because my parents would approve her. Then I am very much afraid that he may have let them convince him that your sister is not suitable." She gazed at him in dismay.

Something enigmatical in his regard made her fear that she had offended him. His next words increased her chagrin.

"If that's so, it's not for me to induce Lord Roworth to accept her as an eligible bride. The best I can do for Fanny is to take her away from here at once."

"No! At least let me talk to Felix. Surely I can persuade him not to sacrifice Fanny's happiness and his own to Mama and Papa's antiquated notions! He is out riding, but I shall give orders that I am to be notified the moment he returns."

As she turned away to ring for a footman, she received a distinct impression that he was both admiring of her resolve and, for some reason, amused. She did not always understand him, yet she had to admit to herself that, besides her concern for Felix, she did not want Captain Ingram to leave Westwood. He filled a void in her lonely life.

Somehow, against all the odds, he had become a friend.

When word came that Felix had ridden into the stable yard, Constantia hurried there to accost him before he could disappear again. She attacked at once, the wait for his return having increased her indignation at his perfidy.

"Fanny is very unhappy. How can you treat her so? I had not thought you so weak-willed as to crawl like a worm at Mama's and Papa's bidding."

"A worm!" With a repressive glance at an eavesdropping stable boy, Felix drew her through a brick archway into the English garden. "Their disapproval has nothing to do with it."

"They have nothing to disapprove of any more, since you have been treating Fanny like a stranger for three days. This morning, Mama went so far as to commend her neat stitches. Have you changed your mind, Felix, as you did with Lady Sophia?"

He groaned. "I am deeper in love than ever. When I see her I want to . . . well, that's not the sort of thing a fellow can discuss with his sister."

Her face hot, Constantia turned aside to inhale the fragrance of a pink and yellow honeysuckle. Bravely she persevered. "Is that why you are avoiding her? You are afraid of . . . of losing control?"

"Good Lord, no! I hope I have more command over myself than that."

"Then why?"

"Because she doesn't need me any more, Con. I'm telling you this in confidence, mind. It turns out that she and Frank are closely related to the Duke of Oxshott and they have come into a fortune."

"A fortune? And a noble family?" Her mind whirled, but she refused to let herself be distracted. "Then what has she to be miserable about except your determination to avoid her?"

"Perhaps I have been too aloof," he conceded warily. "After all, we are good friends."

"Felix, you dear, blind idiot, she loves you. Did you tell her you love her?"

He thought for a moment. "No," he admitted. "I told her I'd adopt Anita and that I don't care a fig for my parents' opinion. And we were interrupted."

"There you are, then. It is all a stupid misunderstanding, I vow. You wait here in the honeysuckle bower and I shall send her to you."

By the time she found Fanny in the nursery, Constantia's confidence was fading. She had assured Felix that Fanny loved him, but both she and the captain might be wrong. How dreadful if her interference only led to more pain for Felix and a shocking embarrassment for Fanny!

Vickie and Anita were walking about the room with books balanced on their heads, under Miss Bannister's strict but benevolent eye. Vickie's usually boisterous carriage was much in need of improvement, and Anita loved to copy whatever she did. Constantia's arrival made both girls lose their concentration and books at once. They fell into a fit of giggles.

Fanny smiled, but with such an effort that Constantia knew she had to risk trying.

"Fanny, may I have a word with you?"

"Of course." She followed Constantia out into the passage. "Connie, is Frank . . . ?"

"Captain Ingram is better every day. I'm sure he is too much recovered to have a sudden relapse. Fanny, I feel like a horrid busybody but I must speak. My brother . . . You and Felix . . . Oh, dear, I am making a dreadful muddle of this."

Fanny flushed, then turned pale. "Felix?"

"You and he have unfinished business, do you not? He is waiting for you in the English garden. Will you go to him?" she begged, praying that she was doing the right thing.

"The English garden? Waiting for me?"

She seemed so dazed that Constantia gave her a little push. "Go on."

Fanny started towards the stairs at a sedate pace, then suddenly picked up her skirts and began to run. Reassured, Constantia followed.

Now she could concentrate on what Felix had told her about the Ingrams. And she had talked of Felix giving in to persuasion that Fanny was unworthy to be his bride! No wonder the captain had been amused.

Her pace, too, quickened. By the time she reached the long gallery she was positively marching along, her mood as militant as her step.

Constantia was furious.

CHAPTER 6

Frank was half sitting, half leaning against the stone balustrade of the terrace when Lady Constantia came storming out of the house. He'd never have guessed she was capable of such wrath. She had forgotten her bonnet. Lightning flashed in her blue eyes and her face was a thundercloud.

Grinning, he glanced up at the sky and held out his hand, palm up, as if checking for rain.

"Don't laugh at me, you wretch! How could you let me spout away about eligibility like the veriest ninnyhammer when all the time you and Fanny are . . ."

He raised a finger to his lips. "Please! It's a secret. I couldn't tell you because I'd agreed with Fanny not to tell anyone. Roworth let the cat out of the bag, I take it?"

"Yes." She came to stand nearby, beside a great stone urn, angrily nipping sprigs off the trailing lobelia. "If she trusted Felix, you could have trusted me."

"I do trust you. You know that. But it wasn't quite that way." He explained how Felix had interviewed Taggle first, before allowing him to see Fanny, lest he bore a threat rather than a promise.

"So you are wealthy?" The storm had passed as quickly as it had arisen. She plucked a geranium head and thoughtfully denuded it of scarlet petals, one by one. "And related to a duke?"

"So we've been given to understand."

"The Duke of Oxshott, Felix said. Now where have I heard . . . Oh, I know. Oh dear."

"Fanny said she'd heard a story about him recently, from which he emerged as an arrogant, cross-grained blusterer."

"I fear so, and worse, easily bested by Mr Rothschild." She related Felix's story. "You are closely related?"

"Grandchildren of the late duke," Frank confirmed. "Nephew and niece of the villain of your tale."

"Closely related to a duke! But why are you keeping it secret?"

"Is not our new-found uncle's character reason enough?" he teased.

"No. Dukes are permitted to be . . . eccentric. You should disclose the connexion. Mama and Papa will change their tune altogether when they hear."

"Precisely," he said dryly, and saw comprehension flicker in her eyes. He had no desire to distress her by dwelling on her parents' shortcomings. "More to the point, we don't want to start bragging until the lawyer has confirmed Taggle's report."

Constantia laughed. "Very wise. When will you be able to brag?"

"Mr Mackintyre should be here within the week."

"So you do not have to rush off to London. Good."

"As my nurse, would you have allowed me to go?"

"Certainly not — as if you would take the slightest notice of my orders if they did not suit you!" Her face darkened. Dropping the remains of the geranium, she clasped her hands tightly before her. "But perhaps Fanny will wish to leave Westwood. Oh, I do hope I was right to intervene."

Placing his hand reassuringly over hers, he at once realized that her usual chaperon was absent. Suppose he were to kiss those sweet, tender lips, now drooping, just to comfort her?

He had the status of a gentleman now, he

hastily reminded himself, as well as the character of a gentleman. With a quick squeeze, he let his hand fall to the sun-warmed stone of the balustrade and said, "Your only concern was for their happiness and I fail to see how you could have made matters worse than they already were. What happened?"

She described her interviews with Felix and Fanny, her lovely face brightening as she did so.

When she told how Fanny had flown down the stairs, Frank said with a smile, "I wager they'll be smelling of April and May next time we see them."

"If not," Constantia declared, "if they somehow still misunderstand each other, I shall continue to interfere until they come to their senses!"

Though heartened by his encouragement, she was left in a horrid uncertainty for the rest of the afternoon. Not until she was changing for dinner did the pair put in an appearance.

When the knock came upon her dressing-room door, she was in her chemise. Joan draped her Paisley shawl about her before answering the knock.

Fanny swept in, eyes starry, cheeks flushed, radiant. She flung her arms around

Constantia and kissed her. "Bless you, Connie. I can't thank you enough."

"It is all settled?" Constantia grabbed the shawl as it slipped, hugged it around her in an automatic defensive gesture. "I am so very glad. Now you will be my sister." And Frank would be her brother, or near as fourpence to a groat. He was not going to vanish into the great unknown from which he had appeared. The thought was cheering.

"Con, you saved my life." Felix wore a complacent, self-satisfied grin. He, too, kissed his sister's cheek, then reached for Fanny's hand and held on to it as if he'd never let it go. "When Frank described you as a ministering angel, I thought he was exaggerating just a trifle, but I see he spoke no more than the truth."

Constantia blushed. "Without the captain's support, I'd not have been so bold."

"So you two were plotting together against us, were you?"

"*For* you. Have you told him yet?"

"Yes; I had to ask his permission to address his sister — after the event, admittedly."

They all laughed. Joan smiled in sympathy, but she also glanced at the clock.

"Come on, Felix," said Fanny. "We must

change for dinner."

"I'll come and help you in a minute, miss," said the maid, and added in her prim way, "May I be the first to wish you happy?"

"Thank you, Joan." Endearingly impulsive, Fanny kissed the abigail. "Don't tell anyone else, will you, either of you. We've decided to wait until Mr Mackintyre has come."

She and Felix left. Constantia heaved a satisfied sigh.

"I do believe his lordship has chose well, my lady," Joan said, folding the blue shawl and taking up a sea-green dinner gown. "Ever such a nice lady, Miss Ingram is, if a bit free in her ways. But there, it's a hard life she's led and no mistake."

"I suppose every detail of her life is common knowledge in the housekeeper's room, if not the servants' hall," said Constantia resignedly as the gown was placed carefully over her head. "I cannot imagine how, since they brought no servants."

"Not every detail, by no means, my lady. Mr Trevor's not one to spread gossip."

Of course, Felix's valet was the source, having been with him in Brussels, in lodgings with the Ingrams.

Joan fastened the darker green satin ribbon beneath Constantia's breasts, and straightened the falls of Honiton lace that filled the low neckline right up to the throat. Hairbrush in hand, she said casually, "Mr Mackintyre, he'll be the lawyer?"

"Is there anything you don't know?" Constantia had to laugh. So much for secrecy.

"Lots, my lady. That Mr Taggle, close-mouthed as a miser's purse he was. All he'd say was he brought good news, with a nod and a wink and broad hints as 'twas a lawyer sent him after the captain and miss."

"Joan, do my parents know so much?"

"Now, my lady, you ought to know better than that," said the maid severely. "There's none of us will carry tales to his lordship or her ladyship."

"I beg your pardon. Still, you must not mention to anyone my brother's and Miss Ingram's betrothal, if you please."

"As you wish, my lady," Joan agreed with a tolerant glance. "Not that anyone with eyes in their head won't guess, them smelling of April and May like they do."

That was the captain's phrase. Constantia was suddenly impatient to share her delight with him. "My hair will do very well, thank you, Joan," she said. "You may go to Miss Ingram."

She hurried down to the gallery, but to

her disappointment Captain Ingram had already retired to his bed. For a moment she had almost forgotten that he was an invalid.

The week that followed was difficult. Inevitably the earl and countess noticed the improved relations between Felix and Fanny, however circumspect they were. The happy couple were far too happy to pay much heed to remonstrance on the one hand or snubs on the other. Constantia suffered more.

Lady Westwood discovered that she owed morning calls to a dozen acquaintances in the vicinity. Constantia had to accompany her. Lady Westwood had the headache. Constantia was called upon to read to her. Lady Westwood decided that the family's improved finances justified the purchase of new summer gowns for herself and her daughters. Constantia and Vickie drove with her into Bath one hot day, to a fashionable modiste on Milsom Street, and spent hours standing in their chemises being jabbed with pins.

Constantia wore a special chemise Joan had made for such occasions, high-necked, of a stout, opaque linen. The modiste clucked despairingly but, in the face of Constantia's adamant refusal to try a fash-

ionable décolleté, was forced to concede. Fortunately, Lady Westwood did not much care what her daughter wore in the seclusion of the country, as long as it was not positively dowdy. In fact, in view of Captain Ingram's presence at Westwood, at present she was much in favour of modesty of dress.

Still, it was an agitating and tiring occasion. Nor did a visit to her grandmother, a crotchety invalid who never wearied of describing her symptoms, sooth Constantia's ruffled sensibilities. In fact, it added guilt. One ought to love Grandmama, but how difficult it was!

As soon as she arrived home, she changed into a thin, cool muslin chemise and a favourite gentian-blue jaconet evening dress. She took the back stair down to the ground floor and hurried to the gallery.

Despite her enforced absences, she had ensured that Captain Ingram was supplied with frequent refreshments as well as three square meals a day. When she managed to snatch some time with him, she urged him to eat well and exercise, and he had promised to obey. She was glad she had come to know him a little before discovering his noble antecedents. She'd never have ventured to treat an aristocratic gentleman with such an indecorous lack of reserve.

He was out on the terrace, seated on one of the marble benches, a light evening breeze ruffling his brown hair. Seeing Constantia, he stood and bowed.

"I'm sorry I don't have a plumed hat to flourish," he said with a smile.

"Who cares for plumed hats! I am just pleased that you are able to bow now without falling flat, and surprised that you recall my gooseish comment." She sat down on the end of the bench and he joined her.

"Not gooseish at all, since it was intended to set me at my ease. The very first thing you ever said to me. How could I forget?" He studied her face. "You look tired."

"I have had the horridest day, but we shall not talk of that, if you please. You do not look tired, which is more to the point. You are feeling well today? Have you been drinking your stout-and-milk?"

"Religiously." He grimaced. "I confess I'm growing rather sick of it. It tastes more like medicine every day."

"You may stop drinking it when you can walk as far as the fountain and back." She pointed to the far end of the Italian garden.

"I'm game." He rose. "Can you go with me?"

"Yes. Mama will have just gone up to change for dinner and I have already changed. I have at least half an hour before she comes down. Are you sure you wish to go so far? You usually retire at this hour."

"Nothing venture, nothing gain."

He descended the broad, shallow stone steps without difficulty and together they strolled along the straight gravel path. On either side, ill-weeded beds of heavy-scented lilies were surrounded by low, ragged box hedges, a columnar cypress at each corner. Here and there ground ivy and chickweed encroached on the path. The statue of Apollo in the centre of one square bed had greenish patches of lichen in the nooks and crannies of his person.

The mechanism of the fountain ahead of them had failed two summers past. A pair of sadly dry dolphins cavorted above a marble basin filled with scummy rainwater.

"The garden is not at its best," Constantia apologized. "It has been sadly neglected this age, but Papa says he will soon be able to hire more gardeners."

"To tell the truth, I don't greatly care for this style of garden," the captain admitted. "It's too formal for my taste, or would be if it were properly trimmed."

"I much prefer the English garden, at the other end of the house. If I had a garden it would all be like that, with winding paths and all sorts of flowers, scattered about, not in rows, and a honeysuckle arbour. Besides," she added on a practical note, "it does not show neglect half so badly."

He laughed. "I hope you will have your garden one day."

As they reached the fountain, she examined him covertly, wondering whether to suggest that he rest awhile on its broad marble rim. His step had slowed, but his cheeks had a healthy colour. He looked well, not to say contented.

They circled the fountain. Turning back along the way they had come, they saw Anita running towards them.

"Uncle Frank! Aunt Connie! I've come to say goodnight."

She sped full-tilt at the captain, arms held out, as if she expected to be picked up and swung into the air. He opened his arms to catch her. Constantia saw his jaw tighten with pain as he clasped the child to him. He made no attempt to pick her up.

His strength increased every day, yet whatever ailed his shoulders still troubled him. She recalled Fanny's telling her that he might be crippled but for Mrs Cohen's medical skill. Jewess or no, Miriam Cohen should henceforth be mentioned nightly in her prayers, Constantia vowed.

In the meantime, she must check that the captain was performing his prescribed exercises regularly.

He and Anita were contemplating the dolphins. "Why has those fishes got holes in their heads?" Anita enquired with interest.

"Partly because they're a fountain," he explained. "I imagine the water spouts up from their heads?"

"It is supposed to," Constantia confirmed.

"And partly because dolphins are animals, not fish, though they live in the sea. When they come up for air, they breathe through those holes. A sailor told me a story about dolphins . . ."

"Tell me, tell me!" Anita begged.

The captain smiled at Constantia and gestured at the fountain's rim. "Will you be seated, Lady Constantia?"

She regarded the dirt-spattered marble doubtfully, then realized that if she did not sit, he would not. He might be more tired than he appeared.

He was before her, spreading a handkerchief. She sat, Anita settled beside her, and he beside the child, who leaned one elbow on his knee and gazed earnestly up into his face. He told her an exciting tale of a shipwrecked sailor who was borne up by dolphins and carried to an island, where he lived on coconuts until the dolphins led a ship to rescue him.

As he finished, the nurserymaid called from the terrace. "Miss Anita, it's bedtime and past!"

She gave them each a kiss and scampered off. Constantia and the captain followed more slowly. In the evening light, the geraniums in their urns glowed vivid red and the lobelia had a rich, purplish cast. Like flame, the sun reflected from the mansion's windows, row upon row. The lilies scented the air with a languid fragrance. Somewhere in the park beyond the garden, a nightingale sang.

Reaching the steps, Constantia turned her head to glance up at the captain. He was gazing down at her with a contemplative air, a slight smile curving his resolute mouth.

She looked away quickly, her breath catching. He laid his hand on her arm.

"No more milk-and-stout!" he said.

Constraint banished, she laughed and they went into the long gallery.

Felix and Fanny had already come down and were entertaining the vicar and his wife and the curate. Constantia had forgotten that the vicarage party were dining at Westwood. She left Felix to perform introductions before Captain Ingram retired to his chamber.

The sight of the curate fixing her as always with his languishing gaze had reminded her of Miss Bannister's advice on how to discourage him. "Avoid tête-à-têtes and strolls in the garden," the governess had said, "and never ask after his health." Where Mr Jones was concerned, Constantia had followed her advice to the letter.

Where the captain was concerned, she had done precisely the opposite.

Not that she cared. She was not trying to discourage Frank Ingram. After all, he never sent languishing glances her way, she thought a little sadly.

The next morning Mr Mackintyre arrived.

Constantia had escaped Lady Westwood's surveillance by retreating to a back scullery to arrange flowers. Mama was not to know that the last vase, delphiniums and marguerites, was delivered to the long gallery. She had just straightened a few blooms, topped up the water with her little watering can, and sat down to talk to the captain when the lawyer was announced.

Captain Ingram, asking the butler to inform his sister and Lord Roworth, rose to greet Mr Mackintyre. He was a short, tubby, energetic man with a jovial face between bushy white sidewhiskers, not at all what Constantia expected of a lawyer, or a Scot. However, he shook the captain's hand with all the solicitous care she could have demanded of him.

"My dear Captain, I am delighted to see you up and about. That rogue Taggle had you confined to your bed, if not at death's door." He had the very slightest of Scottish accents, a faint rolling of the rrrs.

"Captain Ingram has been very ill," said Constantia proprietorially, "but he is rapidly recovering. I am Lady Constantia Roworth. How do you do, sir. I expect I ought to leave you to your business."

"No, stay," the captain urged. "Lady Constantia is aware of the facts of the matter, Mr Mackintyre, and her brother, Lord Roworth, is to marry my sister."

"Splendid! Simply splendid!" The lawyer beamed and rubbed his hands. He could not have appeared more elated had he arranged the match himself. "We shall wait for his lordship and Miss Ingram, then."

He put on a pair of gold rimmed spectacles, took a sheaf of papers from his valise and started to leaf through them. Constantia, on tenterhooks, saw that Frank was tense, a trifle pale. His entire future depended on what Mr Mackintyre had to say, though surely the inheritance must be substantial. The lawyer would not have travelled all this way for a pittance.

Bethinking herself of her duty as a hostess, she offered him refreshments and ordered madeira and tea. A glass of wine would do the captain good, she decided.

She had just poured each of the gentlemen a glass, and tea for herself, when Felix and Fanny came in. Her natural self-confidence restored by her certainty of Felix's love, Fanny had proved to be a lively, cheerful young lady. Constantia admired her sunny temper and friendly openness.

A spring in her step, Fanny crossed the gallery and presented to Mr Mackintyre two documents, which he studied with care.

"Excellent," he said, "quite excellent. Taggle has his faults, but he knows his business, my dear Miss Ingram. He has informed you of your relationship to his grace, the Duke of Oxshott, I believe, and given you some idea of the nature of your inheritance?"

"We'd be glad of your confirmation, sir," said Frank bluntly.

The lawyer regarded him over the top of his spectacles. "Of course, Captain. Your mother was the second daughter of the late

Duke of Oxshott, sister of the present duke." He selected a paper from his sheaf.

The numbers he read meant little to Constantia, but watching Frank's face she could tell that his hopes were met, or exceeded. In fact, by the end of the recital, both he and Fanny appeared a trifle stunned. Constantia refilled his glass.

Felix looked positively grim. "I've no wish to figure as a fortune-hunter," he said. "I suppose you can arrange to settle everything on my wife and her children, Mr Mackintyre? Including the child we intend to adopt."

"Naturally, my lord. I shall be happy to meet with you and Captain Ingram at any time to discuss the disposition . . ."

"Fustian!" Fanny exclaimed. "I shall decide what to do with my money."

"I'll not stand in your way, m'dear," said Frank, grinning.

"Fanny darling, you shall decide except that I absolutely refuse —"

Fanny opened her mouth to interrupt.

Mr Mackintyre's gentle cough stopped the argument in its tracks. "The matter can be resolved at another time and place," he suggested. "To continue, there are two small estates in Hampshire. The late duke acquired them when a distant relative, owner of Upfield Grange, married his neighbour, who subsequently inherited Heathcote from her father, the couple dying without issue."

"Never mind the history," said Frank impatiently.

"It is relevant, Captain," the lawyer said with a reproachful glance. "Upfield Grange is separated from Heathcote by another small property. The late duke wished to purchase this property, combining the three into one estate of considerable size, worthy of a more impressive house than either of the two existing manors. Though the owner of the intervening property proved recalcitrant, his grace continued to hope that the son might sell. He therefore refused to permit any expenditure on repairs to the existing manors."

"You mean we've inherited a pair of ruins?" Frank asked. Constantia could not guess whether he was amused or dismayed.

"By no means, Captain," said Mr Mackintyre. "Both estates — Upfield has three tenant farms and Heathcote two — produce some slight income, though the duke's agent only visits two or three times a year. They could, I am told, make a good return with the application of modern agricultural methods. However, both parks and gardens have been woefully neglected. Upfield Grange, where the couple to whom I alluded resided, is habitable."

"And Heathcote?" Fanny demanded.

"The house at Heathcote, I fear, will require considerable funds to render it fit to be lived in. Your income will permit restoration of the houses and parks, but unless you realize a part of your capital, which I cannot advise, you will be unable to afford both that and an entry into the first circles of Society."

"Society!" Fanny and Frank looked at each other and burst out laughing. Constantia had to smile, but Felix said almost angrily, "As my wife, Miss Ingram will most certainly take her place in Society."

Fanny patted his arm. "Of course, love. It just sounded such a ridiculous choice when Frank and I have never had a home of our own."

Again Mr Mackintyre intervened with a gentle cough. "There is one more regrettable circumstance which I feel it my duty to draw to your attention. Naturally I have informed the present Duke of Oxshott of my success in finding his sister's heirs. His grace, unhappily, had convinced himself that I should fail. He told me, in . . . er . . . no uncertain terms, that he regards both

127

monies and real property as his own."

"The devil he does!" Frank looked as if he was about to jump to his feet and Constantia wondered if the second glass of madeira had been such a good idea after all. But she saw that he had not touched it. He noticed her glance, flushed, and said, "I beg your pardon, Lady Constantia. My tongue ran away with me in the heat of the moment."

"Most understandable, Captain Ingram." She gave him a forgiving smile and turned to Mr Mackintyre. "Surely, sir, the duke cannot prevent our friends' inheriting?"

"If it should come to a legal battle, ma'am, I shall be obliged — most reluctantly! — to represent the duke. However I have made and shall continue to make the most forceful representations to his grace that he has nothing to gain from taking the matter to court. Having made exhaustive enquiries as to your antecedents, Captain, Miss Ingram, I am perfectly satisfied that you are the legitimate offspring of the late Lady Frances Kerridge. I drew up the will myself, and I am not accustomed to having my wills overturned in Chancery, I assure you. All that his grace can expect from public scrutiny is public broadcast of the late duke's . . . er . . . intemperate language."

"Nincompoop," said Frank with a broad grin.

"Taggle, I presume?" Mr Mackintyre sighed. "Taggle must be admitted to have his occasional lapses from perfect discretion."

"This is all very well," Felix said impatiently, "but I have reason to know that the present Duke of Oxshott is no more temperate in his language than was his sire. I will not have my betrothed subjected to his abuse."

Fanny took his hand. "My dear, I'm not such a weakling that harsh words will shatter my bones."

"No," he said with a rueful smile, "but you must give me leave to protect you now."

The loving look that passed between them constricted Constantia's heart. She had believed herself resigned to never knowing the joy of a loving husband, but their happiness reawoke the pain. Her hand crept up unconsciously to press against her chest where the hidden ugliness lay.

The lawyer called them all back to business. "We must hope his grace will heed the dictates of reason. For the present, I have a great many documents which need signing."

At Felix's suggestion, he, Mr Mackintyre, and the Ingrams repaired to the library where papers could be spread on the long table. Constantia could not help feeling excluded, though she had no conceivable reason to go with them. After telling the butler that Mr Mackintyre would stay to luncheon and Captain Ingram would eat with everyone else in the dining-room, she went up to the schoolroom.

Finding the schoolroom party about to walk down to the stream, Anita's favourite place, she decided to join them. She fetched a bonnet and gloves and met them in the great hall.

Vickie and Anita dashed ahead across the grass, hand in hand, skirts, ribbons, black hair and blond flying.

"I fear Lady Victoria will never attain your self-restraint and poise, Lady Constantia," said Miss Bannister with a sigh. "Sometimes I wonder whether anything I say has even the slightest effect on her conduct."

Constantia was about to console the governess with the likelihood that Vickie would suddenly recall every precept when she made her come-out under Lady Westwood's stern eye. Then she realized that Vickie's emancipation from the schoolroom would force Miss Bannister to seek a new post. Whatever the difficulties of her present situation, that could hardly be a pleasant prospect.

But Anita was nearly old enough to need a governess, and Fanny and Frank were now in a position to hire one. Indeed, Felix meant to adopt the child and would certainly expect to have a governess for her. She already knew and liked Miss Bannister. What could be better?

Not wanting to raise any false hopes, she resolved to say nothing until Felix and the Ingrams had been consulted. However, she saw no reason to keep their news a secret any longer.

Like the rest of the household, Miss Bannister had been expecting to hear that Felix and Fanny were betrothed. The Ingrams' inheritance was more of a surprise, though everyone knew that an odd little man had brought them good news and they were presently closeted with a lawyer.

"Two estates as well as a fortune?" she said. "No doubt they will leave Westwood very soon, then. Lady Victoria will be sadly distressed to lose her little companion. I daresay Lord and Lady Roworth will live at her estate when they are married?"

"Perhaps . . . I daresay . . . I don't know." Constantia's heart sank. In her pleasure at the Ingrams' good fortune, she had not considered their next actions. Of course they would wish to see their properties at once. Mr Mackintyre had said one house was habitable, and the captain was well enough for the short journey into Hampshire.

A short journey, but for Constantia too far. Felix and Fanny probably would choose to live there — Fanny had had a poor enough welcome at Westwood. No doubt Constantia would be invited to visit them, and when she was there she might expect to see Frank occasionally.

Desolate, she felt she had already lost a friend.

CHAPTER 7

The cold luncheon spread on the sideboard was lavish and appetising, but Frank was too weary to appreciate the sight. If he had guessed signing papers could be so arduous, he'd not have agreed to join the others for the informal meal.

Except that Fanny needed his support. Roworth was going to announce their betrothal and the Ingrams' newly discovered connexions. He had arranged for Lady Victoria to be present, and had even ordered champagne.

Sinking into a chair at the table, Frank hoped his future brother-in-law was not going to take it into his head to challenge his parents. If he told the earl and countess of the engagement first, before they learned that Fanny was the wealthy granddaughter of a duke, fur would fly. Frank felt too tired to face a brangle, and he didn't want his sister hurt.

Too late to give Felix a hint. Lord and Lady Westwood entered the room and instantly the temperature dropped several degrees. Even Vickie stopped chattering. The atmosphere cooled still further when Mr Mackintyre was presented to them. A lawyer to take luncheon with the family!

If they were puzzled as well as offended by his presence, neither deigned to enquire the reason.

Fanny brought Frank a plate of cold meat, bread, and cheese, and sat down beside him. He was about to eat, hoping to recruit his strength, when Lady Constantia came in.

Her dispirited face jolted him. She'd been happy for him and Fanny. What had happened to distress her?

She looked at him, and at once her expression changed to concern. His weariness must be as obvious to her as to his sister. Not for the first time, he wondered at the joining of so much compassionate sympathy with such loveliness. Beauties were supposed to be spoiled and selfish. He smiled at her and started to eat, knowing she'd be pleased and reassured.

As soon as Lady Constantia had served herself and sat down at the table, Felix rose from his place beside Fanny. "Mama, Father, Vickie, it gives me the greatest pleasure to acquaint you with capital news."

The earl frowned. The countess's pale, chilly eyes grew icy. Evidently they expected to hear of a betrothal between their only son and an insignificant nobody.

Lady Victoria clapped her hands. "Do tell, Felix."

"First," he continued, "Mr Mackintyre has been kind enough to come down from London —" He paused, and Frank guessed he was enjoying his mother and father's bafflement at the lawyer's part in the affair. Thank heaven he'd decided to make that report first. "— from London, to confirm that my dear friends, Captain and Miss Ingram, are the grandchildren of the late Duke of Oxshott."

"A duke!" Lady Victoria squealed, drawing all eyes. "Oh, splendid!"

Lord Westwood appeared frankly flabbergasted. If Lady Westwood had lost her countenance, she had already recovered enough to reprimand her younger daughter.

"Victoria, pray restrain your enthusiasm." She turned to Frank and Fanny. Her own enthusiasm, if any, was so restrained as to be undetectable, but though there was no warmth in her look or tone, the iciness had thawed to mere hauteur. "Captain, Miss Ingram, allow me to felicitate you on this singular discovery."

Frank and Fanny murmured their acknowledgement of her condescension.

"Oxshott, hey?" said Lord Westwood, almost genial. "The present duke is your uncle?"

"He is, sir." Frank wondered whether Felix was going to disclose their inheritance, or if he himself should. Perhaps money was not an acceptable topic. He foresaw an unexpected need to learn the complexities of fully-fledged gentlemanhood.

"The Ingrams are Lady Frances Kerridge's children," Mr Mackintyre informed the earl. "His late grace left them two estates and a pretty penny besides," he added.

Lord Westwood ignored all but his first words, thus proving to Frank that lawyers, like artillery officers, dwelled on the fringes of gentlemandom. "Lady Frances Kerridge," he mused. "I recall . . ."

Felix, probably for the first time in his life, interrupted his father. "I beg your pardon, sir, but I have a further announcement, to me infinitely more important." He looked down at Fanny with a smile of such warmth and tenderness that Frank had to close his eyes and fight down his envy of their love. "Miss Fanny Ingram has done me the inexpressible honour of agreeing to be my wife."

Lady Victoria thrust back her chair, jumped up, and ran round the table to hug her brother and kiss Fanny. "Splendiferous!" she crowed. "Anita will be my sister."

"Near enough," said Felix indulgently.

The Westwoods offered their more temperate good wishes, and Felix called for the champagne. He prevailed upon his mother to allow Vickie a taste and Constantia a glass of the sparkling wine. The earl forestalled Frank in calling for a toast, and they all drank to the health, happiness, and prosperity of the betrothed couple. Felix and Fanny, arms entwined, drank to each other.

Constantia blinked away tears, blaming them on the champagne bubbles. Frank was regarding her with concern. She smiled at him, raised her glass, and silently mouthed, "Your health!"

"Your happiness," he silently replied, and they both sipped their wine.

She was a peagoose to fear losing a friend. Whatever happened, she could not expect to go on seeing him daily for ever. Without his inheritance, without his sister's engagement to her brother, she might never have seen him again once he left Westwood. Now he was going to be part of the family. She would seize any chance she was offered to visit Fanny and Felix in their new home.

As everyone returned to their luncheons, Felix said, "We have decided to leave the day after tomorrow to inspect the estates Fanny and Ingram have inherited." He explained the situation to his parents.

So soon! Constantia thought, dismayed.

"Miss Ingram has no chaperon," Lady Westwood pointed out. "Not even so much as an abigail, I collect."

"I have always managed very well without, ma'am," said Fanny.

"Indeed! But now you are connected with one of the first families of the realm and betrothed to my son."

"Fanny is under my protection," Frank said firmly.

"In her present circumstances a brother is insufficient," the countess rebuked him with a frigid glance all too familiar to Constantia. "Miss Ingram requires a female companion."

Fanny turned eagerly to Constantia. "Connie, will you come? I have been wishing for your company, though I didn't like to invite you until we have set the houses in order."

"A splendid notion," said Felix.

"Please, do come, Lady Constantia." The

captain's voice was quiet but his sincerity decided her.

"I should love to go with you," she said.

"You most certainly shall not," her mother at once forbade her. "It is out of the question."

Perhaps emboldened by the champagne, Constantia argued. "I shall take Joan, Mama, and Felix will be there."

"I'll go, too, Connie." Vickie entered the lists, unabashed by the lack of an invitation. "I can help to look after Anita."

"Then Miss Bannister shall go with us, to chaperon us all," said Constantia triumphantly — and quickly, before her mother could squash the proposal so thoroughly it was beyond reviving.

Lady Westwood's next protest suggested a weakening resistance. "I hardly suppose, Constantia, that having invited you the Ingrams will be eager to accommodate your sister and a retinue."

"They will be most welcome," Fanny assured her, "if there is sufficient room at Upfield Grange." She looked an enquiry at Mr Mackintyre.

"Plenty of room, Miss Ingram, plenty of room."

"Lady Westwood," Frank added his plea, "I shall be most grateful if you will permit your daughters to accompany Fanny. Quite apart from the need of a chaperon, I know my sister will be glad of feminine company."

The countess looked from him to Constantia, then exchanged a significant glance with her husband. "Very well, you may both go for a short visit, until it is time to prepare for the Little Season."

Even as she rejoiced, Constantia had qualms. She was sure her mother hoped that the captain, now well-connected and wealthy, might offer to take her recalcitrant daughter off her hands. Constantia had no reason to suppose he liked her well enough to want to marry her. She prayed he would not propose, for if he did she would have to refuse and she could not bear to hurt him.

Grey rain pattered on the roof of the Westwoods' landau as it turned, squelching, from the muddy lane into the equally muddy drive of Upfield Grange. An avenue of elms dripped on either side. One had fallen, doubtless some time past for no leaves showed green on the bare branches of its crown and the exposed roots were washed clean of soil.

"I'm surprised no one has used that for timber," said Frank, peering out into the gloom, "or at least for firewood."

Constantia smiled at him, glad that the evidence of neglect did not depress his spirits. He had borne the journey very well, sitting up rather than reclining on the seat, which was fortunate as Vickie and Miss Bannister shared the carriage. Anita spent half her time with them, too, alternating with Felix's new phaeton.

"I daresay the duke would have had anyone transported who was so bold as to appropriate his wood," Constantia suggested, "even if he did not want it himself."

"Or hanged, drawn, and quartered," Vickie proposed with relish, bringing a faint protest from her governess. Travel disagreed with Miss Bannister; she was out of curl though they had taken two leisurely days to cover the eighty miles.

"Bloodthirsty wench," Frank said with a grin. "My grandfather may have been a tyrant, but things are going to change now that I'm master here. I hope there's good fishing," he added as they crossed a bridge over a murky stream.

"You have definitely decided that you shall have Upfield Grange, and Fanny Heathcote?" Constantia asked.

"Simply because your mama insists it's not proper for Fanny to play hostess to her betrothed, and the Grange is in better repair for immediate occupancy. So I shall be your host."

"I wager Mama didn't like that much either," Vickie observed.

"She didn't, but apparently it's acceptable since Fanny, your brother, and Miss Bannister will be in residence. I don't believe I'll ever really understand the ins and outs of propriety."

"It sometimes seems a great deal of fuss over nothing," Constantia agreed. "Thank heaven she gave her permission before she realized precisely what is involved. Oh, look, here is the house. Good gracious!"

The landau jolted to a halt before a large house in the most fantastical Gothic style. Towers and turrets, battlements and buttresses, arched windows and oriel windows, even gargoyles leering down from the roof parapet, nothing was missing.

Heedless of the rain, Vickie jumped down from the carriage, not waiting for the footman to descend from his damp perch to let down the step. "Oh!" she breathed in an ecstasy, "isn't it heavenly? Does it not bring to mind mad monks and persecuted maidens? I'm sure you must have a ghost, Captain, or even two!"

Frank went off into peals of helpless laughter. Constantia eyed him uncertainly, wondering if he were more tired than she had supposed and growing hysterical.

With a gasp, he stopped laughing and said, "To think I expected to retire to an unobtrusive life in a modest country manor! Anyone residing in that must surely be destined to figure as either an ogre or a sorcerer — or possibly a mad monk."

"Or an enchanted prince, or an Arthurian knight," Constantia proposed. "It is certainly neither unobtrusive nor modest. Vickie, you will be soaked to the skin. Run to the porch at once. I cannot wait to see inside."

Vickie scampered across the potholed, weed-grown gravel to the shelter of the porch, the open-arched ground floor of a tower superimposed on the façade of the central block. There she seized in both hands a massive iron door-knocker in the form of a dragon's head. With it, she beat a zestful tattoo.

By the time Thomas had escorted the rest of the travellers under his black umbrella to the porch, the iron-studded and banded door was slowly creaking open. A small, balding man in a rusty black coat peered at them myopically.

"Us wasn't expecting so many," he quavered in a voice full of doubt.

Frank looked as if he was about to dissolve in laughter again, so Constantia took charge.

"I am Lady Constantia Roworth," she said briskly, moving forward so that the butler — if such he claimed to be — was forced to retreat. "You must have received the letters regarding our coming, and in any case I am sure my brother and Miss Ingram have arrived already. They were well ahead of us upon the highway."

"They'm come," he conceded grudgingly.

"Are there dungeons?" Vickie demanded.

"For heaven's sake, Vickie, the dungeons can wait. Miss Bannister is unwell, and I for one want nothing so much as a cup of tea."

"And tea you shall have," Fanny promised, emerging from an archway, "if you don't mind drinking it in the kitchen. The drawing-room is all in holland covers, and goodness knows what is under them. Frank, are you . . . yes, you look well but you ought to sit down. My dear Miss Bannister, pray come and see if a cup of tea will not revive you. The kettle is on the hob."

Before following the others through the archway, Constantia threw a glance around the chamber they had entered from the porch. To her delight, it was a Tudor Great Hall, smaller than Westwood's had been, but with all the proper appurtenances: elaborately carved panelling, chimneypiece, and staircase; high, vaulted ceiling; and a gallery around three sides. On either side of the entrance tower, tall, leaded windows under pointed arches admitted a minimum of dull daylight through their grimy diamond panes. The woodwork was dingy, sadly in need of polish, and cobwebs hung from the gallery and ceiling beams, but that could be put to rights.

Frank was waiting for her by the archway under the gallery at one end of the hall. "I'm sorry," he said, chagrined, as they proceeded along a dusty corridor. "I'd not have dragged you here for the world had I known what a shocking state the place is in."

"I'd not have missed it for the world. The Gothic façade must be a quite recent addition since the hall is undoubtedly sixteenth-century, and just what I particularly like."

"Is it, truly?" he asked, gratified. "It looks deuced — dashed — grim to me. Not that I haven't been in some odd lodgings in my time, but I daresay Westwood and Nettle-dene have raised my expectations! To have to invite you to take tea in the kitchen is mortifying, to say the least."

She touched his arm consolingly. "You will

need to hire servants, that is all. There are bound to be women in the village who will like to earn extra money by coming in to help put everything in order to start with."

"Mackintyre did warn us there is no one but an elderly couple, Mr and Mrs Biddle, as caretakers. I had not realized, though, just how much care a house needs. I'm glad you are come, for Fanny won't have the least notion how to go about hiring servants."

Constantia was pleased that he took it for granted she would assist his sister, but she said doubtfully, "I will do what I can. Our housekeeper and butler hire most of our indoor servants. Though Mama had me attend several interviews, some years ago, so that I would know how to go about it, the only servant I have ever chosen myself is my abigail, Joan."

"That's more than Fanny's ever done. Where does one start?"

"With the vicar's wife. She will know of respectable people in need of work."

"Let's hope the vicar is married, then. Oh Lord, I've just thought: if Mackintyre judges this place habitable, what condition do you suppose the house at Heathcote is in?"

At that moment they reached the kitchen. The spotless cosiness of the large room suggested that the Biddles spent most of their time there, but just now they seemed to have vanished. Miss Bannister was already seated at the well-scrubbed whitewood table, where Anita knelt on a chair with bread-and-jam in her hand and jam on her face. Vickie wandered about exclaiming over bright copper pans, wooden spoons, and other kitchen equipment unfamiliar to the daughter of an earl. At the wide fireplace, Fanny was swinging a hook bearing a steaming kettle off the fire.

The young footman, also steaming by the fire, sprang to help her. Felix was there first, potholders in hand.

"Do you remember, Fanny," he said, lifting the kettle, "how once in Brussels I went to the kitchen to ask Henriette for tea and I claimed to be domesticated? You told me I must learn to make the tea for myself. The moment has come. What do I do next?"

Fanny laughed, plainly not in the least dispirited by her surroundings. "The teapot is already warmed and the tea-leaves measured into it, so all you need do is pour on the water. Connie, Frank, do sit down. Are you hungry? I can offer bread and jam."

"So we see," said Frank, grinning at Anita.

"It's good jam, Uncle Frank." Catching a drip, she licked her hand.

Soon they were all seated about the table with cups of tea, except Thomas, who bashfully accepted a mug but continued to stand steaming at the fire.

"Well," said Frank, regarding his guests with a rueful air, "what can I say but welcome to Upfield Grange? I believe I can safely promise you all an unusual visit."

They were laughing when Biddle reappeared. He was accompanied by a little old woman, bent with rheumatism, in a white cap and a grey gown with the wide, quilted skirts of a former age. Peering around the company, he spotted Frank and marched up to him, his wife in tow.

"You be Cap'n Ingram, the new master, sir?"

"That's right."

"Us can't do it, sir, not nohow." He made a helpless gesture at the horde invading his haven. "Us be caretakers, sir, me and the missis, not butlers and housemaids and cooks and such."

Mrs Biddle nodded her crooked head and a tear trickled down her wrinkled cheek.

Frank took her hand in his. "My dear Mrs Biddle, you shan't be expected to do anything beyond your strength. I hope you and Biddle will consent to stay and help as you can until I'm able to hire a proper staff, but whenever you choose to go, you shall have a pension."

Constantia, sitting beyond Frank, saw the light of hope enter the old woman's faded eyes. "Us'll help, sir, to be sure." She faltered. " 'Ee won't bawl at un, like his grace do? I han't made up but two beds yet, sir."

"Fanny," Constantia exclaimed, eyeing the twisted hand engulfed in Frank's, "surely you and Vickie and I can make up the beds ourselves?"

Frank's look of gratitude was reward enough for any amount of unpleasant labour.

"Oh yes!" Vickie appeared to regard the whole situation as a splendid adventure. "You'll have to show us how, Fanny."

"It won't take long."

"Joan should be here soon, too," said Constantia, "with the luggage, and your man, Felix."

"I shouldn't dare ask Trevor to make beds," her brother declared.

Fanny wrinkled her nose at him. "No, he is quite the most disobliging person. Mrs Biddle, have the linens been aired?"

"Oh, aye, miss, that they have."

"Excellent. Thomas, if you are nearly dry, pray carry —" She stopped as the kitchen's back door opened.

The Westwoods' coachman and Felix's new groom came in, the former with a decidedly grumpy expression. Though he seemed a trifle abashed to find the kitchen full of gentry, he addressed Felix in no uncertain terms. "Beggin' your pardon, m'lord, but them stables is fit for neither man nor beast."

Felix grimaced, then gave Frank an apologetic look. "I know," he said to the coachman, "but you are to return to Westwood tomorrow with the landau. Dutton, have you managed to make my pair reasonably comfortable?"

Before the groom could answer, young Thomas stepped forward. "Please, my lord," he cried, "Don't make me go back to Westwood. My lady!" He turned to Constantia and begged, "Let me stay. I asked special to be let come to serve you. I'll do anything, honest. I'll make beds or . . . or even clean out the stables."

Astonished, touched, even a little flattered, Constantia said, "Yes, you may stay, Thomas. Felix, did not Mama say Fanny and Vickie and I must take a footman to wait upon us?"

"She did." He grinned. "However, I believe what she had in mind was your consequence, not my horses' comfort."

Frank groaned. "If anything is certain," he said, "it's that Lady Westwood would never have let you come, Lady Constantia, if she'd had the slightest notion of the state of things at Upfield Grange."

Constantia smiled at him. "So we can only be grateful, Captain, that she did not know."

By the next morning, Constantia's theoretical knowledge of running a large household and Fanny's practical experience of providing necessary comforts had together resulted in a plan. Frank's house was to be refurbished from attic to cellar. To start with, Felix had agreed to drive them into King's Wallop, the nearest village, to call at the vicarage.

It had taken the efforts of both ladies to persuade Felix to postpone riding over to Heathcote to inspect his and Fanny's future home. Their efforts had been less successful where Frank himself was concerned. He refused to spend the morning abed, recuperating from the journey. Thomas and Dutton had carried a chaise longue out to a sheltered corner of the overgrown courtyard garden behind the house, and there the captain consented to recline in the sun. Constantia and Fanny left him poring over an account of Upfield's tenants and rents that Mr Mackintyre had given him.

Miss Bannister, still suffering from a slight headache, was resting in her chamber at their insistence. Vickie had taken Anita off to explore the house.

Having put on their gloves and bonnets, the ladies descended the three steps from the bedroom passage to the gallery, crossed the gallery towards the main stairs down to the hall. Voices came from below, where Anita and Vickie were studying the wonders of the ornately carved chimneypiece.

"Look, Aunt Vickie, there's swans. I like giving bread to swans."

"We'll have to see if we can find some near here," said Vickie. "Look at these little tiny fishes."

"Bless her." Fanny squeezed Constantia's hand. "And bless you, too. What should I do without the two of you?"

"We are both enjoying ourselves immensely. You cannot imagine how wonderful it is to have something useful to do."

As they approached the head of the stairs, the great oak front door crashed open. The man in riding dress who appeared on the threshold was so large, his posture so belligerent, that Constantia would not have been surprised had he roared, "Fee, fi, fo,

fum, I smell the blood of an Englishman."
Had not Frank said the Grange resembled
an ogre's abode?

"Where is he?" bellowed the unpoetical
ogre, glaring around the hall.

Vickie emerged from under the gallery,
her bluebell-sprigged white muslin already
dusty around the hem. "I don't know who
you are looking for," she snapped, "but I
wish you will go away. You're frightening
Anita."

"No, he's not," Anita piped up bravely.
"My daddy was a so'jer."

"I've no desire to frighten women and
children." The ogre had ceased to roar, but
he added in a fiercely threatening tone, "You
can tell him that if he sets foot on my
property he'll be shot on sight."

Constantia clutched Fanny's arm. "It
must be your uncle, the duke," she whispered in horror, "and he is after your
brother's blood!"

CHAPTER 8

"I shan't tell him anything of the sort." Vickie's belligerence equalled the ogre's. "It's his property, the lawyer said so. I daresay he could shoot you, or at least have you thrown in gaol."

"Lawyer!" The ogre sounded aghast. He stepped forward. "What trumped-up roguery is the villain up to now?"

As the light fell on his scowling face, Fanny said, "He's no older than I am, nearer your age, Connie, much too young to be my uncle. Sir," she called, starting down the stairs, "pray calm yourself. I believe you and Lady Victoria are at cross purposes."

"Cross purposes?" The young giant ran a bewildered hand through his dark hair. He looked from Fanny to Constantia, a step behind her, then to Vickie and Anita, and back to Fanny. "Lady Victoria? And who the deuce are you, ma'am? Begging your pardon."

"I am Fanny Ingram. My brother is the new owner of Upfield Grange. And you, I collect, own the property between here and Heathcote?"

"I do," he growled, "at least, so I supposed until . . . Lady Victoria? . . . said that the duke's lawyer —"

"I thought you were the duke!" Vickie went off into a fit of giggles.

He grinned at her sheepishly. "No, ma'am, just the squire. Sir George Berman, of Netherfield." He bowed, then added with a return to pugnacity, "And I'm not selling!"

They took Sir George out to the courtyard garden. He required considerable re-assurance from Frank and Fanny before he believed that neither had any designs upon Netherfield. The Ingrams' inheriting Up-field and Heathcote was a godsend for him, as he did not scruple to say. The late duke had plagued first his father and then himself mercilessly, and the present duke continued the harassment.

Constantia had scarcely recovered from her alarm on taking Sir George for the duke when she heard this evidence of his grace's implacable nature. All his hostility must now be directed at the Ingrams. She could only hope that he might think twice about persecuting them when he learned of their coming close connection with her own noble family. Surely Felix would be able to protect Fanny, and Frank, too, until he recovered his full strength.

She looked at the captain and smiled. He was laughing as he waved a handful of papers at the squire. "I wager you're the very person I need, Sir George. I know nothing of estate management and I cannot make head nor tail of this twaddle. I'll pick your brains if you'll give me half a chance."

"So shall I," said Felix, who had joined them in the courtyard in search of his passengers when the phaeton was ready to go. "I daresay you have a fair idea of the condition of Heathcote?"

Sir George, an ingenuous young man when not incensed, flushed with pleasure. "I do know this area and the land pretty well," he said modestly. "I'll be glad to advise you."

Both Frank and Felix at once started to question him.

"Felix," Constantia expostulated, "you promised to take us into the village."

Her brother waved a dismissive hand. "In a minute."

"Or an hour," said Fanny with a resigned shrug. "Well, I for one don't mean to spend another night in a chamber where every blink raises a cloud of dust. Come on, Connie, Dutton shall drive us."

As they headed for the stables, Constantia glanced back. Frank was listening to Sir George with a serious, intent expression, his determined chin very much in evidence. He looked not at all like an invalid. For the first time since she had met him, she could picture him as an officer, commanding his troops with authority.

Vickie hovered on the edge of the group, attracted by the engaging young squire yet conscious of her responsibility for Anita, now exploring the tangled shrubbery. Constantia felt a moment's qualm at leaving her sister unchaperoned, but after all, Vickie was still a schoolroom miss and Felix was there.

"Connie, are you coming?" Fanny called.

"Yes!" She had fallen behind. As she turned to follow, Frank looked up and waved to her, and her heart gave a little skip. He was going to have the most comfortable home imaginable, she vowed to herself.

The next three days were a whirlwind of activity. Mob-capped and aproned, Constantia, Fanny, and Miss Bannister supervised a swarm of village women as clouds of dust flew. Young Thomas laboured mightily, building and tending fires in each room to drive off the damp of disuse — though strictly speaking he was Lady Constantia's footman, he willingly joined in. Furniture emerged from under dustcovers, some in good condition, some moth-eaten or worm-eaten but repairable, some fit only for the bonfire. Aromatic odours filled the air as woodwork thirstily drank in beeswax, lemon oil, and turpentine until it gleamed. The sun once again found its way through the diamond-paned windows.

Frank and Felix escaped the chaos with the excuse of inspecting the estate and visiting the tenant farmers. Sir George accompanied them, performing introductions and pointing out desirable improvements. From the ladies' point of view, he made himself still more useful by inviting Vickie and Anita to spend the days at Netherfield with his mother and two sisters. The girls returned each evening with reports of puppies and kittens, Lady Berman's kindness and Pam and Lizzie's good nature.

Late on the fourth afternoon, Felix dropped Frank at the front door before driving round to the stables. Entering the great hall, Frank found Constantia admiring its now pristine glory.

"Look, even the chairs and settles and the sidetables have polished up well," she pointed out, turning. Her apron was a smeary grey; a cobweb decorated her mob cap; and above the smudge on her cheek her blue eyes sparkled. "They are centuries old, Jacobean I believe, and magnificently carved. Did I not say this is a splendid hall?"

"You did." He was torn between mirth, dismay, and a sudden urge to drop a kiss on the tip of her nose. "However, I hardly expected you to be used as a dust-mop in the cleaning of it, Lady Constantia. Indeed, I never dreamt you'd take an active rôle in the process, merely that you'd advise Fanny."

"But I am having such fun." She took off the cap and saw the cobweb. "Though I cannot say I care for spiders, alive or dead. Fanny and I, and Miss Bannister, don't actually do a great deal, you know, we just tell the others what to do."

"As an officer I appreciate the distinction, but I also know that if Lady Westwood saw you now she'd drag you home and never let you set foot in the Grange again."

"You cannot imagine how glad I am that Mama is not here!" She glanced down rue-fully at her filthy clothes. "I must go and change for dinner. I am not fit to appear even in the kitchen." He watched her move to the stairs, her graceful dignity no whit

159

impaired by her disarray. Who'd have thought that the sheltered daughter of an earl would take on so cheerfully the menial tasks of housekeeping?

Despite her contentment and his gratitude for her assistance, he was beginning to think it had been a mistake to invite her. Now that the world might consider him a worthy suitor, he found it more and more difficult to control his attraction to her. She was adorable, irresistible!

He could hardly ask her to leave, however. Sternly checking his thoughts, Frank turned away towards the small downstairs room converted to be his chamber. Lady Constantia had shown no embarrassment at being seen in all her dirt, which made it plain that she regarded him as a friend, not an admirer. And that, of course, was precisely what he wanted. Wasn't it?

At the unfashionably early hour of six, they all gathered around the kitchen table. The white tablecloth was darned, the glasses unmatched, the silver still tarnished, but after the day's exertions Constantia was too hungry to notice, let alone to care.

Though they dined in the kitchen, Thomas served the simple dinner — a piece of gammon, a dish of mushrooms stewed in but-

160

ter, plenty of bread and cheese, fresh damsons sent by Lady Berman, ale and cider. After the long, rootless years, three days had not diminished Frank's relish in the rôle of host in his own house. Constantia smiled at his satisfaction as he made sure everyone had what they wanted.

"Me and Aunt Vickie picked the mushrooms," Anita announced. "They grow in Uncle George's field."

"Uncle George?" Fanny exclaimed.

"It's all right, Fanny," Vickie assured her. "Sir George says he's honoured to join the ranks of Anita's uncles. We helped to pick the plums, too."

"You have been busy," said Frank. "You have all been busy. You ladies shall take a holiday tomorrow."

"Not tomorrow," Fanny protested. "The dining-room will be fit to eat in tomorrow if I just —"

"Tomorrow shall be a holiday," he commanded. "I wish to stay at home without being chased from room to room by hordes of maids with feather dusters."

Constantia was instantly remorseful. "Oh dear, you must find it dreadfully tiring being out and about all day, Captain. Though I must say," she added tartly as he helped himself to a thick slice of baked gammon,

161

"you seem very well and your appetite is just what one would wish."

"My dear Lady Constantia, I was teasing! I am not in the least tired. Roworth does all the driving, and we are constantly invited in for refreshments at every farm and cottage, besides stopping to rest at Netherfield in the afternoons. No, I simply feel you three have more than earned a holiday."

"Connie and Miss Bannister certainly have," Fanny agreed, "but I want to keep at it, Frank, and I've already asked the women to come in."

"I believe Mrs Tanner is quite capable of directing the others," Constantia proposed. Turning to Miss Bannister, she asked, "Do you not think so, ma'am? Indeed, Captain, as she is a widow, you might consider hiring her as your housekeeper." She guessed from Fanny's startled dismay that her brother's need to hire a stranger to run his home had not crossed her mind. "He will have to have a housekeeper when you are married," she said gently.

"I suppose so, but for now I —"

"For tomorrow, at least," Felix declared, "you and I are going to drive over to Heathcote. If we don't set repairs in train soon, we'll be living with your brother long after we are married. I don't mean to wait forever."

"Yes, you two go to Heathcote," Frank seconded him. "Not that I've any desire to be rid of you, but I'm sure Sir George is right to say you ought to have the roof and the windows repaired before winter comes."

"Sir George says Heathcote had a ghost," Vickie reported, "but it left when the roof started to leak. He says perhaps it will come back when the roof is mended," she added hopefully, disregarding their laughter. "He says the Grange never had one, Captain, nor dungeons."

"I'm sorry to disappoint you, but you relieve me greatly! Your sister is troubled enough by spiders without the fear of coming across skeletons strewn about the cellars. Lady Constantia, will you give me your advice about the gardens tomorrow? I cannot guarantee you won't meet a spider or two, but I'll be there to rescue you."

"I like spiders," Anita announced.

"Then you must come with us," said Constantia, "and I shall feel perfectly safe." Quite apart from the hazard of eight-legged assailants, the thought crossed her mind that a small chaperon would not come amiss.

The jungle that had once been the gardens of Upfield Grange provided spiders by the dozen. Anita was fascinated, scurrying from web to web. Constantia preferred the red admiral butterflies swarming about a straggling buddleia, and Anita agreed that they were very pretty. She was thrilled when one settled on her arm. As it slowly opened and closed its patterned wings, she stood quite still and held her breath, her eyes round.

Unfortunately, a patch of nettles also attracted butterflies — and therefore Anita. Constantia's "Don't touch!" came too late. Her hands stung, Anita ran to Frank, tears welling from those dark eyes.

"They bited me!"

"Poor sweetheart." Incautiously he picked her up. He drew in his breath sharply and his face paled.

"Let me see." Constantia hurried to take the child from him. He had been so much improved, so full of energy, the past few days, she had almost forgotten his injuries. So, evidently, had he.

She examined the red rash on Anita's hands. "Don't cry, darling," she said, "it was just the nettles stinging. It will soon get better, I promise. Dock or dandelion, the juice of either will soothe it."

Frank looked around vaguely. "Is there any here?"

"Plenty! Both are common weeds and of weeds you have a most excellent crop."

"I do, don't I? Ah, that yellow flower is a dandelion, isn't it?"

Anita was intrigued by the white juice squeezed from the dandelion, and by Constantia's explanation that the jagged-edged leaf looked like a lion's teeth. Then Frank found a dandelion clock. In blowing away the seeds, Anita forgot the nettlerash.

"I daresay she's spreading next year's crop of dandelions," Frank said with a sigh. "Still, there are so many it hardly matters. I can see it's going to take a hell of . . . a vast amount of work to restore the gardens." He held back a branch to allow Constantia to proceed along the path.

"Yes, I'm afraid so. You will need dozens of gardeners to make any impression in less than several years." Emerging from a pink wilderness of rosebay willowherb, she found herself at the edge of the park, at the top of the slope leading down to the bridge over the stream.

Dropping the remains of her dandelion clock, Anita ran to take her hand. "Can we go to the bridge, Aunt Connie? Please?"

"Yes, certainly." She glanced back at Frank. "I shall take her, Captain, if you wish to go and rest awhile."

"No, I'll come. It will be good to walk properly after floundering through the jungle, and I don't think there's any point struggling any further."

"Rather than trying to prune and weed, you may find it easier to clear everything and start anew. That way, you will only need to hire labourers for the present, not skilled gardeners."

"Labourers are hard enough to find, let alone gardeners, or grooms, or indoor menservants." He frowned as they started down the hill. "It seems all the local men either have work on the farms or have left the area in search of work. You have had better luck with hiring maids."

"For the most part, yes, but we cannot find a cook who admits to being competent at more than the plainest of fare."

"We have been eating well," he said, surprised.

"Compared to what Fanny has told me of the wretched provisions you had in the Spanish mountains, perhaps! But unless you mean to be a recluse, your neighbours will expect the owner of Upfield Grange to

166

entertain in reasonable style."

"A recluse! Good Lord, no."

Constantia smiled. "I thought not. So a decent cook must be found, by an advertisement in the newspapers if necessary."

"Not to mention a butler and footmen, I suppose."

"One or two. And you ought to have a gentleman's gentleman."

"I don't want a toplofty valet like your brother's Trevor peering over my shoulder!"

"Then we shall try to find you someone more agreeable. I am not sure how to set about hiring a valet, but Felix will probably know, though he has had Trevor since he left school." She hesitated. "I sound like a horridly managing female, do I not? I hope you will tell me if I encroach."

"My dear Lady Constantia, I have asked for your advice. A fine fellow I should be to complain when you give it."

More than his words, the warmth of his smile reassured her. His eyes crinkled at the corners when he smiled, in the most delightful way. She noticed that his threadbare coat no longer hung on him as on a scarecrow: his shoulders, though they still pained him, had filled out. Before Quatre Bras, he must have presented a vigorous, stalwart figure.

His quizzical look made her flush. To

excuse her staring, she said, "Since you have asked for my advice, I will be so bold as to say it is time you augmented your wardrobe."

"Or replaced it?" he said with a grin.

"Or replaced it," she agreed, and turned her head away before asking what now seemed a shockingly personal question: "Do you still perform Mrs Cohen's exercises . . . Anita, wait!"

The child had run ahead, and the bridge had only open wooden rails on each side. Now, as they approached it, Constantia saw a shabby man plodding down the opposite slope. Tales of tramps and gypsies and kidnapped children raced through her mind. Picking up her skirts, she dashed after the little girl.

"Anita, come back!"

But after pausing on the bridge and staring at the man, Anita sped on. "It's Hoxins!" she cried. "Hoxins, it's me!"

Behind Constantia, Frank exclaimed, "By Jove, so it is!"

She slowed her pace as the stranger stopped, a huge grin splitting his unshaven face. Anita dashed into his arms and he raised her high over his head, then set her on his shoulders and continued down the hill, his step jaunty.

"Hoxins?" said Constantia uncertainly.

"Corporal Hoskins, my batman." Frank, too, was beaming. "A splendid fellow. How the dev . . . on earth did he find us?"

He hurried on. Constantia lingered on the near side of the bridge and watched the meeting of the two ex-soldiers. She was not surprised to learn that Frank had been the kind of officer who earns his troops' loyalty — and to whom they turned in times of trouble, she discovered as they came closer.

"So you see, Cap'n, sir, I did hope as you might have a spot o' work for me."

"Corporal, there's no one I'd rather employ."

"There's just one thing, sir." Hoskins blushed a fiery red. "I don't s'pose you remember Henriette?"

"I 'member Henriette," Anita assured him.

"The cook at our Brussels lodging? Hoskins, you never . . . !"

"Man and wife, sir. She's waiting at the inn in the village, being as she ain't what you might call much of a walker."

"Congratulations, Corporal! Lady Constantia?" Frank turned a laughing face to her. "Hoskins has solved two of our problems at one blow. Behold my gentleman's gentleman, and his wife is an excellent cook."

Corporal Hoskins was not exactly what Constantia envisaged as a gentleman's gentleman, but then, Frank did not want one of that starchy breed. Nor was she quite used to being formally introduced to servants, but she recalled Fanny's telling her how Hoskins had helped nurse Frank when he was first wounded.

He further endeared himself to her when Frank told him she was Felix's sister. "Lord Roworth?" he said. "The finest of fine gentlemen, m'lady. I don't know as Miss Fanny and me could 'a' pulled the cap'n through wi'out his lordship."

"Hoxins, Hoxins," Anita cried from her perch on his shoulders, "Uncle Felix is going to be my papa and then Aunt Fanny will be my mama."

"Is that so, missie? Well now, I'd a notion the wind were blowing thataway." He winked at Constantia. "I'll be that glad to dance at Miss Fanny's wedding."

She smiled at him as they continued towards the house. "Indeed, Corporal, you come at a most opportune moment. How did you find Captain Ingram?"

"That were his lordship's doing, my lady. Afore quitting Brussels, he gave me Mrs Cohen's direction. Me and Henriette, we went to Nettledene and she weren't there

170

— well, I can tell you that gave me a nasty turn. But seeing as his lordship sent us, the folks there told us where to find her in Lunnon. A right kindly lady, Mrs Cohen is, my lady. She'll be a friend o' yourn?"

"I hope she will be one day." Constantia no longer had the least intention of letting her parents' prejudice stop her from knowing Miriam Cohen.

"She put us up in her own pa's house," Hoskins continued. "She'd just got a letter from Miss Fanny saying as the cap'n was here in Hampshire, and Mr Cohen gave me and Henriette our fares for the stage. So here we be."

"And here, I hope, you'll stay," said Frank. "What's more, you've given me a bang-up notion. No doubt there are plenty of soldiers discharged from the army without family or money or work. Lord knows, Fanny and I nearly found ourselves in that case, but thanks to Roworth and the late Duke of Oxshott we're in need of servants instead. I'd like nothing better than to take on some of our fellows, if only we can find them."

"I knows where to look for a couple o' the lads, Cap'n, and they'll likely know more."

"Artirelly," insisted Anita, a true child of the regiment. "Artirelly's best. Did you know Miss Bannister's artirelly, too, Uncle

171

Frank?"

"She is?" he said, startled.

After a moment's puzzlement, Constantia burst into laughter. "You are quite right, Anita, of course she is. Her papa was a canon. With one *n*," she explained to Frank. "A cathedral clergyman."

Frank grinned. "That just goes to prove artillery is best. Do what you can to find some of our fellows, corporal, and I'll hire them."

"Splendid!" Constantia clapped her hands. "With a household staffed by soldiers, you and Fanny will have nothing to fear from the odious duke."

The cleaning was done at last. Constantia and Fanny decided to go into Winchester on a preliminary foray to investigate the shops and tradespeople. New furniture was needed; new upholstery for old furniture; new bedding, especially for the servants' quarters; paint and wallhangings; linen, china, and glassware; and, last but not least, new gowns for Fanny and above all a new bonnet.

"Felix bought this for me in the Brussels market," said Fanny with a sigh, tying the ribbons of her daisy-bedecked chipstraw hat. "I'm not sure that wasn't when I fell in love with him, but you're right, I do need another."

"It is pretty," Constantia said, "but not quite appropriate to the granddaughter of a duke."

"I still find it hard to believe I can afford to buy clothes! You will teach me to keep household accounts, won't you? I've never before had more than enough money for the basic necessities."

"I will. Your brother actually seems to enjoy Sir George's lessons in estate book-keeping."

"Frank's good with numbers. You have to be in the artillery, with angles and distances and trajectories to be calculated. You wait, one of these days he'll bore you to tears on the subject of parabolas."

"Then I shall take my revenge with the subject of parasols."

"I've always wanted a parasol. Oh no!" Fanny stared at her glove in dismay. "The seam has split. I don't want to waste time mending it."

"I shall lend you a pair, and you must buy some more, as well as a parasol. Those gloves already have darn upon darn. Come on, Fanny. We are going to have a wonderful day."

With Dutton to drive them and Thomas

to watch over them and carry their parcels, they did have a wonderful day. They returned to Upfield tired but content, full of ideas for refurbishing the Grange. The phaeton drew up at the front door. Thomas handed the ladies down and Dutton drove off to the stables.

They entered the house and Fanny went upstairs to give Anita a doll she had bought. Constantia lingered in the great hall, her favourite place, to admire the rich gloss on the carvings in the evening sun, slanting in at the northwest-facing windows. Inspecting a vase of purple Michaelmas daisies she had scavenged from the garden, she dropped her gloves on the table and nipped off a few fading blooms.

"I'll toss 'em out for you, m'lady," offered Hoskins, crossing the hall at that moment. A burly man in his thirties, now shaven, hair cut and combed, his blue-and-red uniform jacket cleaned and pressed, he resembled neither tramp nor gentleman's gentleman, but a plain soldier.

"Disposing of dead flowers is not among a valet's duties," Constantia teased. She was on excellent terms with Frank's old batman, much better than she had ever attained with her brother's Trevor.

The two men's mutual scorn, begun in

Brussels, had by no means dissipated upon renewed acquaintance. "Begging your pardon, m'lady," Hoskins snorted, "but niffy-naffy fussing 'bout who does what is what I don't hold with."

Laughing, she handed over the drooping flowers. A crash behind them cut short her laughter. She and Hoskins swung round to see the heavy front door rebounding from the wall. On the threshold stood a stout gentleman in a caped overcoat, purple-faced and grey-whiskered, breathing heavily.

"I'll soon make you laugh on the other side of your face, missie!" he roared, advancing on them.

Constantia flinched. Another ogre! And this time she surely was not mistaken: here was the Duke of Oxshott himself.

CHAPTER 9

As the corpulent bully stormed towards
Constantia, Corporal Hoskins stepped
forward to defend her. "Who you be I don't
know," he growled, no less belligerent than
his adversary, "but the king hisself don't
threaten her ladyship whiles I got two fists
and a pair o' legs to stand on."

"Her ladyship! So the hussy's added a title
to her fraudulent claims?" The duke, if such
he was, sneered contemptuously but ceased
to advance. "And I suppose you call yourself
'my lord,' you vulgar upstart?"

"Me?"

Hoskins' stunned face almost made Constantia smile despite her terror. Wishing she
were braver, she drew herself up and nerved
herself to say in her mother's most haughty
manner, "I am Lady Constantia Roworth,
daughter of the Earl of Westwood, and this
good fellow is Corporal Hoskins, late of the
Royal Horse Artillery. I do not believe I

have your acquaintance?"

"Corporal? Westwood?" He looked taken aback but quickly rallied and blustered on. "I am the Duke of Oxshott, ma'am. What Westwood is about to let his gal consort with shameless charlatans I can't imagine. Give me leave to tell you that if you choose to lend countenance to such rabble I shall make sure you bitterly regret it."

"Captain and Miss Ingram are not charlatans," Constantia said, clasping her hands to stop their shaking.

"Impostors! Thieves! Brigands! But I daresay you're no better. I'm none so sure you're who you claim to be." Advancing again, he peered at her beneath scowling brows and snarled, "Can you prove you're Westwood's daughter, eh? Eh? You're the swindler's doxy, I wager. I'll have you clapped up in gaol along with anyone else who tries to cheat me."

Hoskins raised fists like hams.

"Touch me, you misbegotten cur, and I'll see you hanged!" bellowed the duke.

"Enough!" Frank's voice slashed like cold steel. Every inch a military officer, though he had exchanged his shabby uniform for buckskins and a shooting jacket, he strode into the hall, eyes hard, his resolute chin very much in evidence. He looked perfectly capable of handling a dozen irate dukes. Constantia realized he was no longer the invalid she had cosseted, no longer in need of her care. A hint of regret mingled with her admiration. Now he was the protector. His very presence made her feel safe.

She sank onto the nearest chair as Oxshott swung round. "So you're the —"

"I am Frank Ingram," he said curtly. "Since you, I believe, must be my uncle, I shall forbear to give you my opinion of so-called gentlemen who insult and try to browbeat blameless females. Your quarrel is with me."

"Quarrel! I don't quarrel with insolent whelps, I horsewhip them and . . ." The duke began to wilt under Frank's sceptical, unimpressed gaze. ". . . And call in the law," he finished in a weak mumble.

Frank's mouth twisted with suppressed amusement. "To call in the law would certainly appear to be the best solution. In view of your exalted station, sir, no doubt Mr Mackintyre will be willing to post down here at short notice to reassure you as to my and my sister's credentials. That is, I suppose you really are the Duke of Oxshott?"

Constantia bit her lip to hold back a slightly hysterical giggle. His grace's eyes bulged and he gasped in outrage. Afraid he'd suffer an apoplexy, she rose and went to lay a hand on his arm. "Of course, we do not doubt your assertion, Duke," she said soothingly, frowning at Frank.

"That's Oxshott all right." Felix was up in the gallery, grinning as he leaned over the rail. "I'd recognize him anywhere." At a leisurely pace he followed Fanny, who pattered down the stairs.

"Thomas warned . . . informed us," she explained as Constantia rose and went to meet her.

"Fanny, let me present our uncle, his grace, the Duke of Oxshott," said Frank, his gravity belied by twitching lips.

Constantia wasn't sure whether he had deliberately chosen to introduce the duke to his sister, rather than the other way about, or if he simply was not sure of the proper form. It was a nice point. Fanny was a lady, not a young girl, but she was Oxshott's niece and greatly his junior. Judging by the gleam of mischief in Frank's eyes, he was at least aware of the significance of his choice.

Fanny inclined her head graciously as the duke at last removed his beaver to reveal thinning grey hair. Constantia gave her a smile of approval, guessing she was trying to behave as Felix would expect his future countess to behave. She looked charming in her new walking dress, cinnamon-brown with buttercup ribbons, a fortunate find rejected by the lady who had ordered it from a Winchester modiste.

The duke muttered something indistinguishable. Then, turning to Felix, he said with renewed pugnacity, "You recognize me, but I'll be damned if I know who the devil you are."

"I'm Roworth, Duke, Westwood's heir," said Felix cheerfully. "We met at . . . in Town," he hastily changed his words as Fanny and Constantia glared at him. No need to set up his grace's back still further by reminding him of his set-down at the hands of Mr Rothschild. "We weren't actually introduced, but naturally I recall so . . . distinguished a personage."

Oxshott took this flattery as his due, but appeared slightly mollified. Constantia wondered for what epithet her brother had substituted "distinguished." Ludicrous? Rumbustious? Coarse? She had never heard such dreadful language used in her presence without apology.

However, for Frank's sake — and Fanny's — this altogether obnoxious gentleman must be conciliated. He was odious, but he was a duke and a relative. Surely he'd be pleased to learn of his niece's advantageous match.

"My brother is engaged to be married to Miss Ingram," she told him.

"Your brother? That's right, you're claiming to be Lady Something-or-other Roworth, are you not?" He turned his glower on Fanny. "Well, missie, whether you're my niece or not, you've caught yourself a fine fish. If he really is Roworth."

Felix stepped forward angrily, his amusement quenched. Frank stopped him with a raised hand. "Roworth, perhaps you wouldn't mind sending your groom to London to request Mr Mackintyre's attendance at the Grange? This matter must be settled, and the sooner the better. Sir, I assume you'll wish to stay in the neighbourhood in the meantime. The Pig and Piper at King's Wallop is scarcely suitable. I expect we can put you up, can we not, Fanny?"

Fanny cast a panicked glance at Constantia, who nodded. They were still lacking a full staff, but his grace would have to make do with the inadequate service. After all, the wretched man had arrived not only without an invitation but without notice, Constantia thought rebelliously.

"Of course we can accommodate you, sir," Fanny said, her gracious demeanour preserved with an obvious effort. "I'll have a room prepared at once, if you wish to stay here."

"Stay here? Naturally I'll stay here," the duke snapped. "Blood and 'ouns, where the devil else should I stay but in my own house?"

Burning with indignation, Constantia caught Frank's eye. He shrugged his shoulders slightly, conveying to her that he considered it pointless to argue with his uncle. Delight that the gesture did not appear to hurt him superceded her anger on his behalf.

"Will you come into the drawing-room, sir?" he said with admirable calm, continuing to act as host as if Oxshott had not spoken. "I've not had time to lay down a cellar, of course, but Roworth found a madeira at the Pig and Piper that he assures me is quite tolerable. I'd appreciate your opinion."

As he followed Frank from the hall, the duke caught sight of Hoskins. When his captain took charge of the intruder, the practical corporal had taken a tinder box from his pocket and set about lighting lamps and candles against the encroaching dusk.

Oxshott's brows lowered at the sight of the menial who had defied him. Constantia

182

quailed, expecting another outburst.

However his grace merely bellowed, "Hey, you there. Go and tell my servants we're stopping."

The corporal's salute was a marvel of irony. Unfortunately — or perhaps fortunately — the duke wasn't watching.

"Servants!" Fanny gasped. "Connie, how many do you think he's brought with him?"

Constantia thought back to her father's travelling days. "His valet, of course, and the coachman. At least two footmen. Possibly an outrider or two. They are liveried grooms," she explained as Fanny looked blank, "who ride ahead of or beside the carriage, mostly to add consequence. He may have brought a secretary, too."

"How on earth am I to feed so many?" wailed Fanny.

"Henriette will manage for tonight. She is a veritable treasure, is she not? Tomorrow we shall order fresh supplies. Surely Captain Ingram can afford to entertain Oxshott and his entourage for a few days?"

"Yes, easily. I keep forgetting we're rich. It's not that I'm in the least frightened of our uncle, Connie, but I do so dread letting Felix down."

"I know, Fanny dear, but you will not. And your brother was magnificent. He knew just how to treat the horrid creature." Constantia linked arms with her. "Come on, let us go and consult Mrs Tanner."

Arm in arm, they started towards the housekeeper's room, only to halt as Vickie rushed helter-skelter down the stairs. "Oh no, have we missed all the fun?" she cried.

"Mama!" called Anita, following in her nightgown as fast as her little legs would carry her.

"Now, Miss Anita," reprimanded Miss Bannister, descending slowly in her always dignified manner.

"Aunt Fanny, I mean," said the little girl, running to Fanny. "Miss Bannister says I mustn't call you Mama till after the wedding."

Fanny hugged her, smiling. "She's right, darling. I'm still your Aunt Fanny till then. Have you come down to say goodnight? I was on my way to the nursery when I was interrupted."

"By the ogre?" Vickie asked eagerly. "Thomas said a man came in and started shouting threats at you, Con. We came down to help."

"Thank you, but I was in no danger." Constantia met Miss Bannister's gaze and the governess raised her eyes to heaven. Controlling an excited Lady Victoria was beyond her. "The ogre was Fanny's uncle, the Duke of Oxshott."

"A duke! I always thought a duke would be like Papa, only more so. Was he really carrying on like a Bedlamite?"

"I am sure Thomas exaggerated," said Miss Bannister repressively.

"He was a bit excited," Fanny said, "but Frank soon calmed him down. He'll be staying at the Grange for a few days."

"Then Lady Victoria and I will dine in the schoolroom," the governess declared.

"Oh no! I want to meet the mad — his grace, I mean."

"You shall," said Fanny determinedly. "I've no intention of bowing to his consequence to the extent of banishing you from the dining-room, Vickie. Nor you, ma'am," she added to Miss Bannister. "He must put up with our domestic arrangements or find accommodation elsewhere."

"Indeed, Miss Ingram, you need not suppose that I shall take offence. I never aspired to dine at Lady Westwood's table and I am most conscious of your kindness in allowing me —"

"Balderdash! Felix," Fanny called to her betrothed as he entered the hall, "you don't object to Miss Bannister dining with us, do you?"

He grinned. "Recognizing your militant mood, I shouldn't dare say if I did, but of course I don't."

"Connie?"

"Not in the least, but perhaps you ought to consult your brother, Fanny. He is the duke's host, and he may wish to avoid antagonizing his grace further."

"I'm so glad you're here to advise me, Connie. What should I do without you? It's up to Frank, then."

"I'll go and relieve him and tell him you want a word," offered Felix. "I've sent the groom off to London with a message for Mackintyre." He departed towards the drawing-room.

Anita, who had been tugging at Fanny's sleeve for some time, now burst into speech. "I want to have dinner with the mad duke, too," she begged. "Please, Aunt Fanny."

"When you are older, darling," said Fanny, laughing. "It's your bedtime, now. If you're very good and go to sleep quickly, I'll bring up a present to leave beside your bed for the morning."

Satisfied, Anita kissed her and Constantia goodnight and went upstairs with Vickie and Miss Bannister.

"Heavens," Fanny exclaimed, "I still haven't told Mrs Tanner to make up a chamber for the duke. Connie, will you stay here and consult Frank while I speak to her and Henriette?" She hurried away.

Constantia crossed to the vase of Michaelmas daisies and started to fiddle with the flowers. She changed the vase's position on the dark oak Jacobean table, then moved it back. She felt oddly restless, almost fluttery, as if she were in a quake for some reason.

There was nothing to fear, she scolded herself. The duke had been quite frightening but Frank could cope with him. If he attacked her again, Frank would protect her. How splendidly he had routed the bully with his calm, decisive words and manner. He must have been a superb officer. With a single word he had halted Oxshott in his tracks, and then withered him with scorn.

In fact, Frank had showed a formidable side to his nature, one she had not guessed at. Was that why she was in high fidgets?

Fustian! She did not believe for a moment that he would ever try to intimidate her. Why should their relationship change just because she had discovered a facet of his character that she ought to have expected, knowing his profession? Yet it was confusing, disturbing and — somehow exciting.

"Lady Constantia?" Frank's voice was close behind her.

Her heart skipped a beat and she dropped the flower she had just pulled from the vase. "Oh! You startled me. I did not hear you coming."

"I beg your pardon!" He smiled at her quizzically. "I didn't mean to creep up on you. You were in a brown study, I daresay."

Flushing, she pushed the yellow daisy back among its fellows. "Yes, lost in thought, I fear." Thank heaven he could not read her mind!

His face darkened. "You have much cause for reflection. I dare not hope you will stay after being insulted in my house, by a relative of mine."

"How can you suppose I shall desert Fanny just when she is most in need of my support?" Laying her hand on his arm, she added earnestly, "I shall not heed his raving. He cannot harm me. But he will serve you and Fanny ill if he can. Promise me you will beware of him, Captain."

"I promise, though I believe I have his measure, and Mackintyre will soon set him straight. You must not tease yourself on our account."

He looked down at her with such warmth in his dark eyes that the heat rose in her cheeks again. She turned away to pick up her gloves from the table where she had left them. "I shall try not to. Oh, I almost forgot!"

"Roworth said Fanny wanted a word with me."

"She had to go and see Mrs Tanner and Henriette. I almost forgot I am deputed to ask your opinion. Fanny did say to 'consult' you, but I cannot promise your verdict will be heeded should it differ from hers."

He grinned. "Up in arms is she? I thought she was being amazingly restrained. What's the difficulty? Whether to house his grace in the attics or the cellars? What a pity we have no dungeons."

Constantia smiled. "Most regrettable. No, I believe she intends to provide suitable quarters. She is resolved to prove to Felix that she can be a gracious hostess to a nobleman of high degree. However, she is also resolved to stand upon principle and have Miss Bannister dine with the family."

"Why should she not? Who could be more respectable than the daughter of a canon with one *n*?"

"Miss Bannister fears the duke will dislike dining with a governess. Fanny says he must accept her domestic arrangements, and I do agree, but I felt you might wish to avoid arousing his ire over a minor matter."

"His nose is so far out of joint already it

can make little difference. Besides, Fanny is right, it's a matter of principle. I wouldn't for the world have Miss Bannister imagine Fanny and I hold ourselves superior to her. If he'll condescend to dine with us, he must condescend to dine with her, too."

"I wondered whether perhaps she is afraid of being abused to her face," she said tentatively.

"A reasonable fear, alas. Should he choose to display his boorishness at my table, then duke or no, uncle or no, he can remove himself bag and baggage to the Pig and Piper."

Constantia did not doubt for a moment that he was capable of forcing Oxshott to depart, even though the duke claimed Upfield Grange as his own. How much more comfortable they would all be. "Why did you invite him to stay here in the first place?" she enquired.

"I prefer to have him under my eye, rather than stirring up mischief in the village. You don't think I have more regard for Miss Bannister's feelings than for yours, do you?" Frank asked anxiously. "I ought not to have invited him after he was so abominably rude to you."

"I did not take it personally," she assured him. "At first he took me for Fanny, and then for . . ." Her face flamed as she recalled that Oxshott had called her Frank's doxy. ". . . For someone else. Truly, you must not tease yourself on my account. Excuse me, pray, I must go and see if Fanny needs me before we change for dinner." She made a hurried escape.

What an utter darling she was, Frank thought, watching her slim, graceful figure disappear into the servants' quarters. He remembered all too well what his uncle had said to cause her fiery blush. His doxy never, no, nor his wife, though his body ached to hold her. When she said she'd stay, thankfulness had overwhelmed him, but how was he to bear her constant presence?

Constantia — constancy. A name as beautiful as its owner, and if he ever earned the right to use it he'd never shorten it to Connie. Constancy. The only constant was that she was within reach yet ever beyond his reach.

With a bitter laugh he mocked himself as a maudlin fool and turned his steps towards the drawing-room. The battle of wits with his grace, the Duke of Oxshott, would distract him from his woes.

The next morning's post brought a letter from Westwood. Lady Constantia was to

return home at once to prepare for the
Little Season.

CHAPTER 10

"I can't see why on earth I have to go too," Vickie stormed. "Mama doesn't mean to take me to Town until the spring, and I can learn here just as well as at home."

Roworths and Ingrams, together with Anita and Miss Bannister, were seated at breakfast in the dining-room. Constantia's announcement of the contents of Lady Westwood's letter had cast an immediate gloom over the company and roused her sister to rebellion. She breathed a sigh of relief that the Duke of Oxshott was not an early riser.

"You cannot defy Mama in this, Vickie," she said gently.

"Apart from anything else, she would blame Miss Bannister, and maybe even Fanny, for your disobedience."

"Not to mention you and me, Con," said Felix. "Of course you must go, Vickie."

Anita had been looking from one to another, tears filling her black eyes, her lower lip trembling. Now she slid down from her seat and hung on Vickie's arm, wailing, "Don't go, Aunt Vickie!"

"I shan't," Vickie declared stoutly.

"I fear we have no choice, Lady Victoria," her governess said. "Lady Westwood has every right to insist on your return, and I should be sadly remiss in my duty did I not take you back to Westwood."

"Are you going too?" asked Anita. Her little face crumpled and she ran sobbing to Fanny. "Mama, Mama, you won't go away?"

Fanny lifted her onto her knee and held her tight. "No, darling, I'm staying right here. Vickie will come often to visit us, I hope, and Miss Bannister will come back to teach you as soon as Vickie no longer needs her. Will you not, ma'am?"

"Certainly, Miss Ingram," said the governess, flushed with pleasure. "If you honestly wish it."

"Can you doubt it? I don't know how we shall manage without you in the meantime." She turned to Constantia, biting her lip. "This is the worst possible time! I need your support and advice now more than ever, Connie."

Constantia's heart swelled within her. Here she was needed and wanted. To Mama she represented a duty, a recalcitrant daughter to be married off to the most eligible suitor available. Her hand crept to her chest as she envisioned the coming battles over modish décolletés for Town wear.

"I shall stay," she announced.

Fanny's delight stiffened her resolve. "Connie, will you really? Bless you!"

"You're forgetting, Fanny," said Frank. "Lady Constantia's offer is extremely kind, but you can't wish to deprive her of the pleasures of the Little Season."

"Oh drat," Fanny exclaimed. "You're right, I had forgotten. I couldn't be so selfish as to keep you, Connie, when at last you have a chance to go to balls and routs and ridottos."

"But I have no desire to go." Constantia turned to Frank and assured him, "Indeed, I truly would prefer not to go to London."

"It's quite true," said Felix. "She told me the same before you even came to Westwood, so you need not feel the least guilt, Fanny love. You need her support now, and in the spring we'll go up to Town and she'll have our support for the Season, instead of being all alone at Mama's mercy."

"That's not fair," Vickie cried. "I'll be all alone at Mama's mercy if you make me leave."

"You'll have Miss Bannister," her brother pointed out, "and you're only seventeen, so you have to abide by Mama's commands. Connie's of age. She can decide for herself."

"I don't like it." Frank frowned down at the rapidly cooling remains of his bacon and eggs, refusing to meet Constantia's eyes. "We ought not to set ourselves up against Lady Westwood. She's going to be your mother-in-law, Fanny. It'll hardly make for cordial relations if she blames us for keeping Lady Constantia from her."

"I'll take the blame," said Felix cheerfully. "I'll tell her I insisted on Con staying to companion Fanny. After all, she herself said Fanny shouldn't be without another female to protect her against me."

"Nonetheless," Frank persisted with the dogged obstinacy his chin warned of, "to disregard a summons —"

"Connie's not in the army," Fanny reminded him. "She's not going to be court-martialled for desertion."

"I cannot stay against Captain Ingram's wishes," said Constantia flatly, unable to prevent a catch in her voice.

At last he looked at her, the dismay and concern in his eyes mingled with some deeper, unreadable emotion. "Nothing would please me more than to have you

196

stay. It's just . . ." He shrugged his shoulders and continued with a wry smile, "I daresay it's military habit makes me consider all the possible consequences of any action. Please don't leave."

Accepting gracefully, she remained unconvinced. She did not doubt his genuine concern for her feelings, yet she was sure he did not really want her to stay at Upfield Grange, and that hurt.

Frank saw through her attempt to conceal her chagrin and damned his own insensitivity. He had expected her to see his objections as reasonable scruples, but she had guessed that he wanted her to leave. To explain his real reasons was out of the question. The only way to remedy his apparent unkindness was to spend as much time as possible proving to her how much he valued her friendship.

A tempting prospect, yet one that could only increase his torment.

Vickie started to argue again. Her governess appeared reluctant to intervene in her dispute with her brother and sister. However, when Roworth and Constantia continued to hold firm against her, Miss Bannister said severely, "That is quite enough, Lady Victoria. We shall return to Westwood."

Disconsolate, she submitted. "Yes, ma'am.

But not today," she pleaded. "I can't leave without saying goodbye to Sir George. And to Lady Berman, and Pam and Lizzie. And you promised we'd have a picnic at Heathcote, Felix. I haven't even seen Fanny's house yet."

"I like picnics," Anita announced. "Amos does, too."

"We could go today," said Constantia impulsively. How like her to sympathize with her sister's disappointment, Frank thought, glancing at the window. Outside the golden September sunshine gave promise of near-summer warmth. "Papa is sending the carriage and he expects it to arrive this evening, so you cannot leave until tomorrow, in any case, Vickie. We could invite the Bermans to go with us to Heathcote."

"What a splendid notion, Con!" Vickie sparkled again. "Sir George has a splendid farm wagon that he fills with cushions to take his family on outings. We'd all fit in, I'm sure, even with Lady Berman and the girls. Well, almost all." She counted heads.

Miss Bannister smiled at her. "I shall not go, Lady Victoria. You know how poorly travelling suits me. And I daresay your brother will ride or drive."

"I'll drive Fanny," said Roworth, exchanging a fond glance with his betrothed.

"And me," Anita begged.

"Won't you want to spend every possible minute with Aunt Vickie?" Roworth suggested slyly.

Frank wondered whether he was wise to let his sister spend so much time alone with her beloved. On the other hand, he knew full well he couldn't stop her.

Roworth's ploy worked. "Oh yes," cried Anita, filled with remorse. She jumped down from Fanny's lap and ran to hug Vickie.

"Wait a minute." Looking ruffled, Constantia turned to Frank. "There are two matters we have not taken into consideration. It is your servants, Captain, who will be responsible for preparing the food. Perhaps you do not care for a picnic."

"What a spoil-sport you must think me!" he said ruefully. "I'm perfectly prepared to enjoy any picnic that's better provisioned than our bivouacs in the Spanish mountains, and I, too, want to see Heathcote. You know Henriette will be happy to oblige just as long as she's not asked to leave her kitchen. What's your second difficulty?"

Her smile faded. "The duke."

Dismayed faces around the table told Frank he was not the only one to have forgotten his unwelcome guest. "Dash it," he groaned, though his interior language was considerably stronger. "We can hardly go off and leave the old . . . dastard alone. I'll have to invite him to go with us, but if he accepts he'll ruin the picnic and if he doesn't I, as his host, will have to stay behind to entertain him."

"Yes, I fear you ought." Constantia sighed. Frank had the impression she was going to say something further, but she bit back the words trembling on her lips. Had she been going to offer to stay with him? No, sheer wishful thinking. Lady Constantia Roworth had been brought up far too properly even to contemplate so indecorous a suggestion.

"If you ask me, you've more need to keep an eye on him than to entertain him," said Felix with a grin. "The old . . . dastard might take it into his head to barricade the place while he had it to himself and refuse to let us back in."

"That he won't!" Thomas had come in with fresh coffee and tea. He stopped with the coffee-pot hovering over Frank's cup. "Begging your lordship's pardon, but me and Corp'ral Hoskins wouldn't never let his grace get away with a trick like that. 'ess your ladyship was wanting me to go along to wait?"

Constantia consulted Fanny with a glance. "No, thank you, Thomas, we shall be quite informal. Oh dear, that is, unless the duke joins us. If so I daresay he will wish to bring his servants to make him comfortable."

"And if he doesn't go, he'll have six men, including himself, to the two of you, Thomas," said Frank grimly. "Remember, Lord Roworth's groom left for London last night."

Felix laughed. "Trevor certainly wouldn't be much use if push came to shove," he said, "but I wasn't serious! Oxshott's a nobleman, not a brigand. He'll take a lot of convincing that you're the legitimate heirs, but he's not going to do anything so outlandish as to take possession of the place and prepare for a siege."

Frank had less faith in the rationality of the aristocracy. "Perhaps not," he conceded, "but I'll still have to be here to entertain him."

"I hope he chooses not to come," said Vickie. "I'll be sorry if you have to miss the picnic, Captain, but he'd ruin the fun. Sir George cannot abide the sight of him."

One way or another, Frank thought, it sounded like an exhausting day. At Upfield Grange he'd be striving to keep his temper with his uncle; at Heathcote he'd be striving to keep his neighbour from his uncle's throat.

"Perhaps we should invite Sir George and his family to join us on another occasion," Fanny proposed.

"No!" Vickie cried. "If you're going to make me go back to Westwood, it will be my last chance to spend some time with him . . . them for an age. Anyway, we need his wagon to take us all there."

"It's time I was setting up my carriage," said Frank. "Fanny, can you believe it? Only a few weeks ago . . ." His voice failed him. Only a few weeks ago, he had been fighting for his life in dingy lodgings in Brussels, with the prospect of a life of struggling poverty before him if he survived. He had not even dreamt of Lady Constantia's existence, and now he was making himself miserable because he could never ask her to be his wife. What a sapskull! He should be revelling in his good fortune and in every moment he could spend with her.

Today he might have to make the best of the duke's company instead, but that was no reason why Lady Victoria should suffer. "I'll send Hoskins over to Netherfield with an invitation," he promised her. "Thomas, tell him to report to me."

Fanny went off to discuss picnic provisions with Henriette. Felix followed her, and the nursery party also left. Constantia, her expression troubled, lingered over a cup of tea. Frank was still hungry, but his congealed eggs looked most unappetizing so he buttered a roll.

"How quickly one grows accustomed to luxury," he said to Constantia, laughing as he indicated his plate. "There were times in Spain when a dish of eggs, hot or cold, would have seemed a feast, yet now I scorn it because I've let it cool."

She smiled. "Be as finicky as you please. When I recall the pains I was at to tempt your appetite, I can only be glad that you are hungry. Captain, I hope you will not think me interfering. I know you are much recovered, but are you sure you will not find this outing too tiring?"

"What could be more relaxing than lounging in a wagon filled with cushions and lovely ladies?" he bantered. "If I go, I shan't attempt to see all of the house, and I may return to the wagon to join Anita for her afternoon nap, leaving your brother to deal with Sir George and the duke."

"You don't believe your uncle has abandoned his efforts to dispossess you? He was quite civil last night — at least, comparatively!"

"My guess is, his improved manners were due to his accepting your credentials, not mine or Fanny's. Let's hope Mackintyre can convince him that we're his sister's children."

"It is shockingly improper in me to say so, but what an unpleasant man he is," said Constantia with a shudder. "I daresay spending a day alone with him will tire you far more than any number of picnic parties. It seems unlikely he will wish to join us, however."

The duke confounded her expectations. He'd take the opportunity to inspect the other half of his property, he declared aggressively. To Fanny's disgruntlement, he displaced her from Felix's phaeton rather than call out his own carriage. He had been cooped up in it all the previous day, he said, announcing his intention in such a way the Felix found it impossible to protest without gross impoliteness.

That left seven people to ride in the wagon, counting neither little Anita nor Sir George, who drove. It arrived at Upfield Grange drawn by two huge Suffolk Punches, the brasses on their harness gleaming scarcely brighter than their chestnut coats. A hamper was tied to the back, and Thomas set about loading Henriette's contribution.

Lady Berman was on the box beside her son. A plump, cheerful woman with iron-grey hair and no pretensions to grandeur, she offered Constantia her seat.

"Oh no, ma'am, I wouldn't dream of taking your place. The back looks vastly comfortable."

"It is, Lady Constantia," Pamela Berman assured her. "We gathered every cushion and pillow in the house."

"And rugs, in case it's chilly later," Lizzie added. The sisters, about Vickie's age, were lively, amiable girls very like their mama.

Regarding Lady Berman with a hopeful look in her eye, Vickie opened her mouth to speak. Constantia quickly took her arm, with a tiny shake of the head. An earl's daughter outranked a baronet's widow, but Lady Berman's years entitled her to the best seat, even if Vickie were not still a schoolroom miss.

Vickie pouted for a moment, then her friends called to her. Megrims forgotten, she lifted the excited Anita into their arms. Sir George jumped down to help her scramble up by the step at the side, and she ensconced herself between his chattering sisters, their backs to the horses, Anita in her lap.

Sir George and Felix handed the ladies

into the wagon and passed up their parasols. Frank climbed up without assistance, stiffly but without pain as far as Constantia could see. He settled in the remaining corner, facing the girls, with Fanny between him and Constantia. There was plenty of room to sit without crowding.

Leaning back against the bright-hued cushions he gazed up into the blue sky and said lazily, "What a perfect day! Don't fret, Fanny, you have the best of a bad bargain. Poor Roworth has not only to do without your company but to put up with our dearly beloved uncle."

"Poor Felix." Fanny sighed. "How mortifying it is to have to acknowledge such a relative."

The Suffolks set the heavy wagon in motion with the greatest of ease and they started down the drive. As they crossed the bridge over the stream, Constantia glanced back. Hoskins was only just bringing Felix's phaeton around the tower at the corner of the house. Not only was the light vehicle faster, they had decided to postpone for as long as possible Sir George's inevitable encounter with the duke.

The short journey passed quickly, along narrow lanes between hedgerows hung with silvery old man's beard, purple-black sloes and elderberries, and the varied reds of hips, haws, and bryony. Sir George had an alarming tendency to leave his team to its own devices while he turned to chat with his passengers. However, the great horses trotted calmly on their way with no more than a hint from the reins when the lane branched. Constantia could not imagine a more delightful way to travel on a fine day.

Approaching Heathcote, a pinewood interspersed with clearings purple with heather hid the house until they were nearly upon it. As they emerged from the dappled shade, a circular carriage sweep led them around a thicket of overgrown roses to stop before a manor in the style of Queen Anne's reign. Mellow red brick edged with dressed stone, white-painted sash windows, carved cornices beneath the eaves — and workmen on the red-tiled roof.

"It is charming, Fanny," said Constantia.

"Not quite as exotic as Upfield Grange," Frank said, grinning.

"Aunt Fanny, is this where I'm going to live?" asked Anita. "Aunt Vickie says you and me and Uncle Felix is going to live at this house."

"Yes, as soon as it's been put in order, sweetheart."

"I like it. What's those men doing up on

the roof? Do they live here too?" She waved back to the waving workmen as the wagon came to a halt before the small, white-pillared porch.

"They are mending it. A chimney-pot fell through in a storm last winter so they have to put on new tiles so the rain doesn't come through the hole. The chimney fell right through the plaster between the joists of the attic floor," Fanny told Constantia, "so there was quite a bit of damage to the top story."

"You said the rest is in fairly good condition though?" Frank asked, descending to the weedy gravel.

"A few broken windows," said Sir George. His patient horses stood still while he lifted his plump mother down as easily as if she were the veriest sylph. "The village lads regard the windows of an empty house as legitimate targets, I'm afraid. All right, Mother?" Helping Constantia and Fanny to step down, he turned to Vickie. "Lady Victoria, if you'll just pass Anita down to . . ." He paused, mouth open, then thundered, "What the deuce is he doing here?"

The phaeton was rounding the curve of the drive. Sir George at once recognized the stout gentleman seated beside Felix, and he was not pleased.

"George, mind your language," said Lady

Berman sharply.

"Sir George," said Fanny, fixing him with a steely eye, "you are my guest at Heathcote, as is my uncle Oxshott. Be so good as to waive your quarrel for the day."

"I'll not start a dust-up, Miss Ingram, but if yon blackguard tries to come the bully over me I'll not take it sitting down. It's more than flesh and blood can bear."

As the girls scrambled down unaided by the irate squire, Felix drew up the phaeton behind the wagon. The duke was glaring up at the workmen on the roof.

"Wasting my money on a house I'm going to demolish!" he howled. "You there, Ingram, what the devil do you mean by it, eh? As soon as I've induced that pigheaded jackanapes of a farmer to sell me Netherfield, this place is coming down, along with Upfield Grange."

"Over my dead body!" cried Sir George, striding forward, his face suffused with rage.

Frank grabbed his arm. "That will do, Berman," he said curtly.

The duke sneered down at the large young man. "Oh, so you're here too, Berman. You're trespassing on my property."

Stepping in front of Sir George, Frank addressed Oxshott in a quiet, courteous, yet authoritative voice. "Sir, the question of

trespass will be settled when Lawyer Mackintyre arrives, I believe. In the meantime,
let us try to make this a pleasant outing for
the ladies."

"I do so enjoy picnics, Duke, do not you?"
Constantia moved towards the phaeton with
swift, light steps. She had not the least
desire for his grace's company — indeed,
she found him disagreeable when he was
not alarming — but she was one of the few
present with whom he had no quarrel. It
was up to her to deflect his attention from
Frank, and the other victims of his rudeness
and ill temper.

The smile Frank flashed at her was reward
enough. Oxshott merely grunted as he
heaved himself down from the carriage.

"I've brought a bottle of that madeira, sir,"
Felix said soothingly. "There's a pleasant
bench on the terrace where we might sit
and indulge ourselves a little."

"Trying to turn me up sweet, eh?"

"Certainly, sir. Constantia, will you take
his grace around that way?" He indicated
the west side of the house. "I'll come as
soon as I've seen to my cattle."

"Shall I go with you?" Frank asked her in
a low voice.

Reluctantly Constantia shook her head.
"Let him calm down first." She looked back

in the hope of persuading Vickie to accompany her.

Vickie was saying to Sir George, with deep sympathy, "I knew you'd be mad as a wet hen. Never mind. Let's go and explore."

And linking her arm through his in the friendliest manner, she drew him towards the house.

Though she was sorry not to have her sister's support, Constantia was favourably impressed by Vickie's tact in removing the wrathful squire. She moved on to join the duke.

A crash behind her coincided with a yell from above. "Watch out below!"

She swung round. On the gravel at Vickie's and Sir George's feet lay a shattered tile.

"Watch out above!" shouted Sir George and charged into the house, Vickie at his heels.

Constantia pitied the unfortunate workman who had dropped the tile.

"What a shame," said the duke with a malevolent grin. "The fellow nearly presented me with Berman's dead body."

Shocked by both his malice and Vickie's narrow escape, she asked, "Surely a tile could not kill someone? It does not look very large, only about a foot by half as much."

"But falling from a height, ma'am, falling from a height. Had the corner hit him on the head —"

"It would have knocked off his hat, I daresay, but had it hit my sister, her bonnet would have given little protection."

"True. A lucky escape."

After that, she found it difficult to come up with any unexceptionable topic of conversation. Fortunately, Oxshott seemed to be in a reflective mood. They sat in near silence on the terrace bench until Felix arrived to relieve her, bottle and glasses in hand.

"Ingram's waiting for you at the front door," he whispered to her.

She hurried back to the front of the house, where Frank was seated on a mounting block. He rose with a smile, and came to meet her.

"Thank you," he said simply. "Our obligations to you and your brother and sister constantly increase."

"It was nothing." She lowered her lashes and twirled her parasol in a sudden access of shyness. "After all, Fanny and I shall soon be sisters. I only wish your uncle had not spoiled today for her and Felix."

"They have the rest of their lives before them." He sounded sad. Looking up, Constantia wondered if she saw a momentary hint of despair in his face, but he smiled again, offered her his arm, and said, "Shall we inspect the house?"

"You are not tired from the journey?"

"Not at all. Only three miles, after all. I'm fit as a fiddle. In fact, I'm going to venture upstairs to the first floor."

They wandered through Fanny's house, admiring the pretty gilt plasterwork of the high ceilings and the elegant columned chimney-pieces after the style of Inigo Jones. The light, airy, beautifully proportioned rooms were almost bare of furniture.

"I expect the best pieces were taken to Upfield Grange when the owner of Heathcote died," said Connie. "Did not Mr Mackintyre say his daughter was already married to Mr Kerridge of Upfield?"

"Yes, that's right. Fanny never mentioned the dearth. She must select what she wants from the Grange. It's odd, don't you think, that the Kerridges chose to live there when this house is so much more modern?"

"Upfield Grange has far more character," Constantia declared.

"Mr and Mrs Kerridge were already quite elderly when her father died." Lady Berman had entered the room where they were and overheard their words. "They decided that

213

removing to Heathcote was more trouble than it was worth, and besides, Mr Kerridge was very much attached to his ancestral home. I remember visiting here as a young bride." She strolled on with them, reminiscing.

From a first floor window, she pointed out a Grecian temple gazebo on a small knoll behind the house. It was the perfect place for the picnic which, since the duke did nothing worse than sit and glower, everyone else enjoyed. Afterwards, Anita fell asleep with her head in Frank's lap. Oxshott also nodded off, his muffled snores punctuated now and then by a jerk into near wakefulness, a truculent glare around, and a redescent into somnolence.

Lady Berman announced that she meant to sit and admire the view while the others explored the grounds. She offered to watch Anita but Frank, too, admitted himself ready for a rest. Constantia stayed behind in the gazebo to chat with them. She told herself she wished neither to race around with Vickie, the energetic Sir George, and his lively sisters, nor to play the gooseberry to Felix and Fanny now that at last they could be together.

At last Anita began to stir, and the duke's periods of wakefulness grew longer. "It's time we were heading for home," said Lady Berman in a low voice. "I am in dire need of a dish of tea. I should like to invite you all to Netherfield to take tea, since we must pass the gate anyway, but I know poor George will not have his grace in the house."

"Who can blame him?" said Frank with a sigh.

Constantia thought tea at Netherfield would be a delightful way to prolong a delightful day. "I'll ask Felix to take the duke straight back to the Grange," she proposed hardheartedly. "As you said, Captain, he and Fanny have the rest of their lives before them."

So it was arranged, after a few groans from Felix.

Netherfield was just as Constantia had expected, not quite either manor or farm-house, untidy but sparkling clean, comfort-able and welcoming. Vickie was perfectly at home there, and Constantia suspected the greater part of her objection to returning to Westwood was the prospect of parting from the Bermans. In fact, when Sir George brought the wagon round to the front door to take the visitors home, Pam and Lizzie insisted on going too for a last goodbye even though he had invited Vickie to join him on the box.

Constantia found herself seated between Fanny and Frank. As the wagon rolled down Netherfield's well-kept drive in the golden light of late afternoon, Frank drifted into slumber. Gradually he inclined towards her until his hat fell off and his head rested on her shoulder.

"Do you mind?" Fanny whispered.

"Oh no," said Constantia, her heart filled with a vast tenderness.

And then, as if of its own accord, her hand crept towards her chest in a harsh reminder of reality.

CHAPTER 11

Mr Mackintyre arrived that evening, shortly before dinner. Fanny put back dinner a quarter of an hour to give him time to change out of his travel-worn clothes.

Constantia expected the duke to take exception to dining with his lawyer but, though he appeared decidedly disgruntled, he said nothing. Of course, after sitting down with a governess he would look idiotish objecting to a respectable lawyer, besides not wishing to suffer another defeat. When his grace had cavilled at Miss Bannister's presence last night, Frank had prevailed.

The noble duke's bluster was no match for the commanding manner of a military officer. Frank was amazingly imposing when he chose.

Naturally no business was discussed at the dinner table. Mr Mackintyre, a beam on his genial face, admired the improvements to the Grange and enquired as to those at

Heathcote, while Oxshott grew more and more morose. In fact, the duke wanted to put off the business until the morning, but Mr Mackintyre insisted he absolutely had to leave early.

"I must appear in court the day after tomorrow," he said, "and my preparations for the case are incomplete. For no one but your grace could I possibly have left London at this time at such short notice."

This mild flattery did not perceptibly lift Oxshott's gloom. No doubt he was all too well aware that the lawyer had bad news for him. Constantia did not quite understand what he had hoped to gain by coming to Upfield Grange, unless he had really believed he might intimidate the Ingrams into abandoning their inheritance. To a bellicose nobleman used to having his own way, a woman and a wounded soldier must have sounded like feeble opponents.

Frank looked tired. She hoped his grace would be quickly convinced of the futility of his claim.

Fanny was perfectly self-possessed at the dinner table, but when she led the ladies to the drawing-room she clung to Constantia's arm.

"It doesn't matter so much to me," she said. "Felix is able to support a family, and though we should have to live at Westwood, I should not mind once we are married. But Frank . . ."

"If the captain were unable to return to military life, Felix would certainly invite him to make his home at Westwood," Constantia reassured her, sitting down by the fire on the faded loveseat soon to be recovered with blue brocade.

Fanny sat beside her. "But Frank will hate to hang on Felix's sleeve. I daresay he will refuse."

"Not 'will,' Fanny dear. 'Would.' I am sure you need not fret yourself into flinders. After heartily commending your improvements to the Grange and Heathcote, Mr Mackintyre cannot intend to say they are not yours after all."

"Perhaps you're right. I'm behaving like a ninnyhammer, I know. Simply having my uncle in the house has me in high fidgets. I cannot wait for him to realize he is mistaken and go away!"

"Indeed, he is not precisely the ideal guest! The sooner he departs, the happier we shall all be."

The gentlemen did not dawdle over the port, an inferior wine of which Felix had reluctantly acquired a small quantity at the Pig and Piper, lacking time to go into

Winchester. Though appreciating a good vintage, neither he nor Frank was a dedicated toper who must without fail take his glass after dinner. Whatever their usual habits, the duke and the lawyer evidently did not find the Pig and Piper's port an irresistible draw.

When they entered the drawing-room, Miss Bannister removed the unwilling Vickie. Constantia was about to follow when Mr Mackintyre stopped her.

"Pray stay, my lady, if you will be so good," he said softly. "I know you to be in the Ingrams' confidence and I shall be glad of another witness."

"If they have no objection," she assented, somewhat alarmed. Witness to what? She returned to her place by the fire, a small one, for the evening chill had not yet ousted the day's warmth from the south-facing room.

When the gentlemen came in, Fanny had gone straight to Felix. Constantia saw Frank glance after his sister, his face forlorn. For so many years the twins had confronted the world together. Now she had abandoned him for the man she loved.

A wave of longing swept over Constantia, for Frank to regard her with the same fond, possessive gaze that Felix was now bestowing upon Fanny. Yet if she ever read so much as hope in his eyes, she must dash it, or flee. She was a fool to seek out his company, to treasure his friendship when she wanted so much more. Yet when he came to take Fanny's place beside her, she smiled up at him, glad of his choice of seat.

The duke planted himself heavily on an elegant Hepplewhite chair that had barely been reprieved, having a middling case of woodworm. It was Fanny's favourite, but she was slight, delicate in appearance if not in fact. Constantia held her breath as Oxshott's large rear end descended. The chair creaked but survived.

Thomas brought in Mr Mackintyre's valise. The lawyer set it on a table, opened it, and armed himself with a sheaf of papers. He went to stand with his back to the fireplace.

"Your grace," he said deferentially, Scottish *r*'s rolling, "I understand you desire to inspect the proof that Captain and Miss Ingram are the legitimate offspring of your late sister, Lady Frances Ingram, née Kerridge."

"Of course I do, my good man," snapped the duke. "You don't think I'm going to hand over two properties and all the ready to m'sister's by-blows."

Frank's mouth set in a grim line, but he held his peace. Felix sprang to his feet, his handsome face wrathful. Fanny grasped his sleeve and held him back. "His grace might have chosen his words better," she said with disdain, "but his concern is natural. Do sit down, Felix."

"Quite so, ma'am." Mr Mackintyre put on his gold-rimmed spectacles and selected a paper from his sheaf. "Here is a copy of the entry in the parish register of the church where Lady Frances wed Captain — then lieutenant — Thomas Ingram of the Royal Horse Artillery, according to the rites of the Church of England and the laws of the land. As you will see, your grace, it is certified as an exact copy by the present incumbent and a churchwarden."

He stepped forward to hand it to the duke, who bounced up to grab it with an agility remarkable in one of his size and age.

After a brief glance, Oxshott thrust the paper back at the lawyer. "Pah!" He dropped back into his seat. Constantia winced as the abused chair creaked again.

"I have also a witnessed statement from one of the witnesses to the marriage," the lawyer continued urbanely, riffling through the documents. "An elderly lady, I am informed, who still sighs over the romantic runaway match of the dashing young soldier in his smart uniform. Naturally there is more than one copy of each. My investigator is extremely thorough."

"Good for Taggle," said Frank, grinning. Mr Mackintyre's eyes twinkled at him over the gold spectacles.

This time the duke waved away the proffered paper. "So she married the rascal," he growled. "What's to say this fine pair are really her children and not impudent impostors?"

"I could show your grace a number of affidavits from officers acquainted with the family at various times and places, covering overlapping periods. All expressed their willingness to identify Captain and Miss Ingram under oath in court if necessary. However, perhaps their baptismal certificates will suffice to persuade your grace. Captain?"

"I have them here." With care, Frank extracted two faded documents from his coat pocket.

The lawyer nodded. "If you would not mind showing them to Lady Constantia, Captain? My lady, his lordship your brother has already examined these certificates and is prepared to swear to having done so, but one can never have too many witnesses."

Frank passed them to her with a curious reluctance. She perused the first: born to Frances Cynthia Ingram and Thomas Ingram, man and wife, on the twelfth of May 1790, in Nilgapur, India, a daughter Frances, baptized two days later, and the regimental chaplain's signature. The second was almost identical right down to the date: born to . . . Nilgapur . . . a son, Francis Cynthia, baptized . . . Francis Cynthia?

As she turned to Frank, she caught sight of Felix's grin and her lips began to quiver.

"Don't you dare laugh," Frank breathed through clenched teeth, his still-thin face scarlet. "I'll explain later."

Biting her lip to hold back a giggle, she nodded. She held out the parchment pages to Mr Mackintyre, and said with only the tiniest tremor in her voice, "Here, sir. I have read and will remember them."

"Let me see." The duke leapt up and seized them from her hand. Moving closer to the light of the candles on the mantelpiece, he squinted at the certificates, holding them at arm's length.

And then he dropped them. Surely he could not have deliberately thrown them towards the fire, but they landed right beside a glowing log feathered with white ash. At once one corner of the heavy parchment began to scorch.

With an inarticulate cry, Constantia flung herself on her knees and snatched them away.

All but the first word of Fanny's was still legible. As she sat back on her heels, satisfied, Frank dropped to his knees at her side. He tossed the certificates aside, and grasped her hands, turning them palm upward.

"You're not burnt?" His voice shook. "My dear girl, of all the idiotish risks to take!"

Her hands trembled in his. Though no flame had touched her, his touch sent a searing heat flaring through her body. Her pulse raced. Did he hear her heart madly beating?

"Well done, little sister." Felix had already retrieved the documents. He looked down benignly on Constantia and Frank, who dropped her hands abruptly, as though they were indeed afire. Her brother reached down to help her up, then gave the certificates to the lawyer.

"Thank you, my lord," said Mr Mackintyre. Stroking his white sidewhiskers with one forefinger, he aimed a bland smile at Oxshott. "It would have been a pity to lose these, but of no great importance. Admittedly, Lord Roworth and Lady Constantia might be considered biased witnesses, despite their consequence. However, I have copies in the safe in my office, attested as true copies by myself and my investigator, the estimable Taggle. You have finished your examination, your grace?"

As the duke turned away with a snarl, Mr Mackintyre returned the parchments to Frank. Flustered, Constantia had sat down without seeing him rise from his knees. She did not know whether he had managed it himself, or if Fanny had helped him.

Fanny sat beside her now, saying, "Bless you, Connie. They may not matter to Mr Mackintyre but they are precious to . . ."

Creak, crack, CRASH! One rear leg of the Hepplewhite chair had finally surrendered under the assault. His grace, the Duke of Oxshott toppled over backwards with his feet in the air.

In unison, Constantia and Fanny gasped and clapped their hands to their mouths. Over their hands, their eyes met, brimful of mirth. Fortunately Felix's shout of laughter was almost drowned by the duke's howl of rage. Felix and Mr Mackintyre rushed to the rescue, while Frank looked on, grinning.

His grace righted and deposited upon a stout sofa, the lawyer brushed him down, murmuring solicitous tut-tuts. Oxshott pushed him away. His face was suffused with blood and Constantia feared he was about to suffer an apoplexy.

After gaping wordlessly for a moment, the duke manifested his mangled sensibilities in a roar. "You needn't think you've heard the last of this! I shan't be robbed without a fight. I'll go to law!"

"I cannot advise such a course, your grace," said Mr Mackintyre, unmoved. "It is highly unlikely that the testament I drew up will be overturned, but even if it were, the suit might take many years to come to judgment. Though I should be the gainer thereby, I must warn you that both parties are likely to be ruined by attorneys' fees in the process. I have known many such cases."

"I'll see you all ruined!" thundered the duke, and rushed from the room.

Mr Mackintyre heaved a sad sigh. "There is no arguing with his grace in this mood," he observed. "I shall try to have a word with him in the morning. At least he now recognizes that he cannot simply dispossess you, my dear Miss Ingram, or you, Captain."

"We might really be ruined, even if we won in the end?" asked Fanny in dismay.

"I fear so."

"What can we do?"

"Wait until morning," advised the lawyer without much hope.

"I believe, Fanny," said Constantia, feeling utterly limp, "you had best ring for the tea tray."

Tea and Henriette's crisp, wafer-thin, almond biscuits revived them all a little. However, Mr Mackintyre was forced to admit that Oxshott was by no means always susceptible to reason. The fact that he'd ruin himself in the process of ruining the Ingrams would not necessarily weigh with him.

Constantia realized that Frank was not joining in the discussion. He was seated a little way apart, his head resting against the high back of his armchair. His eyes were closed and he looked exhausted. However splendidly indomitable he appeared when he stood up to the duke, he was still convalescent.

As if he felt her gaze upon him, he opened his eyes and gave her a tired smile. She went to him, stopping him with a gesture as he made to stand up.

"Will you take more tea? Or a glass of madeira? Or milk and stout?"

His smile turned wry. "Tea will do very well, thank you, though I am a little weary. I confess I'm glad I don't have to climb the stairs to my chamber."

"It has been a difficult day."

"You never spoke a truer word. It's far more difficult to hold my temper than it would be to retaliate in kind, yet descending to his level can only make matters worse. If Wellington taught us anything, it's to hold one's fire until it will do the most good." He sat up straighter, his expression grim. "But had anyone other than my mother's brother impugned her morals as he did, I'd have called him out on the spot."

"I cannot for a moment suppose he really believed what he suggested," Constantia said soothingly, though she had been excessively shocked when the duke claimed his sister had borne children out of wedlock. "He simply says whatever comes into his head that he hopes might help his cause."

"Such insults are not to be endured, whether intended or not." Nonetheless, he relaxed again.

Taking his cup, she refilled it and her own, balanced two biscuits on the edge of his saucer, and went to sit beside him. She refused to let the strange sensations his touch aroused in her become a barrier between them. What she needed was a cheerful, amusing topic of conversation to return their friendship to an agreeably lighthearted level.

The duke's tumble had been the funniest

thing she had seen in a long time. However, she wanted to banish him from Frank's mind for the moment. "You promised me an explanation," she said tentatively, "but I shall not press you if you do not care to tell me."

"Explanation?"

"Of your name."

He groaned, flushing. "If I'd guessed Mackintyre meant to show you that paper . . . ! I'll satisfy your curiosity if you swear on all you hold dear never to reveal my middle name to a soul."

On all she held dear? Felix, Vickie, Fanny now, and Anita — and Frank himself. Her blush matching his, she said quickly, "Of course I swear. I should never have told anyway."

"I know, I do trust you, but it's a sensitive subject," he said ruefully. "It was all my father's fault. Fanny and I were born in the middle of the monsoon floods and Father was distracted with worry for Mama and for his guns. Fanny was supposed to be christened first, named for Mama, but he handed me to the chaplain by mistake."

"So you were christened Frances Cyn . . . My lips are sealed." And as solemn as she could make them.

"Father realized what had happened as

soon as he took me back. Though the chaplain agreed to use the masculine spelling of Francis on the certificate, he refused to leave off Mama's middle name, saying he couldn't revoke the solemn sacrament of baptism."

"Oh dear! But why was Fanny also christened Frances?"

"Poor father was in such a state by then he couldn't think of any other female name he liked. As we're twins, most people don't consider it odd that we share a name."

"I always considered it a charming notion. With Frank and Fanny there is no confusion."

"Now you know, you won't snicker every time you see me?"

"Heavens, no," she promised. "Only occasionally."

"Wretch!" he said, grinning.

They were back on their old, comfortable footing. Yet, as she sipped her tea, she felt that her sense of intimacy, of significant matters left unspoken between them, had not been lessened as she intended, but reinforced.

Whether he felt the same, she could not guess. At least he looked less worn to the bone, crunching an almond biscuit with relish. She had succeeded in distracting him from his uncle's animosity.

Fanny soon reminded him. She came up to them and said to him, "Frank, Mr Mackintyre says there's absolutely nothing we can do to prevent a lawsuit, short of handing over lock, stock, and barrel."

"That we shan't do. Nor shall I leave Upfield Grange unless a bailiff comes to throw me out," he said stubbornly.

"We can stay, and the income is still ours, until the suit is settled, which may be years and years."

"Splendid." Frank squeezed his sister's hand. "There's no sense leaving more than we must for his grace to set his greedy hands on. Until we're ruined, let's enjoy ourselves."

"With him in the house?" Fanny shuddered. "He still believes it's his. He may stay forever."

"He has nothing to gain by staying," Constantia pointed out, "now he realizes you are not easily cowed. Hotheaded as he is, he will want to set his lawsuit in train without delay. I daresay he will be gone by noon tomorrow."

"Besides," said Frank, "he's used to much grander surroundings. He only wants the Grange in order to tear it down, remember."

"Dreadful man!" Fanny exclaimed. "I'll

be heartily relieved to see the back of him."

In the morning, Mr Mackintyre joined the family at breakfast prior to going up to Oxshott's chamber to make a last attempt at reasoning with him. It was a gloomy meal. The lawyer felt he had failed the Ingrams, and Vickie and Miss Bannister were packed and ready to leave for Westwood. Anita sat on Frank's lap, fearful of losing him, too. Constantia watched as he coaxed the little girl into drinking her milk and eating tidbits from his plate.

Lord Westwood had never taken any of his children on his knee, let alone fed them with his own hands. What a wonderful father Frank Ingram would be! Constantia sighed.

The dining-room door opened. Anita looked round, then shrank back against Frank's chest as the duke came in. Yet his grace's face was not distorted into a scowl, nor a frown, was not even wearing its habitual petulant expression. His grace's face was twisted into a smile, more grimace than grin. He looked as if it hurt him.

"Good morning, good morning!" he cried with a horrid approximation to geniality, rubbing his hands together. "All up with the lark, I see. Excellent."

Thomas, who had followed him in, hurried to set another place and pull up a chair. He served the duke from the sideboard, poured him coffee, and left with a backward glance, torn between curiosity and eagerness to inform his fellow-servants of this latest start.

"Excellent," Oxshott repeated, regarding his devilled kidneys and cold tongue with real satisfaction. He looked around the table at the flabbergasted company. His eyes held no warmth, Constantia noted. "Well, now, I expect you're all wondering what brought me down so early. I wanted to tell you I've decided Mackintyre has the right of it. No one will profit from a lawsuit but the lawyers, ha ha."

"So it would seem, sir," Frank said cautiously.

"Call me uncle, my dear fellow! I'm determined to be better acquainted with my niece and nephew, dear little Frances's children."

"How . . . how kind of you, Uncle." Fanny forced the words through stiff lips.

"So I'll stay here at Upfield as long as I can be spared from business elsewhere."

Fanny blenched. "Pray don't put off urgent business for our sakes, Uncle."

"No, no, I insist. What could be more

important than newly discovered relatives, eh? You have been isolated from the family far too long. My son — your cousin Mentham — and his sister will be delighted to make your acquaintance, and your aunts also. I shall write this very morning and direct them to come and join us at once."

CHAPTER 12

"They couldn't possibly all be like him, could they?" With a moan, Fanny dropped onto the one of the Jacobean hall chairs as the duke disappeared into the bookroom to write his letters.

"The odds are against it," Felix opined.

"Have you never met any of them in Town?" Constantia asked.

"It's a good many years since I took much part in London Society." He frowned in thought. "Come to think of it, I believe I've met the Marquis of Mentham at my club. He's a bit of a slowtop as I recall. I may have come across his sister and your aunts, too, but I don't remember them."

"Cheer up, Fanny," said Frank. "Among so many, surely one or two will turn out to be agreeable."

Fanny moaned again. "Sisters, aunts, cousins! It's all very well for him to wave his hands and say airily he's sure I'll find room for them, but where?"

"Lay 'em out in rows in here," said her betrothed, glancing around the Great Hall. "Plenty of space."

"Do be serious, Felix."

"It's not my problem, thank goodness. That's what females are for. Come on, Ingram, let's go and consult my father's coachman about the sort of carriage that will best suit your needs. He'll be off in half an hour."

"Men!" said Fanny in disgust as they turned to leave.

"Perhaps I ought to go with Vickie," Constantia suggested hesitantly. "That would give you an extra bedchamber."

"No!" Fanny clutched her arm. "Now of all times, don't leave me in the lurch, Connie, pray don't."

Frank's footsteps paused, and then he turned back. "I can't blame you, Lady Constantia, if you choose to flee my uncle's unamiable presence and a houseful of what I fear may prove equally disagreeable company. But, for Fanny's sake, I wish you will not leave."

For Fanny's sake, not his. Once again his desire for her to stay was less than wholehearted. Constantia was torn. She anticipated no pleasure from the coming house-party; her chamber was needed; Fanny would have sufficient chaperons without her. On the other hand, she ought to be relieved that Frank showed no sign of becoming a suitor, since she would not be forced to reject him. She hated to turn tail and run from the challenge of the duke and his family. And as well as the practical support she could give Fanny, the friendship of an earl's daughter was bound to make her new relatives less likely to condescend to her or try to intimidate her.

Felix echoed her thoughts. "Lord, Con, you can't go. How is Fanny to manage a horde of starchy, stiff-rumped females without you?"

"Fanny is equal to anything, but I daresay I can help. We had best go and talk to Mrs Tanner, Fanny."

Fanny gave her a grateful smile. "I'm afraid it will be a perfectly horrid affair, but perhaps they won't all come," she said hopefully. "How sadly mistaken I was to assume that being betrothed to Felix and inheriting a fortune was the end to all my troubles!"

As they made their way towards the housekeeper's room, Constantia was struck by a dismaying possibility. Suppose Fanny proposed that the two of them share a chamber? She would never be able to keep her scar hidden. Fanny might mention it to Felix, from whom Constantia had so carefully guarded her secret all these years.

Nor could she ask Fanny not to tell Felix. Fanny would want to know why, and loving Felix as she did, it would distress her to think he considered himself responsible for that long-ago accident.

"You will take Anita into your bedchamber, I expect?" Constantia suggested hastily.

"I meant to do that anyway, even were we not about to be invaded. Her room is too far from mine, and she is so sad to lose your sister and Miss Bannister, she needs a little extra cosseting."

"Her room is quite small. If I remove thither, we shall be able to fit two into the chamber I have now."

"If you truly don't mind, that will help. I wish we hadn't given the room which will be Frank's to the duke. It's quite the largest, and with the dressing-room connected, too, but I'm too craven to ask him to move or to share with Lord Mentham."

"Heavens, so am I! I own I am curious to meet the unfortunate young man who has the duke for a father."

"Since the late duke was as quarrelsome as his son, no doubt his grandson is a chip off the same block. Can you imagine what it will be like having two of them in the house? Oh, Connie, if you decide to leave I'll quite understand."

"I shall not desert you," Constantia promised.

So she was not among the unwilling passengers borne away by the Westwood carriage. Vickie leaned from the window waving madly, her sorrows only slightly mitigated by the five golden guineas Felix had pressed into her hand. On the porch, Anita waved her little hand until the carriage disappeared from sight.

Later, Constantia took the child down to the bridge to play. She hoped Frank might go with them, but he had to interview a couple of ex-artillerymen who had turned up looking for work.

Though sad to lose her friends, Anita was philosophical, for her short life had been full of partings.

"Aunt Fanny's the only one who never goes away," she explained to Constantia, holding her hand and walking sedately at her side down the elm avenue. "Even Uncle Frank goes away sometimes, when Duty calls, but then he comes back. He says you have to go away one day."

Constantia read a question in her grave, dark eyes. "Yes, I shall, sweetheart. I hope to visit you often at Heathcote when Aunt Fanny and Uncle Felix are married."

Anita smiled and gave a little skip. "They'll be my mama and papa then. Amos already has a mama and papa. Aunt Miriam and Uncle Isaac. He has a sister, too, only she's just a baby so she can't play prop'ly with him. D'you think I'll have a sister one day?"

"I should not be a bit surprised." She quelled a blush, recalling one or two warm embraces she had observed when chancing unexpectedly upon her brother and Fanny. What was it like to be held in the arms of the man you loved, knowing he desired you? She would never find out, for she must never let Frank come close enough . . . let *any* man come close enough. She shivered.

"Are you cold, Aunt Connie?"

"No, love. It is another beautiful day, is it not?"

"I like it when the sun shines. Can I . . . Please may I pick up that stick? Aunt Vickie teached me a game."

As they continued down the hill to the sparkling, rush-edged brook, Anita collected a bundle of twigs in her pinafore pocket. She set them in a careful pile on the bridge's deck. The heavy timbers were in good repair, which was more than could be said for the wooden railings. Constantia vowed to herself not to take her eyes off the child for a moment.

Anita chose two twigs and gave her one. "Yours has a fork, see? You gots to remember it. Then we drop them in the water on this side and see which one comes out first, mine or yours."

Hopping with excitement, Anita tugged Constantia to the upstream side of the bridge. They dropped their twigs into the clear water, every pebble in its gravel bed visible, and hurried to the other side. Anita flung herself on her stomach, the better to see her stick amidst a school of darting minnows a few feet below.

"It's mine. Mine's first. P'raps you'll win next time, Aunt Connie." She scrambled up, her white pinafore already grubby.

The little girl was far too absorbed in the game, and Constantia in keeping her from falling in, to notice the duke's approach until he hallooed.

Stumping onto the bridge, cane in hand, he tipped his hat. "A fine morning, ladies. Now do you know, ma'am, no one has explained to me who is this pretty little thing. Come here, my dear." He held out his hand as if to a suspicious dog.

Anita stood her ground, hands behind her back, eyeing him warily.

"Why, you are not afraid of me, are you?"

"No. My daddy was a so'jer. He was artirelly, like Uncle Frank."

"Artillery, eh? A fine body of men, I make no doubt."

Constantia trusted his geniality no more than did Anita, but she decided his request for an explanation was reasonable. "Anita's father was a fellow-officer of Captain Ingram's," she told him. "When she was orphaned, he and Miss Ingram took responsibility for bringing her up."

"So she is no legal connexion?"

"I believe not. However, when my brother and Miss Ingram marry, they will adopt her."

"I wonder whether my dear niece and nephew have thought to make their wills in the child's favour?"

She did not for a moment suppose that he was concerned for Anita's future. In her opinion, his last question was not reasonable but inquisitive. Yet she had no wish to antagonize him — in fact, she had to admit to herself she was a little afraid to be virtually alone with him at some distance from the house. If he were to start shouting at her, she might display her cowardice by picking up Anita and running away.

"I think it most unlikely that they have

243

made wills at all," she said, "since until very recently they had no possessions to bequeath. Now I daresay it is hardly worth the trouble until Felix and Fanny are wed."

"Excellent, excellent." The duke rubbed his hands together. "Well, child, are you going to catch a fish for dinner?"

He moved towards Anita, and she took an involuntary step backwards. However, he merely gazed down into the water, leaning against the rail.

"Take care!" Constantia exclaimed, too late.

The rotten wood did not crack and snap, it simply disintegrated. With a surprised squawk, his grace splashed paunch first into the brook. His hat floated serenely downstream, twirling in an eddy of the current.

Anita giggled. Constantia raised a warning finger to her lips, though she could not suppress a broad smile. The Duke of Oxshott appeared to be unusually prone to accidents.

Her eyes sparkling with excited delight, Anita ran to Constantia and tugged on her arm until she leaned down.

"Will the ogre drown?" she demanded in a whisper.

"Ogre!"

"Aunt Vickie did tell me he's an ogre, like

in *Jack and the Beanstalk*. That ogre went tumbling down, too."

"The duke is not an ogre," Constantia reluctantly disillusioned her. "And the stream is too shallow to drown a grown man, I fear . . . I am sure."

Indeed, his grace had already turned himself over. Spluttering, he sat there submerged to where his waist would be if he had one. A strand of bright green water-weed draped across his chest like the sash of some foreign order. From his draggled locks and whiskers, rivulets ran down his stormy, burgundy-red face.

Cautiously Constantia approached the edge of the bridge. "Are you hurt, Duke?"

"Devil take it, get me out of here!" The duke had recovered his breath, though not his temper.

"Anita, run up to the house and . . . Oh, thank heaven, here comes your uncle."

Frank increased his pace from a stroll to a stride as Constantia hurried to meet him. "What's happened? What has he done now? If he's insulted you again, I'll make him sorry he ever heard of Upfield Grange!"

He held out his hands to her and she gave him her own. For a timeless moment their gazes locked, and it seemed to Constantia his yearning matched her own. Then Anita pulled at his sleeve.

"Uncle Frank, the ogre fell in the water but Aunt Connie says she fears he won't drown."

Constantia gave a breathless gasp of irrepressible laughter. "Oxshott leant on the fence and it gave way."

"Dash it, I missed the show. I must have been behind one of the trees when he went over. Hoskins told me he had come down after you and I thought I'd better join you."

"He's sitting in the stream yelling for help."

"I hear him."

The duke's imprecations floated up to them. "Damn your eyes, you buttock-broker, where in frigging hell have you taken yourself off to?"

Frank winced. "Somehow you don't expect a duke to have a mouth as foul as a trooper's. I can't say how sorry I am to expose you to such unpleasantness, Lady Constantia."

"I cannot hold you responsible, unless you hold me responsible because my parents were not precisely all amiability to you and Fanny? Gracious!" she exclaimed as a further flood of Billingsgate reached her ears.

"What's he talking about, Uncle Frank?"

Anita enquired with interest. "I can't under-stand all the words."

"Nor can I, I am happy to admit," Con-stantia told her. "You must never, under any circumstances, repeat what his grace is say-ing."

"Never! Will you take her up to the house? I'll see what I can do for my beloved uncle."

"You will not try to pull him out?" said Constantia anxiously.

He flexed his shoulders. "No, perhaps not. Luckily I've just hired a couple of brawny gunners. Tell Hoskins to send them down."

" 'Fore Gad, I'll have your gizzards for garters! I'll flay you alive, stap me if I don't!"

"Something tells me he's not going to be pleased when I tell him I can't help him," said Frank with a grimace.

"We shall make haste. Come, Anita."

She glanced back from further up the slope. Frank was seated on the edge of the bridge, his legs dangling. The duke's clam-our reached her, but fortunately distance muffled the words.

Whatever names he was called, Frank survived them without injury. To everyone's relief, the duke retired to his bed to ward off a chill. By the time he reappeared at noon the following day, he had recovered his composure and his dubious cordiality.

He even proposed taking Fanny and Constantia into Winchester in his carriage one day soon to purchase much needed household effects.

"I'll be damned if I'll go on swigging the Pig and Piper's swill any longer," he added, somewhat detracting from the generosity of his offer. "There's bound to be a respectable wine merchant in Winchester with all those clergymen swarming around the cathedral."

"Still," Fanny said optimistically to Constantia later, "he might just as well have gone without us. Perhaps he really has resigned himself to our inheriting and wishes to make up for his rudeness. Only I wish he had not invited all our relatives to stay!"

The trip to Winchester was set for four days hence. In the meantime, the first of the relatives arrived.

Thomas ushered him into the drawing-room, where Fanny and Constantia were entertaining the vicar and his wife to tea. Adolphus Kerridge, Marquis of Mentham, heir to the Duke of Oxshott, was a small, scrawny young man. His clothes were of the first stare, superbly tailored, but he was oddly dishevelled, a button unfastened, a collar turned up on one side and down on the other, a loose end of his neckcloth dangling.

As Fanny rose and crossed the room to greet him, he peered around with a hunted air. "M'father here?" he blurted out.

"I'm not sure where the duke is, Lord Mentham, but Thomas will find him and inform him of your arrival."

"Oh no! Mean to say, thank you, ma'am. Came as quick as I could. You'll tell him I came as quick as I could?" the marquis entreated.

"Certainly," said Fanny, surprised but sympathetic. "Will you take tea with us, or would you prefer to go to your chamber first?"

He glanced down at himself in a helpless way and muttered something about "travel dirt."

"Pray don't consider it. After all, we are cousins and I hope you'll make yourself at home here. Mrs Watchett," she addressed the vicar's wife, "you don't object?"

Mrs Watchett was only too pleased to meet a marquis, the duke having so far eluded her. Constantia poured him a cup of tea. He sat down beside her and drank thirstily.

"Didn't dare stop on the way," he confided. "M'father's a regular Tartar when he's crossed."

"So we have noticed," she murmured, refilling the cup. She pitied the unhappy son of such a father. Lord Mentham was clearly no match for the duke. "Would you care for a madeleine?"

She passed the plate of small, rich cakes, one of Henriette's specialities.

Quietly contented, he consumed three and was reaching for a fourth when Oxshott came in. At once he jumped to his feet, his face resuming its timorous expression.

"So, Mentham, you're here at last and already making up to the ladies," boomed the duke.

"Yes, sir. Mean to say, no, sir. Wouldn't do that, sir. Cousins," he squeaked.

"Lady Constantia is not your cousin, looby."

"Not my cousin? Could have sworn you told me to come to stay with my cousins." He stared at Constantia in puzzlement, then turned to Fanny. "Didn't you say so too, ma'am? Cousins, you said. Make yourself at home."

"I did indeed, Lord Mentham. I should have made plain that while I am your cousin, Lady Constantia is not."

"So that's it," he said, relieved. "Mean to say, deuced confusing. Not that I don't wish you was my cousin, ma'am," he added politely to Constantia. "More the merrier. Hope you'll call me Dolph. Everyone does."

"Mooncalf," snorted his sire.

His low opinion of his offspring, while regrettable, was undeniable. Lord Mentham was possessed of more hair than wit.

"Poor Dolph's understanding is not powerful, but he is perfectly amiable, is he not, Fanny?" Constantia said kindly when she and her brother and the Ingrams met in the drawing-room before dinner. On her way down, passing the duke's chamber, she had heard Dolph say in anguished tones, "But I don't want to. I like Cousin Fanny." To which the duke had replied in the hectoring voice she had come to hate, "What the devil has that to say to the matter, you noodle?" She had hurried on.

"The poor lad seems good-natured enough," Fanny agreed, "and that's better than I'd bargained for. I'm not dreading the arrival of the rest quite so much."

Felix smiled at her. "A good-natured knock-in-the-cradle is a vast improvement over a cross-grained surlyboots."

"If you ask me," said Frank, "he's not just a slowtop, he's touched in the upper works. When I told him a fellow's bringing a carriage over for me to inspect with a view to

251

purchase, he tried to dissuade me. He has a bee in his bonnet about the danger of carriage accidents."

"Perhaps the duke mentioned your injured shoulders to him," Fanny suggested. "I must admit, I'm a trifle concerned myself. Are you sure you're ready to drive, Frank?"

"No," he said patiently. "That's why Felix lent me Dutton to scour the countryside for a suitable vehicle. Sir George sent him to a friend of his, Parslow, a gentleman-farmer over towards Alton. I did tell you all about it."

"Fanny has a great deal on her mind at present," Constantia pointed out. "When shall you see the carriage? Tell us about it."

His face lit with enthusiasm. "It's a barouche-landau, in good condition though in need of paint. It will carry four passengers in comfort and it has a box for a coachman, yet it's light enough for me to drive it myself when I'm able. Parslow's bringing it round first thing the day after tomorrow. He'll sell me his horses, too, if I want them."

"It sounds quite perfect for you," said Constantia, "But that is the day we go to Winchester. I hope we shall have time to see it before we leave."

Oxshott, entering, had overheard them.

"Plenty of time, plenty of time," he assured her, adding with a chuckle, "I'm no early riser, as you know."

Though Constantia and Fanny had hoped for a full day to make their purchases, they once again expressed their appreciation of his offer to take them into the town. He assured them gaily that it was his pleasure. Indeed, his cheerfulness seemed unforced that evening. Poor Dolph, on the other hand, was misery incarnate. No doubt the duke relished having someone defenceless to harass.

By the morning post next day, Constantia received a letter from her mother. She set it aside to be perused later, for the contents were bound to be distressing.

The barouche-landau arrived an hour after breakfast. Fanny was busy about her household duties, consulting Mrs Tanner and Henriette, but she no longer needed Constantia's advice at every turn. Donning a warm pelisse over her walking dress, for it was a grey, chilly day, Constantia wrapped Anita up well and took her out to see the carriage and pair.

"Come for a drive to try it out," Frank invited, as excited as a child with a new toy. "We'll be back long before my slug-a-bed uncle comes down."

Felix helped them in and joined them, and Frank climbed up on the box with the hopeful seller, a lean, weathered country squire. They tooled around the lanes, through King's Wallop, and back again. Fanny came out as they pulled up before the house.

"Are you going to buy it, Frank?" she asked.

"I'm not sure," he said cautiously. "I want to check the hoods."

Fanny went in again, but Anita begged to stay to see the leather hoods raised fore and aft, turning the hybrid vehicle into a closed carriage. They were in poor repair, so Frank requested a reduction in price. While he and Mr Parslow stood at the corner of the entrance tower, bargaining, Constantia took Anita to talk to the horses, a sturdy, easygoing pair of greys.

Coming to an agreement, Frank shook hands with the satisfied seller. Felix offered to take the carriage round to the stables and fetch his phaeton to drive Mr Parslow home.

As the barouche-landau disappeared around the corner of the house, Constantia congratulated Frank on his purchase.

"What colours shall you paint it?" she asked.

"Blue and red," said Anita promptly, "like

your uniform, Uncle Frank."

"Blue picked out in red would be excessively smart," Constantia agreed with a smile.

"Blue and red it shall be," said Frank, and requested Mr Parslow's advice on where to go to have the body repainted and the hoods replaced.

"It's good it's got hoods to keep you dry," Anita observed. "Look, Aunt Connie, it's beginning to rain." She held out her hand.

The four of them moved into the shelter of the porch, just as a carriage appeared from the direction of the stables. It was not Felix's phaeton but the duke's travelling chaise. As it drew up close to the porch, Oxshott emerged from the front door.

He scowled when he saw them. "Are you ready to leave, Lady Constantia?" he snapped.

"I must fetch my reticule. I shall not keep you above three minutes. Come, Anita."

The child obediently took her hand and followed, looking back over her shoulder. They were on the threshold when there came a splintering crash behind them, followed by a roar of rage from the duke.

"My carriage!" he howled. "Destroyed!"

CHAPTER 13

With a cry of fright, Anita ran to Frank. He picked her up and hugged her. Constantia was far more interested in the fact that he did not wincc in pain than in the wreck of the duke's chaise.

"It's all right, sweetheart," he soothed the little girl in his arms. "You're quite safe. Let's go and see what happened to Uncle Oxshott's carriage." Still holding her, he took a step forward, then stopped. "Good Lord!"

Constantia watched the dawning realization on his face. "Your shoulders do not hurt?" she asked.

"The merest twinge!" His lips curved in a joyful smile, his eyes glowing. "No more than a touch of discomfort. I'll be driving in no time."

"You can't drive his carriage." Anita, sangfroid restored, pointed at the duke's chaise. With deep satisfaction she said, "It's got a big hole in it. It's 'stroyed."

"I heard a crash but I cannot see any damage," said Constantia doubtfully.

"I saw it. Let's go and look, Uncle Frank."

The duke was stamping about, gibbering, his voice for once suppressed by outrage. His coachman wisely stayed stolidly on the box, in firm control of his alarmed team. Mr Parslow stood to one side, gazing upward, his hand shielding his eyes from the spitting rain.

"What did you see, Anita?" Frank asked as they left the porch.

"I did see a stone falling from the sky and it hit the carriage."

"The child's right," said Mr Parslow. "You've lost a gargoyle, Ingram. Up there on the corner of the tower, see? There's one missing. Deuced lucky it didn't hit anyone, begging your pardon, my lady." He crouched to peer under the carriage.

"Lucky!" Oxshott found his voice, his most stentorian. "Lucky! Your damned gargoyle went right through the roof and then the floor, Ingram. I hold you responsible."

"Fustian!" Fanny had come out unobserved, dressed for the shopping expedition, followed by Thomas. "If the house is falling to pieces, our grandfather, your late father,

257

is responsible, Uncle. Frank has not had time to put all in order after years of neglect."

Taken aback by her sharp rebuke, the duke gaped at her.

"All the same," said Frank peaceably, "I'll have to have the roof checked. I thought it was in good repair. Someone might have been killed."

"They might well." Mr Parslow had dived under the carriage and now emerged with a piece of carved stone in each large, leather-gloved hand. He stuck them together and a hideous, leering demon stuck its tongue out at them. "It weighs a fair bit, more than enough to dash your brains out, or mine. I was standing just there not a moment earlier. Lucky all it hit was the carriage," he reaffirmed dourly with a glance at the duke. "There's no damage that can't be easily mended."

Oxshott glared at him, turned, and stalked into the house. They heard him yelling for his numskull of a son.

"Oh dear," said Constantia with a sigh, "I am afraid poor Dolph will suffer for his father's frustration, though how the duke can possibly hold him to blame I fail to see."

Frank apologized to Mr Parslow for his narrow escape, but the man brushed aside his apologies. "No one's fault, these things happen. I daresay the rest of the roof is perfectly sound."

Felix drove up in the phaeton just then and had to hear the whole story. The rain was beginning to fall in earnest, so Constantia and Fanny left the men to get wet and took Anita into the house. Constantia abruptly found she had to sit down.

"How silly," she said faintly, dropping onto the nearest chair, "my knees feel quite weak all of a sudden. Anita and I and your brother were all standing quite close together. Any of us could have been hit."

"Connie, you're white as a sheet. Let me take off your bonnet. Put your head down between your knees. I haven't any smelling salts. Anita, run to Henriette and ask her for tea."

Thomas had followed them in. "I'll fetch the madeira, my lady," he cried and departed on the double.

"No, no, I am perfectly all right." Bent double in her seat, Constantia felt an utter peagoose. After all, no one had been hurt. Why should her head swim so horridly? "I shall go upstairs and take off my pelisse and perhaps lie down for a moment."

"Fanny, do you want to take my new carriage to Winchester? Felix has gone off with . . . Lady Constantia! What's wrong?"

"She's just a little dizzy, Frank. You and I are accustomed to close escapes but it's alarming if one is not."

Fanny's light pressure on the back of Constantia's neck eased, and she ventured to raise her head. Frank looked down at her in consternation.

"I never thought! My dear Lady Constantia, forgive me."

She managed a shaky laugh. "No, forgive me for such absurd behaviour, Captain. I did not expect to swoon — I have never done so before! — so how should you foresee it? It is a most peculiar sensation."

Thomas rushed up with a decanter and a glass. A few sips of the strong wine greatly revived her, and again she declared her intention of going up to her chamber.

Anita had returned from her errand. "Don't you want some tea, Aunt Connie?" she asked, disappointed. "I did tell Henriette to make some."

"Yes, I should like tea, but you will not mind if I drink it in my room, will you?"

"No, I don't mind. Are you feeling better?"

"Much better, darling." She stood up, still a trifle wobbly, with Fanny's hand beneath her elbow.

"Take my arm, my lady," said Thomas anxiously.

Frank intervened. "I shall help Lady Constantia," he announced in a tone that brooked no denial.

"Yes, do, Frank," his sister approved. "Thomas, tell Joan her mistress needs her, if you please."

Though Constantia's knees no longer resembled jelly, she was glad of Frank's arm to steady her for the dizziness returned as they started up the stairs. She was aware of a certain awkwardness in his gait, but he did not falter. He was rapidly regaining his full strength and vigour. How ironic, how unbearable, if he had been killed by a falling gargoyle after surviving Bonaparte's efforts to slay him!

As they climbed, he told her Felix was to return via Heathcote and ask his builder to come and inspect the roof of the Grange.

"I hope he won't find any more unsafe gargoyles," he said. "If I have to have them all taken down, Lady Vickie will rake me over the coals when next she visits. Perhaps it's just as well she left," he added ruefully as they approached the door of the duke's chamber. "I'd not wish her to take my uncle's abuse as a patterncard."

"Sapskull! Lobcock!" Oxshott's voice

might easily have penetrated two inches of oak, but the door was ajar so they heard Dolph's bleated response.

"C-couldn't help it, Father. Took longer than I thought, then I couldn't stop it."

"You're a bungling blockhead! What did I ever do to be cursed with such a simpleton for a son?"

"What on earth has the poor milksop done wrong now?" Frank wondered aloud.

"The duke does not need a reason to take out his ill-temper on poor Dolph. Is there nothing we can do to help him?"

"Nothing but to give him a chance to escape now and then. In the future, I'll invite him to visit Upfield whenever he chooses. In the meantime, I'll see whether he'd like to go with me about the estate. I'll soon be able to ride about my business."

Reaching the door of the small chamber which had been Anita's, she turned to face him. "I am so glad, so very glad, you were able to lift the child."

He grinned like a carefree boy. "I must write to tell Miriam. Will you advise me on the proper wording again?"

"Of course, if you wish. Thank you for lending me your arm up the stairs."

"Not so long ago I doubted I'd ever climb

262

stairs again unaided. You are recovering from the shock, aren't you? The roses are back in your cheeks."

Though he spoke matter-of-factly, not at all as if addressing a compliment to a young lady, under his approving gaze her face grew warm. "I feel much better already," she said hastily and escaped into her room.

She took off her pelisse and sat down at the makeshift dressing table to stare at herself in the mirror. Roses in her cheeks? Yes, and ringlets of spun gold, though a little disordered now, and eyes of cerulean blue, but what did they avail her?

Sometimes she thought Frank was falling in love with her, sometimes that he barely tolerated her presence. She did not know which she wanted. When he insisted on helping her to her chamber, Fanny had sounded delighted. She would be happy to see her brother marry her betrothed's sister. Would she, too, be hurt if it came to the point where Constantia had to refuse, without explanation, an offer from Frank?

Bowing her head, she hid the deceptive beauty in her hands. Better, perhaps, that it should have been destroyed, and she with it, by the falling stone.

Joan bustled in, clucking like a mother hen. "What a horrid fright you've had, my lady! Why anyone would want those nasty gargles stuck up on their house I'm sure I can't guess. There now, let me help you out of that gown and you lie down on your bed for a bit."

"I feel quite well now, Joan," Constantia said as her abigail unfastened the walking dress. The last thing she wanted was to be left alone to brood. "I shall change and go down. Oh, I must drink a cup of tea, first, since Anita ordered it for me specially."

"Young Thomas'll bring it up any moment. Is it true, my lady, as the captain picked up Miss Anita with never a second thought?"

"Yes, is it not wonderful?"

"That it is, my lady, when I think how he was carried into Westwood like a bundle of laundry, thin and pale as a wet sheet and fragile as old lace." Joan lifted the gown over Constantia's head. "Mr Trevor says it was a Jewish lady, his lordship's friend, physicked the captain and set him on the road to recovery."

"Yes, a Mrs Cohen." Returning to the stool at the dressing table, she ran her fingertip along the scar. The puckered skin felt as ugly as it looked. Miriam had cured Frank, saved him from life as a cripple. Was it possible she might have some remedy for so hideous a blemish?

Did she dare write and ask? She had heard enough about Miriam, from Felix first and then from Fanny and Frank, to be sure her secret would be kept. Nor did she suppose Miriam would take offence at being consulted by a stranger. She could write about Frank's recovery and add her question as an afterthought, as though it did not really matter to her, as though she were asking for a friend.

"Joan, I want to write a letter."

"Then you'll have to put on a dress and go down to the bookroom, my lady. There's no room in this cupboard for such things." The abigail sniffed. "It's not right your ladyship should be stuck in here."

"Now, Joan, you know quite well that I offered to take this chamber. It is perfectly adequate, though I do miss the window seat. I trust you will do what you can to help Miss Fanny through this difficult time."

"You know I will, my lady. We all will," said Joan, injured. She added tartly, "But it's to be hoped the rest of miss's grand relations is somewhere between nasty-tempered blasphemers and hapless halfwits."

Thomas arrived with the tray of tea. While she sipped at a cup, Constantia noticed her mother's letter, lying unread on the dressing table. She slit the seal and unfolded the page.

Vickie and Miss Bannister had arrived safely at Westwood. Miss Bannister was laid up after the journey, leaving Vickie on her mother's hands. Vickie was a hoydenish romp, quite unfit for a London Season. Constantia, on the other hand, was a perverse, disobedient miss. Her brother's support of her insubordination only showed that he, too, was lacking in the most elementary sense of duty to his parents. Lady Westwood was displeased.

Constantia sighed. Maybe it would be best for all if she yielded to Mama and went home.

Finishing the tea, she dressed and left her chamber. Fanny and Anita were coming down the passage towards her, hand in hand. Anita ran to her.

"Are you awright, Aunt Connie? Me and Aunt Fanny's coming to ask."

"I drank a cup of tea, and now I am right as rain."

"Good." Beaming, she took Constantia's hand.

Fanny studied her. "Are you sure you are fit to go down?"

"Yes, truly. I must write a letter. I have just read Mama's."

"Connie, you won't leave? You promised."

So, once again, she allowed herself to be persuaded to stay. "I shall tell her Oxshott's heir is here," she said wryly. "If she believes I have a chance to contract so desirable a match, perhaps she will stop demanding my return. She has been out of the world for so long I doubt she is aware of his deficiencies, and if she is she may not care."

"You wouldn't marry poor Dolph!"

"No. I shall never marry." She had not meant to say that, but perhaps it was for the best.

"That's what I thought until I met Felix," said Fanny wisely, though she looked disappointed. She must imagine that if Constantia had not yet found her true love, then Frank was not the man.

Constantia hoped Fanny would find a way to tactfully dissuade her brother should he show signs of attempting to fix his interest — unless Miriam came up with a remedy for the scar.

She was not destined to write to either Miriam or her mother that morning. As she and Fanny and Anita reached the gallery above the hall, a brisk rat-tat on the front door brought Thomas at a run. He opened the door. A tall, lean, elderly lady in a huge puce bonnet surmounted by black plumes marched in as if she owned the house.

"I am Lady Elvira Kerridge," she snapped. "Where is my brother, my good man?"

Thomas at once put on the impassive face of the well-trained footman, abandoned since leaving Westwood. "I believe his grace is above stairs, my lady, and not wishful to be disturbed. I shall inform the master of your ladyship's arrival."

"Master? Master? I suppose the Duke of Oxshott is master in his own house."

"I don't see why he should be," drawled a sneering male voice, "since he ain't master at home. At any rate, not now you are here, Aunt."

An elegant gentleman in immaculate morning dress had entered behind Lady Elvira, forestalling Thomas's effort to close the door. On his arm leant a plump lady in black with a veil hiding her face.

"Godfrey, my poor head," she moaned in a failing voice. "I shall have a Spasm."

"You shall lie down at once, Mama, with a tisane."

"Hypochondriac!" snorted Lady Elvira.

After a moment of frozen dismay, Fanny had started down the stairs, leaving Constantia to follow, if she so chose, with Anita. She crossed the hall to the group by the door.

"I am Fanny Ingram," she said brightly, "and you, I believe, must be my aunts and my cousin?"

Godfrey — the Honourable Godfrey Yates, Constantia remembered — performed an elaborate bow that was somehow a masterpiece of mockery. Lady Elvira produced a lorgnette and eyed Fanny from head to toe, and back again. Lady Yates moaned.

"And I'm your uncle Vincent, missy," said a hearty gentleman with a brick-red face. Thrusting himself between the ladies, he enveloped Fanny in an embrace that made her squeak and surreptitiously rub her rear end. Then he turned and shouted, "Alicia, come and meet m'new niece!"

A small, meagre, fluttery lady in grey trotted after him, babbling. "Vincent, pray do not . . . My dear Miss Ingram . . . Too kind . . . So sorry . . ."

Constantia hesitated on the stairs. She ought to go down and help Fanny deal with the influx, but Anita's presence could only complicate matters. The child was peering through the bannisters, fascinated by the newcomers.

And yet another newcomer appeared in the doorway, a smart young matron in an olive green carriage dress with epaulets and military frogging. She stood there regarding the scene with a sardonic expression. "La, all my charming relations," she drawled. "My apologies for adding to their number, Miss Ingram, but when Father summoned me I was overcome by curiosity."

Joan came hurrying along the gallery towards Constantia. "Thomas said the captain's guests is come, my lady. Shall I take Miss Anita? You'll be wanting to go down."

"Yes, please, Joan. I am needed."

Thomas must have made his escape to warn the household as soon as Fanny reached the hall, for Frank, Felix, Mrs Tanner, and Hoskins all came in as Constantia descended the stairs. Hoskins went out to deal with the visiting servants. Once introductions had been performed, Frank and Felix took Lord Vincent off for a glass of madeira before luncheon. Mr Yates, his contemptuous air slightly modified by Felix's presence, said he'd join them as soon as he had assisted his mama to her chamber. Accompanying Lady Yates, Fanny invited Lady Elvira to go with her and confided Lady Vincent to Mrs Tanner's care. Constantia was left with the remaining guest, Lydia, Lady Warrington, Lord Mentham's sister.

"I daresay poor Dolph is here already?"

she enquired in her fashionably languid drawl as they started up the stairs. "He left the moment Father's letter arrived."

"Lord Mentham arrived yesterday. He was staying with you?"

"Lord, no. We are all of us come straight from Telver Park, country seat of the Dukes of Oxshott since sixteen something or other. The rest all live there, leeching on Father. I'm staying because Warrington had to go to Paris on government business."

"You were not able to go with your husband?"

"No, you see I'm . . . Wait just a moment and let me catch my breath," she said as they reached the top of the flight. "You see, I'm in the family way."

"Oh!" Constantia blushed. "I beg your pardon, we did not know. Ought you to climb the stairs?"

"Lord, yes, I'll just take my time about it. You say 'we.' You know my cousins well?"

"I have not known them long but I have seen a good deal of them since first we met."

"Father was mad as fire, I vow, when his lawyer announced he had found two nobodies who claimed to be heirs. I must say it's a surprise to find they have acquaintance among the Ton. Tell me about them. I suppose you like them or you would not be here."

"Fanny is betrothed to my brother," Constantia explained. She was about to launch into a paean of praise of her future sister-in-law when a squawk of outrage rose from the group stopped at a door just ahead of them.

"Share?" Lady Elvira sounded exactly like her brother the duke, only an octave higher. "Share my chamber? With Millicent, and her pills and potions?"

"Perhaps you had rather share with Uncle Vincent," suggested Godfrey Yates mockingly.

"Godfrey, my head!" gasped Lady Yates, drooping. "If I am forced to share a chamber I shall not sleep a wink, and you know how shockingly ill that makes me."

"I'm sorry," said Fanny resolutely, "but this house is no mansion. Every bedchamber will be occupied."

"My dear aunts," said Lady Warrington, "pray recall that Cousin Fanny did not invite us! But perhaps one of you would prefer to share with me? I suffer horridly from morning sickness, alas."

Lady Elvira gave her a venomous glance and stalked into the room. Lady Yates, transferring her clutch from her son's arm to Fanny's, pressed the other delicate hand to her heart and stumbled after her sister. As Fanny followed perforce, she turned her head and rolled her eyes at Constantia.

"We thought it best to put them together," Constantia said anxiously to Lady Warrington as they continued along the passage. "They are sisters, after all."

"And have been at daggers drawn since before I entered this world. Am I to share with you, or with Cousin Fanny?"

"No, you and I each have a very small chamber to ourselves, much too small to share, and Fanny has Anita with her." She explained Anita's presence in the household.

"La, what a shame I did not bring my son with me. David is just three and would be *aux anges* to have a playmate. Still, I imagine you might have found it difficult to accommodate him and his nurse. Tell me, Lady Constantia, is Dolph in a room with Cousin Godfrey?"

"Yes, none of us quite liked to ask your father . . ."

"Say no more! Poor Dolph. And my uncle and aunt Vincent?"

"They are man and wife!" As long as she could remember, Lord and Lady Westwood had had separate rooms, but Fanny had assumed Lord and Lady Vincent would wish

273

to be together, even if there had been a choice.

"They have not shared a room in a decade or more." Lady Warrington laughed. "This will spike his guns. Your housemaids should be grateful. Not that I imagine Uncle Vincent ever gets much beyond pinching the occasional bottom."

Blushing again, Constantia was glad to reach the door of Lady Warrington's chamber. Showing her in, she said, "We have a cold collation for luncheon at about one o'clock. Shall you come down or would you like a tray up here?"

Lady Warrington glanced around the tiny, shabby room. "I shall come down. I'm eating for two, remember, and there is not space enough in here for all the food I require. Besides, I am eager to see my dear papa, I vow, and discover what he is scheming."

"Scheming?"

"He is not staying here for the pleasure of the amenities, that is certain! My dear Lady Constantia, pray do not look so offended. I allow my tongue too free a rein, I know. I am well aware that my cousins have scarcely had time to realize their good fortune, let alone to refurbish the place. I promise I shall say nothing to them that might be taken amiss. Now, you were asking about Father's scheming."

"The duke said he wished to become better acquainted with his niece and nephew, and to make them acquainted with their other relatives."

"La, how charmingly benevolent! No, he certainly has some nefarious business in mind, but you must not let it disturb you. Though Father makes a good deal more noise than Dolph, he is not much brighter and his plots almost always go astray."

Almost always, thought Constantia, leaving Lady Warrington to the ministrations of her abigail. Ought she to warn Fanny and Frank that the duke's daughter suspected him of plotting against them?

CHAPTER 14

Lady Warrington's warning of future trouble was driven from Constantia's mind by the troubles of the present. As she returned towards the hall, she met Mrs Tanner emerging from the chamber allotted to Lord and Lady Vincent. The usually placid house-keeper was looking decidedly ruffled.

"I don't know what to do, my lady. Her ladyship's in high fidgets because she's to share a bed with her husband."

Constantia blenched. "Where is Miss Fanny?"

"Still trying to stop the other ladies pulling caps."

"See if you can find a truckle bed, Mrs Tanner, but Lady Vincent will have to share a chamber, at least, unless she is willing to move into the servants' quarters. We cannot disrupt all our arrangements at this stage." She braced herself. "I shall go and talk to her."

Lady Vincent Kerridge was a picture of pathos, huddled in a low chair with tears trickling down her face. Her frilled white cap sat lopsidedly on untidy grey hair and an equally crooked brooch on her meagre bosom pinned a grey shawl about her thin shoulders.

"So sorry," she wept. "I simply cannot . . . I do wish . . . But you will think . . . You see, it is . . ."

What it was took Constantia ten minutes of patient probing to discover. At last she elicited a whispered admission that Lady Vincent was afraid her husband would "bother" her.

Constantia put her hands to her fiery cheeks. Really, she had blushed more since Fanny's relatives' arrival than in the rest of her life to date. She wondered if she might have misunderstood.

"Is it not natural," she said tentatively, "for a husband to . . . to bother his wife?"

"Natural?" Lady Vincent blinked at her. "You cannot . . . Not married . . . But men . . . Such nasty creatures . . . At my age . . . To put up with . . . Unspeakable . . . Quite impossible . . ."

Despite her sheltered life, Constantia had some understanding of relations between the sexes, though ignorant of the most

277

intimate details. The only marriage she had ever closely observed, her parents', was not now passionate, if it ever had been. Yet she found it difficult to believe that most women regarded men as nasty creatures to be put up with.

Only consider Fanny, who had seen plenty of life with the army. She appeared to want and to thoroughly enjoy Felix's embraces, and she must have some notion to what intimacies they led.

"And my maid . . . Perfectly understandable . . . Refuses to come to me in case . . . Horrid!"

Constantia had no doubts of her ability to deal with servants. "I shall speak to your abigail, and I have directed the housekeeper to find a second bed for this room," she said hastily, and made her escape.

When the chastened abigail was scurrying to attend her mistress, Constantia wearily made her way towards the drawing-room. In the hall she met Frank. As he approached, she tried to imagine him as a nasty creature bent upon horrid, unspeakable indecencies — and failed. She rather suspected that any indecencies he attempted would prove all too delightful.

His greeting brought her back to earth with a thump.

278

"My dear Lady Constantia, you look as if you had just beaten off an attack by Boney's Imperial Guard."

"You are full of compliments, Captain!"

He grinned. At least he had wiped the bashfulness from her beautiful face. Why was she suddenly shy of him? "Not compliments, but gratitude," he said. "I wish you will not exhaust yourself trying to conciliate my wretched relatives. Come and sit down for a moment. You have had a trying morning." He led her to one of the high-backed wooden settles by the fireplace and sat beside her.

"So far, today seems to have sped from one contretemps to another," she agreed with a tired smile, leaning back.

"I gather all is not sweet conviviality above stairs, either."

"Have Mr Yates and Lord Vincent been difficult?"

"Yates has a damnable — dashed sneering way about him. My skin is impervious, but he had poor Dolph cowering in a corner. My uncle Vincent merely sent the maid who came in to make up the fire screaming from the room."

"Yes, I have learned of Lord Vincent's propensities."

"Surely he did not assault you!" Sudden

anger blazed within him.

"No, no, though I fear Fanny . . . Lady Warrington believes he does not . . . Oh dear, I am beginning to sound like Lady Vincent, never finishing a sentence." She was scarlet from the high neckline of her blue gown to the roots of her golden hair. "Lady Warrington says his . . . assaults are limited to . . . to minor improprieties."

His lips twitched. "That is a relief. My sympathies are with his wife — or has she been equally troublesome?"

"In her way, but I hope I have relieved her concerns." She rushed on as if to prevent his asking the nature of Lady Vincent's concerns. "They all expect to be wrapped in luxury in a palace," she said crossly, "and you did not even invite them."

"Is Lady Warrington very demanding? From what I heard, I'd guess she and God-frey Yates are birds of a feather."

"To some extent, I daresay, though leaning towards mockery rather than contempt, if you consider the difference significant. Her manner is disconcerting, but she appears to accept you and Fanny as her cousins and to bear you no ill will."

"No doubt she is married to a wealthy man and had few expectations from her grandfather's will," said Frank cynically.

"Perhaps." Her satin-smooth forehead wrinkled in a worried frown. "She did mention that she doubts her father has truly abandoned his claim to your properties."

"So do I. Mackintyre warned me that when the duke returns to Town he may find himself another lawyer to contest the will. There's nothing we can do about it until it happens. At least he cannot forward his plans while he is at the Grange."

"For all that, I wish him away!" Fanny joined them, slumping on the opposite settle. "And the rest with him."

"Are your aunts still insisting on separate chambers?" Constantia asked.

"I don't wonder they don't care to share, for I should hate to be confined with either. One cannot speak to Lady Yates without being accused of attempting to hasten her end, which, incidentally, Frank, was our sole purpose in claiming our inheritance. She had her eye on at least one of the estates for her son, I daresay."

"Which would have pleased the duke no better than our inheriting, I wager."

"No doubt. Lady Elvira utterly refuses to accept that you are her host, not Uncle Oxshott. She runs his household at Telver Park, I collect, and expects to run this."

"Oh Lord!" Frank groaned.

"For a start," Fanny continued in despair, "she had her maid strip the sheets off her bed and demanded a different pair because they are darned and fit only for servants. And Lady Yates swears darned sheets will chafe her delicate skin into sores. The few others we possess are all as bad. What am I to do, Connie?"

"Stop letting their complaints distress you," Constantia said firmly. "They are shockingly unreasonable. I shall advise them to remove to the inn for the night. I am quite certain the Pig and Piper's sheets not only have holes in them but are damp!"

Frank laughed. Fanny summoned up a smile. "Shall you really?" she asked.

"Yes. You cannot, because you are their hostess, and because they are your relatives and you must conciliate them." A touch of Lady Westwood's hauteur mingled with Constantia's indignation on Fanny's behalf. "Their opinion is nothing to me. In any case they are not likely to subject me to such Turkish treatment."

What a darling she was, Frank thought. Without her loyal support, even his intrepid sister might founder beneath the weight of the united censure of her toplofty aunts. He shuddered to think of Fanny's plight if Constantia had meekly submitted to her mother's summons. He wanted to take her in his arms and prove to her with kisses how much he admired her.

Instead he stood up. "I had better return to the fray. Felix handles them admirably, of course, but I must keep my hostly colours flying lest they forget who owns the Grange."

He strode off, erect, with head held high, a soldier marching into battle.

Constantia gazed after him. "Your brother handles them admirably, also," she said to Fanny, "and he has not Felix's advantages. I marvel at his patience, at his not losing his temper."

"A good officer must be patient and even-tempered, and Frank is — was a good officer. Connie, where is Anita?"

"Joan offered to keep her amused."

"She and Henriette and Mrs Tanner are very good to her, but it is no part of their duties. I feel I'm taking advantage of their kindness."

"We must look about for a nurse, now that Vickie and Miss Bannister are gone." Constantia was glad of a chance to broach the subject. She had been avoiding it, knowing it would hurt Fanny.

"Yes, I can see I shan't have time to care for her myself," said Fanny sadly. "But nor have I time to find a nurse while my horrid relatives are here."

"Lady Warrington is disposed in your favour, I believe. I shall go up now and see if I can make Lady Elvira and Lady Yates see sense. Or perhaps they will take my advice and remove to the Pig and Piper."

"That is too much to hope for." Fanny accompanied Constantia, enquiring about Lady Warrington and somewhat cheered by the report. As they reached the top of the stairs she said, "I must go and make sure Lady Vincent is comfortable. Do you know how Mrs Tanner fared with her?"

"Not well, I fear."

"Oh Lord! She looks such a meek mouse. What is her complaint?"

Constantia stopped, one hand on the balustrade. "She does not care to share a bed with Lord Vincent. I told Mrs Tanner to try to find a second bed for their chamber. Fanny, Lady Vincent said men are nasty creatures with . . . with unspeakable desires. My parents have had separate chambers as long as I can remember, and I wondered . . . I mean, I . . ."

Fanny touched her hand. "My parents were deeply in love until the day Papa died. You know we often shared the most primitive quarters on campaign, with little privacy. I assure you, they . . . well, Mama never considered my father a nasty creature. I can scarcely wait until Felix and I are married."

Her cheeks were rosy not with embarrassment but with eager anticipation. She leaned on the balustrade, lost in a dream that made her eyes sparkle and her lips curve upward.

Regarding her with envy and sadness, Constantia clasped her hands to her breast.

A sigh announced Fanny's emergence from her dream. They went on together, she to Lady Vincent, Constantia to knock lightly on the door of the chamber grudgingly shared by Lady Yates and Lady Elvira. A hatchet-faced abigail answered her tap.

"I am Lady Constantia Roworth. May I have a word with your mistress and her sister?"

The woman curtsied. "I'll just see, my lady."

From within came the sounds of an altercation. "I tell you, Elvira, I shall take a chill and very likely a putrid sore throat if you insist on having the window opened."

"Balderdash. Fresh air never did anyone harm and since we are obliged to coexist in this wholly inadequate space it is an absolute necessity."

"I'm sure I cannot imagine why Oxshott made us come," said Lady Yates fretfully. "I daresay I shall not survive, for I have never been subjected to such discomfort in my life."

Incensed, Constantia boldly pushed open the door and stepped in. "I fear you find your accommodations unsatisfactory," she said, mimicking her mother's most frigid tones. "May I suggest you repair to the inn in King's Wallop? Or Winchester has many superior hostelries, if you do not care for the Pig and Piper."

"Pig!" said Lady Yates faintly. She was reclining on the vast, canopied bed. "Bidwell, my smelling salts."

"You have them already, my lady," her maid ventured to point out. "Here are the Ward's pills. Shall I send for burnt feathers?"

"No wonder you are an invalid, Millicent," Lady Elvira snorted. "Constantly physicking yourself with quack nostrums. Lady Constantia, naturally I do not hold you accountable for the sorry state of affairs, you being a guest like myself."

"Thank you, ma'am," said Constantia ironically, "but I am as responsible as Miss Ingram for the transformation of this house from a near ruin into a habitable home in a very short time."

"That is as may be. However, there are serious shortcomings in my niece's housekeeping, if she is indeed my niece. I shall attempt to remedy them. I shall stay."

"I cannot possibly remove," Lady Yates moaned. "I shall be confined to my bed for a week, I know it."

"Our bed," said Lady Elvira distastefully. "You have pushed the bolster far beyond the middle line."

"Racked by rheumaticks as I am, I need to be able to stretch my aching limbs."

Leaving them to the battle of the bolster, Constantia departed, closing the door firmly behind her. Her intervention had accomplished little, she feared. The ladies might be resigned to their situation, but they were not at all likely to admit it.

Luncheon passed better than she had expected, for which she gave credit to Henriette's superb spread. Lady Elvira ate heartily despite criticizing every dish. Mr Yates and Lady Warrington sniped at each other. Poor Dolph was silently cowed. The duke appeared to be sulking over the damage to his carriage. Lady Yates took a bowl of gruel in her room.

From Constantia's point of view, the worst was finding herself at the sideboard with

Lord Vincent. She jumped when he pinched her, but managed to restrain an exclamation. She suspected Frank's patience had its limits, and the last thing they needed was for him to challenge his uncle to a duel.

After luncheon, Lady Elvira declared her intention of touring the house with the housekeeper. Lady Vincent hid herself in a corner with her embroidery. Lady Warrington said her doctor had recommended gentle exercise after eating. She invited Constantia and Fanny to take a turn with her in the shrubbery since the rain had stopped, so, leaving Frank and Felix to entertain the gentlemen, the three went to put on their bonnets.

"And pray bring the little girl," said Lady Warrington. "I am fond of children."

Always ready to make new friends, Anita skipped happily along beside them.

Lady Warrington was vastly amused by the shrubbery, which was still a jungle. Fortunately, Fanny was not at all put out by her quizzing. In fact she was far less shocked than Constantia by her cousin's frankness, and far better able to respond in a similar bantering tone. By the time they returned to the house after a half-hour's saunter, they were Cousin Fanny and Cousin Lydia — Aunt Lydia to Anita.

Frank and Felix intercepted them in the hall.

"We're off duty," said Frank. "Uncle Oxshott has sent Yates into Winchester in search of something fit to drink, and he's dictating letters to Uncle Vincent in the bookroom. I didn't realize Lord Vincent was his secretary."

"Since Father is forced to support an indigent brother and nephew," drawled Lady Warrington, "he makes good use of them. If you will excuse me, I shall retire for my nap now."

"It's time for Anita's nap, too," said Fanny.

"I'll come up with you." Felix lifted the child to his shoulders and they all started up the stairs.

Constantia made a move to follow.

"Don't abandon me," said Frank, "now that at last I'm free of pestilential relatives for a while."

"I was just going to put off my bonnet."

"Are you wearied? Busy as today has been, I haven't had my exercise for the day and I hoped you'd walk with me."

"I ought to . . ." She knew she ought to refuse. "Oh, fiddlesticks! Yes, I will come with you. I have been shockingly lax in supervising your exercise of late, but you are so much recovered."

"And you are so much occupied with setting my home to rights." He opened the
front door and they strolled down the drive
towards the stream. "I mean to try if I can
handle the ribbons tomorrow. Shall I take
you and Fanny into Winchester? I want to
talk to the fellow Parslow recommended
about painting and refurbishing the carriage."

"One of us had best stay here. The final
selection is up to Fanny, so she should go."

"But you've discussed it with her, have
you not? Besides, it's my house you're
furnishing at present, not hers. I'll be more
than happy to live with whatever your taste
dictates."

"Beware! You might find yourself saddled
with false Egyptian, all sphinxes and croco-
dile legs; or imitation Chinese bamboo
adorned with dragons; or simply feminine
frills and floral prints everywhere."

He laughed. "No fervent admirer of my
Elizabethan hall is likely to choose any of
those. I trust you to buy me what best befits
a country gentleman of modest taste and
no pretensions to fashion. The Grange's
façade is eccentricity enough for me."

They turned and looked back up the hill
at the absurd towers and turrets.

"You will not let the duke take it away

from you!"

"No." Frank was calm but resolute. "All my life I have been a wanderer perforce, and now I find in myself a deep desire to put down roots, to make the best I can of a little piece of England. I shall not yield up my home without a fight."

As always his force of character impressed Constantia. The physical strength now rapidly returning was less important than the inner strength, the vigorous vitality she recognized in him. What he set his mind to, he would attain.

The idea frightened her a little.

As they continued in silence down the hill, she wondered how she was to make him accept her refusal if he asked for her hand. Was she playing with fire, staying on at Upfield and allowing herself the painful pleasure of his company?

No; she flattered herself. He did not love her, or she would be certain of it by now. At times it was possible to deceive herself but in reality he saw her as no more than a friend, soon to be a sister. He walked beside her without languishing glances, without sighs, without attempts to press her hand, without lavish compliments on her ravishing beauty.

"The leaves of the elms are beginning to

yellow," he said. Did that not prove he had no tender feelings for her? "Autumn is on its way."

Looking up at the tree-tops, she saw a cloud of birds wheel across the grey sky. "Yes, see the swallows gathering. They will soon be gone. A melancholy season."

"Not so! The melancholy comes from consorting with my guests. Evade them tomorrow. The bustle of the Winchester shops will drive away your megrims."

Constantia smiled at him. "I daresay, but I must consult Fanny. She is surely as eager as I to escape, and I have already tested the comfort of your carriage. But you said you mean to try if you can handle the reins," she added anxiously. "Winchester is all of ten miles."

"I don't imagine I'll be able to drive so far at first. I'll take Hoskins."

"He is a coachman, among his many skills?"

"Not exactly a coachman. He has often driven a gun-carriage."

"And you?" she enquired with suspicion.

Frank grinned. "I too have driven a gun-carriage upon occasion. Believe me, after coercing mismatched army horses over road-less mountains, tooling my new team along the lanes will be as easy as hitting the side of a barn at fifty paces."

"Indeed, I hope so!"

"If you are wary of entrusting yourself to my skill, I'll borrow Felix's groom instead of taking Hoskins."

"Oh no, I would not wish to hurt the corporal's feelings. If Fanny does not choose to go, I am willing to risk my life."

"You are quizzing me, I trust, Lady Constantia! It's a staid barouche-landau I've acquired, not a high-perch phaeton, and Felix has pronounced my cattle slugs."

"How shockingly rude. He would not dare so insult any but an intimate friend. I am glad that you and he are become good friends."

"And I that you and Fanny are good friends."

Their eyes met, but neither remarked upon the friendship existing between the two of them.

Reaching the bridge with its broken railing, they commented on the duke's extraordinary run of bad luck, then turned back to the house.

All was quiet. Rather than seeking out trouble, they decided to sit in the hall, where they could be easily found if sought for. And after half an hour or so discussing the house and garden, there they were found by Thomas.

"My lady, if you please, Mrs Tanner'd like a word, when convenient. She's that upset, my lady. Will I tell her to come to you here?"

"Is she in her room? I shall go to her."

Frank followed her to the housekeeper's room, stopping in the doorway as she went in. Mrs Tanner jumped up from her chair, twisting her apron in agitated hands.

"My lady, it's that Lady Elvira. I didn't like to trouble the master or Miss Fanny, seeing she's their auntie, but . . . Oh, Captain, sir, I didn't see you there. If I don't give satisfaction, I'm sure I'm ready to give you my notice, sir." She burst into tears.

"Come, now." Constantia seated the unhappy housekeeper and took the chair opposite her. "I am sure there is no need for that." She raised questioning eyebrows at Frank.

"Certainly not." He turned his head to glance back into the passage. "Thomas, the madeira, and we'd best have tea, too, I daresay. Mrs Tanner," he went on, advancing into the room, "I depend upon you, and there is no question of dissatisfaction. Just what has my aunt been saying?"

Mrs Tanner mopped her eyes with her apron and was about to rise again when he put his hand on her shoulder. "Her ladyship found fault with everything, sir. Leastways, she couldn't say anything wasn't clean, so she kept mum on that — not a word of approval, mind you. But she went through the linen cupboard and there's not enough of anything and what there is is mended. And there's odd dishes among the china, and odd knives and forks and glasses. And the curtains in the morning-room's too short, and the . . ."

"Yes, I remember they shrank when we washed them," said Constantia, cutting off what promised to be an endless list of complaints. "Surely Lady Elvira did not reproach you for the household's inadequacies?"

"That she did, my lady. She said a competent housekeeper'd contrive and she ordered me I must do this and that different till I was that flustered I didn't know was I on my head or my heels."

Frank gave her a smile of singular charm. "In my opinion you are perfectly competent, and my opinion is the only one that counts. If any of Lady Elvira's hints seem useful to you, by all means put them into practice. If in doubt, consult Lady Constantia or Miss Fanny. Ignore the rest. Ah, Thomas, pour a glass of wine for Mrs Tanner, please."

As Constantia left with him, she heard the

housekeeper say to the footman in a loud whisper, "You couldn't ask for a better master, Thomas, indeed you couldn't."

Frank's ears turned bright red.

"You have won an ally for life," said Constantia. She sighed. "Another minor disaster averted. What next, I wonder?"

CHAPTER 15

The rest of the afternoon passed without major crises, though not without minor unpleasantnesses, such as Lady Yates demanding a blend of China tea they happened not to have in the house. Her delicate digestion could stomach no other, she declared.

Before dinner, Constantia changed into a gown of lavender sarcenet, trimmed with lace at sleeves and hem, and with a triple fall of lace at her throat. It was one of the dresses ordered when her mother had taken her and Vickie to Bath, after Felix's windfall. Though that day had been perfectly horrid, with the tryings-on and the visit to Grandmama, she was glad now to have the new clothes. They added to her standing as daughter of an earl, and therefore made it easier for her to protect Fanny against her noble relatives.

After dressing, she went to Fanny's room. Anita was already in her little truckle bed,

297

watching with sleepy eyes as Fanny donned a new gown of rose-pink lustring.

"Hallo, Aunt Connie," she said drowsily. "Isn't Aunt Fanny pretty?"

"Very pretty. Let me help you tie those tapes, Fanny. Has your brother spoken to you about going to Winchester tomorrow?"

"No. I've hardly had a chance to exchange a word with him all day, or with you, or to play with Anita. I'm going to start getting up earlier, so that I can spend some time with her before anyone comes down to breakfast. She wakes early anyway. What is this about Frank and Winchester?" She picked up a hairbrush and began to tidy her brown curls.

"He wants to consult someone about refurbishing his new carriage, and he offered to take us in to town to do our shopping. I fear one of us ought to stay at home, though, to make sure all runs as smoothly as possible."

Fanny wrinkled her nose at the looking-glass. "Smoothly is not possible, but if Frank is going, I must stay and play hostess. You take your chance to escape for a few hours. I hate to ask you to perform our errands, though."

"I shall enjoy it. I have a good idea of the exact patterns and colours you want."

"I'm quite sure Frank will accept whatever you select," Fanny said gaily, glancing over her shoulder at Constantia. "After all, you know far more about elegant furnishings than I, and you guided my choices in the first place."

Despite her explanatory second sentence, Constantia was left with the feeling that Fanny was still hoping to promote a match. She tried to think of a way to convince her that her efforts were futile — without revealing the real reason and without leading her to suppose her brother's myriad virtues were unappreciated.

Joan came in to see if Fanny needed her help. The moment passed, and, after kissing Anita goodnight, the ladies went down together.

Though dinner was a family occasion, under Lady Elvira's unrelenting guidance it was a formal and uncomfortable affair. To Constantia it seemed that the rigorous observance of every nicety of etiquette was a shield against the petty squabbling that would otherwise flare up among Oxshott's family.

As she later learned, as soon as the ladies withdrew after the meal, disharmony had reared its head. When the gentlemen joined the ladies in the drawing-room, Frank came over to her.

"Yates — Cousin Godfrey as my uncle insists on my calling him — brought a couple of bottles of port back from Winchester," he told her in a low voice, "but it was too shaken up to be drinkable. Uncle Oxshott is in a vile temper."

"Is he not always?" she teased.

"Usually," he agreed ruefully. "I'd hoped the port might mellow him. Yates ordered a case of it and one of brandy to be delivered, but my uncle gave him a bear-garden jaw, and then both of them started badgering poor Dolph."

"I thought he was looking even more hunted than usual."

"Should you mind if we took him with us tomorrow?"

"Not at all. A brief respite from the duke's company cannot but do him a world of good."

"And us, too!"

Lady Vincent joined them, embroidery in hand. She eyed Frank with such a mixture of repugnance and misgiving that he soon took himself off. He went to speak to Dolph, while she said anxiously to Constantia, "Tête-à-tête . . . unmarried gentleman . . . so very dangerous . . . Rescued you, my dear."

Constantia swallowed a sigh and admired her embroidery, a bouquet of white, virginal rosebuds. As Lady Vincent chatted on in her disjointed way, Constantia watched, fascinated, Dolph sidling around the room towards her.

Forced at last to abandon the wall and cross an unprotected tract of carpet, he threw a nervous look over his shoulder at his father and made a dash for it. "Lady Constantia!" he gasped, wiping his forehead.

"Yes, Lord Mentham? Will you not be seated?"

He perched on the edge of a chair and leaned towards her, apparently oblivious of Lady Vincent at her side. "Cousin Frank says I may go with you to Winchester tomorrow," he whispered.

"Certainly, if you wish. Did Captain Ingram explain that we are going on errands, not a party of pleasure?"

Nodding vigorously, he assured her, "I don't mind. I'll help if you tell me what to do. But he isn't going, is he? Just you and me and Cousin Frank?"

"Two gentlemen . . . abigail . . . must strongly advise . . ." Lady Vincent broke in, agitated.

"I have every intention of taking my abigail," Constantia promised. "Corporal

Hoskins goes with us, too."

Dolph had fixed his aunt with an anguished gaze, as if he had only become aware of her presence when she spoke. "Won't tell Father, ma'am?" he entreated.

"That man . . . forced to . . . exigencies . . . his house . . . not breathe a word!"

At an hour long before his grace was ever known to stir from his chamber, the barouche-landau rolled down the drive and across the bridge. It was a fine day, though with a crisp hint of autumn in the air, so the carriage was open and Constantia was able to watch Frank at the reins.

She had no real doubt of his competence. Her concern was lest he overstrain his shoulders. Hoskins, on the box beside him, would do his best to stop his captain harming himself, but she knew well how Frank's resoluteness was apt to shade into stubbornness. If he decided to keep on driving when he ought to stop, the corporal might not be able to prevent him. In that case, she hoped he would heed her pleas.

Her pleas were not needed. After a couple of miles, he handed over the ribbons and came to sit beside Dolph with his back to the horses, looking pleased with himself. He drove another stretch later, but let Hoskins take over again when they reached the high road and started to meet with traffic.

Constantia thoroughly enjoyed the day. Having consulted the coach-builder, Frank returned to join her and Dolph in going from draper to upholsterer to furniture-maker to china-shop. Joan's and Hoskins's arms filled with smaller purchases. Dolph proudly treated them to a neat luncheon at the Black Swan — his father kept him short of the ready, he said, but not so short he could not sport his friends a meal.

Weary but content, they returned to Up-field Grange, arriving as the long golden light of late afternoon faded to a rosy sunset glow. One of the duke's puce-liveried foot-men awaited them in the hall.

"My lord, his grace wishes to speak to your lordship immediately," he said to Dolph, staring blank-faced over his shoul-der. "His grace is in the drawing-room."

Dolph quailed. "Im-m-mediately?" he stammered.

"At once, my lord." The footman allowed a hint of commiseration to creep into his voice.

"I'll go with you," said Frank, patting Dolph's shoulder in a fatherly way. "He can't have you shot at dawn, you know."

Poor Dolph looked as if he placed no

credence whatsoever in his cousin's assurance.

"I shall come, too," Constantia volunteered. Not that she had any desire to witness the duke in a rage, but he might moderate his tantrum if she were present. Unlikely, she had to admit, to judge by past performance. Nonetheless, raising her chin, she preceded the gentlemen to the drawing-room.

Oxshott surged to his feet with an inarticulate roar as Dolph followed her in. "What the devil do you mean by it, eh, you wastrel?"

"B-by what, Father?" Dolph sounded bewildered as well as terrified.

"By going off without so much as a by-your-leave, numskull! By gadding about when I had need of you. By . . ."

"Leave him alone, Father." Lady Warrington's drawl had a cutting edge. Quill in hand, she stalked towards them from the little writing table by the window, where a half-finished letter lay. "Dolph is of age. He does not need to beg your leave to spend a day with his cousin."

"Of age! Your brother is a dolt, unfit to make his own decisions."

"How do you know?" Lady Warrington snapped. "Have you ever allowed him to try? You are a tyrant, a brute, a savage!" With each epithet she stabbed at her father with the quill.

"Savage! I'll show you savage, you beldam! The ducking-stool is too good for termagants like you." His abuse descended to the foulest profanities.

His daughter gave as good as she got, though observing certain limits on her language. Constantia was shocked into immobility until Frank took her arm, jerked his head towards the door, and mouthed, "Off you go." He appeared to be amused!

Constantia fled, her hands over her ears. Dolph did not need her feeble protection when he had his sister to champion him.

Lydia Warrington came to her chamber later. "I am prodigious sorry you witnessed our little disagreement," she said calmly. "I have already told Cousin Fanny that I cannot stay any longer in the same house as my father, not even for Dolph's sake. I shall leave in the morning."

"Can he not go with you?"

"La, he is more afraid to leave than to stay. Be kind to the poor mooncalf. I hope to visit my cousins at a later date, when Father is not here. No doubt we shall meet again."

"I hope so," said Constantia, without much conviction, then repeated the words more firmly. "I do hope so." Lady Warrington's heart was in the right place, she believed, and whatever her shortcomings she was by far the best of the Ingrams' relatives.

Departing, Lady Warrington turned as she reached the door. "Two words of advice, Lady Constantia, if you promise not to take them amiss. Pay my father no heed; and snap up Cousin Frank if you can. He is a jewel, I vow."

She sauntered out. After a frozen moment staring after her, Constantia managed to smile and shake her head. The world was full of matchmakers. She must learn to ignore them — unless Miriam came to her aid.

With an effort she diverted her attention to wondering how soon the battle for Lady Warrington's vacated bedchamber would erupt.

Nothing happened that evening, as Fanny had asked her cousin not to mention her plans. It was when Lady Warrington's trunk was carried down to the hall and she bade her family farewell that the skirmishing started, in a form Constantia had not anticipated. No one actually wanted the small chamber. Lady Elvira and Lady Yates each wanted the other removed to it.

The battle raged fierce and hot; it raged but briefly, however. Frank, after consulting Fanny, had already directed Dolph's valet to take possession for his master. He was installed and ready to take on all comers. Dolph did not mind in the least that the room was cramped and shabby.

"He's just glad not to have Yates constantly sneering at him," Frank explained to Constantia. "I couldn't in all conscience leave the poor fellow in such misery. The others can stand up for themselves."

"And Mr Yates is pleased to have the larger room to himself," she congratulated him, "so you have pleased two out of the six, which I had not thought possible."

"And the rest cannot complain quite as vociferously as they otherwise might because Dolph is, after all, the heir to the dukedom."

The complaints were vociferous enough. Life remained a sea of trouble dotted with islands of crisis. Even the delivery, bit by bit, of the goods Constantia had ordered was spoiled by Lady Elvira's endless, automatic criticism. This colour was too pale, that too bright; Wedgwood was vulgar, the truly elegant preferred Royal Worcester or Crown Derby; the style of Chippendale was vastly superior to the chosen Sheraton.

Frank's outspoken delight in everything

was some compensation to Fanny and Constantia for Lady Elvira's disdain.

"All the same," said Fanny to Constantia one evening as they ascended the stairs on their way to bed, "I'd not survive without my hour of peace with Anita every morning before anyone else is up. We go down to the kitchen for bread and butter first and then take a walk if it's fine, or amuse ourselves indoors. It is sheer heaven to be free of carping and quarrelling for a little while. What use is a family that never has a kind word for one another?"

As she answered, Constantia happened to glance up at the gallery. The duke stood there in the shadow, staring at them. He must have overheard Fanny's complaint about his family's conduct, yet he looked more smug than incensed.

She shrugged away her puzzlement. Very little of Oxshott's behaviour made any sense to her.

The following day, his grace decided his port and brandy, delivered several days earlier, had settled enough to be broached. The ladies had to wait considerably longer than usual for the gentlemen to join them after dinner. The duke led them into the drawing-room, carrying a decanter and a glass. Though none of the others was so burdened, they were all bright-eyed and a trifle flushed, even Felix and Frank.

"Are they inebriated?" Constantia whispered to Fanny in dismay.

"Heavens no, merely a little bosky. A cup of tea will soon put them to rights." She rang the bell.

A startled yelp drew their attention to Lady Vincent. As pink-faced as her husband, she glared at him. She had evidently just been pinched, an aberration due to drink, no doubt, since Lord Vincent generally confined his familiarities to anyone but his wife, whatever her fears.

"Disgraceful!" she squeaked. "How dare . . . Shall not stand for . . . Retire at once . . . No tea . . ." And she flounced out, insofar as so meagre a figure was capable of flouncing.

Lord Vincent chortled and came to sit beside Fanny. Felix promptly removed her. Frank slid into the place next to Constantia, shielding her from the would-be roué.

The manoeuvre was so swiftly and neatly accomplished that Lord Vincent, slow on the uptake after several glasses, did not realize in time how he had been outwitted.

"Ouch!" said Frank, and rubbed his buttock.

Constantia clapped a hand to her mouth,

too late to stifle a giggle. "A taste of your own medicine?" she enquired.

"My medicine!" he said in mock outrage, a gleam in his eye. "I'd have you know, Lady Constantia that I've never in my life thus assaulted a respectable female."

"Nor did he, in this case." She felt an alarming urge to ask whether he ever thus assaulted less-than-respectable females. Hastily she reminded herself that she was not the one who was — what had Fanny said? — a trifle bosky.

One of Frank's new servants rescued her, bringing in the tea tray. He was still in his blue and red Horse Artillery uniform instead of livery. Nor had he yet mastered the art of footmanship despite Thomas's drilling. Glancing at the corner to which Fanny and Felix had retired, he grinned and winked at Constantia. "Tha'lt pour, my lady?"

"Yes, Twistlethwaite, please set the tray here."

"I particularly admire," said Frank dreamily as the man left, "the way you say that name. Whistletwaith, Tithleswaite, Swizzleswith, Thistledown and Will-o'-the-withp."

She frowned him down, her lips twitching. "An ancient Yorkshire name, he assures me."

"No, what I really meant to say was, I admire the fact that you know his name. You may not have noticed, but Aunt Elvira, after favouring my sister with a curled lip, was about to demand the right to pour tea. Not having troubled to learn the footman's name, she was stymied by the impropriety of calling out 'You there!' Or possibly 'Hey you.' Or 'Here, fellow.' Or 'Come, my good man.' Or . . ."

"I think you had better drink a cup of strong tea," said Constantia severely.

Dolph came up, eager to be of service. Since his hand appeared steady, she sent him with cups of tea to the ladies, then poured one for the duke.

He waved it away, raising a half full glass of tawny port to her. "Your health, ma'am. There's not much to be said for Godfrey, but he does know his wines." His voice was slurred, his nose beginning to glow.

He kept Dolph by him, talking to him in a low, insistent voice, so Constantia let the rest of the gentlemen fetch their own tea. As the duke's glass emptied, refilled, and emptied again, she noticed poor Dolph's face growing longer and longer.

The rumble of Oxshott's voice died away, returned briefly, then stopped. He slumped back in his chair — a new, solid, Sheraton one with a high back — and a rumbling snore took the place of speech.

The duke was still sound asleep when everyone else was ready to retire for the night. No one quite dared to wake him. Fanny had Twistlethwaite place a branch of fresh, lighted candles beside him, along with his unlit night-candle. Then they left him to his dreams.

Constantia read for a while, then snuffed her candle and fell into a light, uneasy sleep. In her dreams, Frank approached her, the gleam in his brown eyes beckoning her to unimaginable delights. The gleam became a flickering flame, a flaring firestorm, hiding then revealing his face, a crowd of frightened faces, burning beams, toppling towers . . .

She awoke in terror, her heart pounding, shaken by a horrid premonition. Suppose the duke burned down the house? He did not want it, only the land it stood on. He had no affection for his family. Would he care if they perished, along with Fanny and Frank . . . ?

Fustian! she scolded herself. Oxshott was a wealthy man with or without Upfield Grange and Heathcote, a noble peer of the realm, a gentleman of high pride and dignity.

But she found herself feeling with her feet

for her slippers, wrapping her new lavender-blue dressing-gown about her, stealing out into the dark passage.

Trailing her fingertips along the wall, she crept along towards the corner. A floorboard creaked loudly and she froze, but no one stirred. Down the three steps to the gallery, reach for the balustrade, move along it, with more confidence now, to the ball-topped post at the head of the stairs.

There she hesitated. All was still. No smell of smoke, no flicker of flame as she peered into the blackness below. How absurd the terrors that came upon one in the small hours of the morning! The sooner she returned to her chamber the better.

But there! A fitful light over towards the drawing-room, growing brighter . . .

And a heavy tread, heavy breathing, the dishevelled duke stumping into the hall, candle in hand. He was on his way to bed, of course. Or was he moving from room to room setting light to the curtains? She called herself a peagoose yet she lingered to make sure he came up the stairs.

His course meandered as he crossed the hall, but it brought him to the foot of the staircase. He stood there for a moment, candle held high, blinking doubtfully at the ascent as if about to tackle a mountain.

Constantia watched him set foot on the bottom step, then turned away.

"Aaargh!"

At the cry, she swung round, to see Oxshott frantically flailing his arms in the air, tottering backwards. The candle flew from his hand and went out as he fell. In the darkness, a bellow of pain and fury drowned out the thud of his landing.

Clutching the handrail with one hand, holding up nightshift and dressing-gown with the other, Constantia sped down the stairs. She was half way down when a light appeared from the direction of Frank's room. Dressed only in an ankle-length nightshirt, he ran into the hall, lamp in hand.

"Captain!"

Over the flood of vituperation now pouring from the duke's mouth, Frank heard her call. He looked up, slowed his headlong pace, and held up the lamp. "Lady Constantia! What the deuce?"

Her way now lit, she let go of the railing and with both hands raising the hem of her hampering garments she hurried on down. She was nearly at the bottom when her feet flew out from under her.

Headfirst she hurtled down the last three steps.

CHAPTER 16

Frank caught her. Shaking, Constantia sagged against his chest, letting him support her.

The lamp had gone out when he dropped it in his leap to save her. Surely she imagined in the darkness his lips brushing across her forehead as he held her close. Her racing heart was due to shock, not to the strong arms enfolding her, the hard body pressed to hers. The overwhelming desire to throw her arms about his neck was a need to cling to something in her fright, not a disgracefully immodest longing to pull his head down and feel his mouth on hers.

Alarmed by the sensations coursing through her, she drew back. At once he released her, keeping one hand on her arm to steady her. She was uncertain whether she wished she could see his face or was glad she could not.

"Are you all right?" He had to raise his

voice to be heard through Oxshott's curses.

"I think so," she quavered.

His fingers gripped her arm convulsively. "My God, I was afraid you'd break your neck."

"So was I. It sounds as if your uncle has not broken his, either."

"His vocal chords are certainly in good order. The first priority is light, methinks. There's a tinder-box on the mantelpiece if I can find it."

While he shuffled off, cautiously feeling his way, Constantia for the first time listened to what Oxshott was saying. Among the many expressions she failed to comprehend, she gathered that he blamed his son for his accident. Why poor Dolph was as usual picked as the culprit she had no notion, unless it was because he had not wakened his father at bedtime.

A light sprang up by the fireplace. Frank lit several of the candles on the mantel, revealing the duke sitting huddled on the floor. With one hand he tenderly felt the back of his head; the other, clenched into a fist, beat the air in impotent rage.

He glared at Constantia and Frank. "Help me up, jackanapes!" he snarled. "Where's that damned good-for-nothing son of mine? I'll have his blood for this, curse the day he was born. I'm black and blue all over, and so will he be when I lay my hands on him. Well, are you going to give me a hand, you gunner's whelp?"

"I believe you ought not to move further," said Frank coolly, setting down a lighted candle on the table by the stairs, "until we discover what damage you have done yourself. I've rung the bell. Hoskins should be here shortly and he knows a good deal about injuries."

"Why the devil isn't my man here? You two heard me fall, so he must have. If that son of a whore's bastard isn't waiting up for me in my room . . ."

"I shall see if I can find him," said Constantia. Seizing the candle from the table, she fled up the stairs.

She fled with care, grasping the the handrail. In passing she noticed that the third step up appeared to have something spilled on it. That would explain why both she and the duke had come to grief.

Safely attaining the gallery, she hurried to the duke's chamber and tapped on the door. She waited a moment, but there was no response so she knocked harder. After a minute or two, the door opened. Oxshott's valet stood there, fully dressed, peering at her through bleary eyes.

"My lady?" he mumbled.

"His grace has had a fall and requires your attendance."

"A fall?" the man screeched. No doubt years of living with a noisy master had forced him to develop his piercing voice. "What 'orrible news! I trust 'is grace is not badly hurt?"

"Not badly, I think."

"No? What a mighty relief!" The valet dropped his tone to normal. "Where is the old . . . er . . . 'is grace, my lady?"

"Out of earshot," said Constantia dryly. "In the hall. He fell down the stairs. Be careful of . . ."

"What is this disgraceful din?" Lady Elvira appeared in the doorway of the next-door chamber, majestic in voluminous puce velvet, a vast nightcap on her head. "Never in my life have I had the misfortune to visit so ill-run a house."

"Oxshott has fallen on the stairs," Constantia informed her coldly. "He is not seriously injured."

"Nonetheless, it is my duty to go to him at once." She turned her head. "Do be quiet, Millicent. Oxshott has had a fall, but you will be of no use to him whatsoever so you may nurse your spasm in peace."

As she swept by, Constantia remembered

to warn her and the valet, "Take care on the third step from the bottom. It is slippery."

And, feeling she had more than done her duty, she went back to bed.

Constantia was not destined to make up for lost sleep. At an early hour Joan roused her, shaking her gently but with determination.

"I'm that sorry to wake you, my lady. It's Miss Fanny, she said to tell you soon as you was up but I know you wouldn't want me to wait."

"If Miss Fanny is in trouble, you are quite right." She sat up. "What is wrong, Joan?"

The abigail pursed her lips. "I'd best let Miss Fanny explain, my lady, not wanting to speak ill of my betters."

One or more of the Kerridges, of course. Constantia groaned. Quickly she washed and dressed. On the way down to the housekeeper's room, where Joan said Fanny was to be found, she noted that the spill on the stairs had been thoroughly cleaned up, leaving no trace.

Ill-run household, indeed!

Fanny was near tears. She came to meet Constantia at the door of Mrs Tanner's room and clutched her hands as if she were drowning.

"Connie, that dreadful, dreadful woman!"

"Lady Elvira?" she asked though there was no doubt in her mind. Lady Yates and Lady Vincent were irritating but not quite dreadful. "What has she done now?"

"She woke Mrs Tanner in the middle of the night — two o'clock in the morning! — to rail at her about some tallow spilled on the stairs."

"It weren't my doing, my lady," said Mrs Tanner grimly, "nor none of my girls, nor the men, neither. We don't any of us use the front stairs, as your ladyship knows, let alone with tallow candles, for it's not on our way to bed."

"Mrs Tanner has given her notice," Fanny burst out despairingly.

"It's not just being dragged from my bed like a criminal, my lady. That was just the last straw. I didn't want to keep complaining, but her ladyship never stops interfering, poking her nose where it's got no business, do this, do that. And in the kitchen, too. If it weren't for Mr Hoskins refusing to leave the master, Henriette'd be gone long since, and she's the easygoingest creature for all she's a foreigner. And there's three of my girls've only stayed acos I've begged and pleaded and upped their wages out of my own. That Lord Vincent oughtn't to be let loose outside of a place I wouldn't soil my tongue by putting a name to."

"We shan't have any servants left," wailed Fanny, "and Felix will think I'm utterly unfit to run the simplest household, far less an earl's."

"Do not be a goose, my dear Fanny." Constantia hugged her. "Felix is perfectly capable of putting the blame for this imbroglio where it belongs. Mrs Tanner, I quite understand your difficulties. Matters cannot continue thus. It is for Captain Ingram to act and I shall speak to him immediately."

"Yes, my lady." The housekeeper curtsied.

"But what can Frank do?" Fanny cried.

Constantia smiled at her. "Perhaps I have more faith in your brother than you do," she said. "He will contrive."

Frank was dressing when a message arrived that Lady Constantia wanted to see him. He was in the duke's chamber — his own henceforth, he resolved — since it had proved impossible to haul his bruised, bellicose, and still somewhat befuddled uncle up the stairs last night.

Tying his neckcloth with especial care, Frank wondered what she wanted to say to him. He had to admit to a certain consternation. Had she felt the all too brief kiss he had dropped on her silken-soft forehead? How tempted he had been to press on while he held her in his arms, to capture her sweet mouth and damn the consequences! He had fought his passion and won. It would be too ironic if he had nonetheless raised expectations in her that he was incapable of fulfilling.

She awaited him in the book-room, deserted at this still early hour. The small room, with its single wall of books, served also as an estate office. Beside the desk was a shelf of ledgers, and maps of Upfield Grange and its three farms hung on the wall opposite the ceiling-high bookcases. Disregarding all these signs of culture and cultivation, Constantia was pacing restlessly when Frank entered.

No chaperon, he noted, uncertain whether to be relieved or dismayed. Then he saw the rare militant glint in her blue eyes. Since he found it utterly impossible to imagine her trying to force him to the altar, her militancy must be directed elsewhere.

"Captain Ingram, you must act!"

"By all means," he said obligingly. "What shall I do?"

"Well, I am not quite sure, but matters cannot continue as they are. Half your staff are threatening to give notice and Fanny is at her wits' end. Though it is shockingly uncivil in me to criticize your relatives, I cannot stand by and see Fanny driven to distraction."

As always, her loyal, warmhearted spirit captivated him, but he kept his tone even and affable. "I hadn't realized things had come to such a pass. Since I doubt I can change my relatives' troublesome natures, drastic measures are called for. We'll just have to get rid of them."

"Oh!" Rosy lips and azure eyes rounded in dismay. "Drastic? Get rid of them?"

"It shouldn't prove difficult," he said, straight-faced. "There are now several soldiers in my employ who will obey any order I give them."

"Any . . . I believe you are quizzing me, Captain!"

He grinned. "Let's hope I shan't have to put them up before a firing squad to dispose of them. However, something stronger than a hint that their departure would be welcome is called for, I suspect. None of them would recognize a hint if it bit them. We must plot a subtle plot."

Once the foundations of their plot were laid, they recruited Fanny, Felix, and Hoskins into the conspiracy.

"The effrontery of it beats the Dutch!" Felix said admiringly. "Do you really believe they'll fall for it?"

"If anyone can carry it off, Captain Ingram can," Constantia said. "He has only to put on his officer's manner and they will run like Bonaparte's troops before his guns."

Corporal Hoskins enthusiastically seconded the vote of confidence.

The duke was exempted from eviction, on Constantia's advice, to avoid a total break with the Ingrams' newly discovered family, however disagreeable, and also on account of his fall.

Bruised and shaken, Oxshott kept to his bed all day and sent word he would dine there. His absence not only made the plot easier to put into effect, it facilitated the exchange of bedchambers. The duke's belongings were carried down, Frank's carried up, and he was at last in possession of his rightful place.

Upfield Grange was his. His officious aunt Elvira and the rest were uninvited guests who had long outstayed their welcome. He went down to dinner in a jaunty mood, determined in one way or another to prevail.

He took Aunt Millicent in to dinner. She was devilish tedious with her parade of symptoms and complaints of ill-health, but she was not actively malicious. In fact, he decided as he glanced around the table, apart from the duke only Lady Elvira and

Godfrey Yates were utterly unbearable. The rest might be tolerated at a pinch, singly, in small doses. He had even developed a certain affection for poor Dolph, who looked quite cheerful tonight, with his father missing.

So much for the company. As for the setting, let Lady Elvira criticize! To Frank, the table was perfect, draped with new white damask, set with new china, glass, and silver, laden with Henriette's delicious creations. He looked forward to entertaining his neighbours, once he had rid himself of uncles, aunts, and cousins.

Fanny caught his eye. It was time for her to lead the ladies' exodus to the drawing-room — and tonight, time for him to act, as Constantia had imperiously demanded. He smiled at her and rose to his feet.

"Lords, ladies, and gentlemen; aunts, uncles, and cousins," he began. A splendid rhetorical opening provided by Felix, from vague schoolroom memories of the speeches of the noble Romans. When he suggested it, Constantia had giggled and proposed Frank's continuing: "I come to bury Oxshott, not to praise him."

Shakespeare misquoted, apparently. Frank vowed to find time to do some reading.

"Fanny and I are glad to have had the opportunity to become acquainted with our mother's family," he went on. "Now that your visit is drawing to a close, we wish to thank you for sparing us so much of your precious time. Your carriages will be at the door at ten o'clock tomorrow morning. Naturally, if any of you prefers to get an earlier start, that can be arranged. You need not fear that you cannot be ready in time; your servants have already been instructed to proceed with your packing."

Hoskins' notion, that. As soon as their masters and mistresses were well out of the way in the dining-room, he had informed valets and abigails, as well as coachmen, of their departure on the morrow.

Frank beamed round at flabbergasted faces. "It remains only for me to say that I trust you have all enjoyed your stay at my house." He had been going to say Upfield Grange but Constantia had insisted on the change. "And we wish you a swift and safe journey home."

There was a moment of stunned silence. Then, before any of the open mouths could utter more than a squeak of protest, Fanny and Constantia stood up. Such was the power of habit and etiquette that the Ladies Vincent, Yates, and even Elvira followed them from the room as meekly as lambs.

Frank hoped their previously worked out story would save Fanny and Constantia from the worst of the ladies' displeasure. In the meantime, he had the gentlemen to contend with.

Hoskins and Twistlethwaite came in to clear the covers and set out the port, the inferior wine from the Pig and Piper since the duke was incapacitated. Hoskins winked at Frank.

Lord Vincent's face had turned purple, making him look very like his elder brother. He burst into a duke-like roar, but of laughter, not rage. "Damme, that did the trick neatly, my boy," he choked out. "Left us not a leg to stand on. No wonder we beat Boney with sharp fellas like you in the army. Too devilish knowing for the Frogs by half."

Felix grinned. "Rolled them up, horse, foot, and artillery," he congratulated Frank.

"You don't mind, Uncle Vincent?" Frank asked. "You see, the thing is, with guests to be entertained Fanny's not getting any of her wedding preparations completed and she's in high fidgets."

"Bless the child," said Lord Vincent indulgently, signalling to Hoskins to fill his glass. "I know women and weddings."

"If you ask me," said Frank in a confidential tone, "she's afraid Roworth will cry off

327

if he's left to his own devices too long."

"Here, I say, Ingram," Felix protested with feigned indignation. "That's deuced insulting."

"Insulting behaviour appears to be common currency in the army," said Godfrey Yates contemptuously. "I've never in my life seen such an exhibition of vulgar ill-breeding as in this room tonight. If this is an example of the manners of an officer, I shudder to imagine what uncouth conduct prevails among the rank and file."

Hoskins improvised. Standing behind Yates, about to offer the port, he simply emptied the decanter down the back of his neck.

Yates jumped up with an incoherent exclamation.

"Beg pardon, sir, I'm sure," said the corporal. "I were that int'rested in what you was saying, I forgot what I was at. But there's no need to take on so, sir. It's not the good stuff. Here, let me dry you off." And he attempted to stuff his napkin between Yates's close-tied, port-stained cravat and his neck.

"Are you trying to strangle me now, ruffian?" yelled the hapless gentleman, twisting away. He glared at Frank. "Believe me, I'll be glad to shake the dust of Upfield Grange from my feet." He stalked from the room.

Lord Vincent was laughing so hard, he too spilled his port.

Frank sent Hoskins to refill the decanter. "I hope Yates won't make trouble with the duke," he said, frowning.

"He can't," said Lord Vincent candidly. "Godfrey's tied to his mother's apron-strings and Millicent hangs on m'brother's sleeve. They've neither of them a ha'p'orth of influence there. Truth to tell, no one does. A law unto himself is his Grace of Oxshott, and so was your grandfather before him, nevvy. Now, where's that port? Pigswill it may be, but for want of anything better . . ."

"I'll put some decent wines in Frank's cellar before your next visit, sir," Felix promised. They chatted vintages.

As soon as Yates stormed out, Dolph had sneaked around the table and taken the chair beside Frank. He had the bewildered, apprehensive air of a new recruit from Yorkshire being shouted at by a Cockney sergeant.

"Do I have to go away, Cousin Frank?" he quavered.

"Don't you want to, Dolph? The duke will stay here for a while at least, so you'll be free of him."

"Mustn't go before he tells me. Besides, like you, like Cousin Fanny, like Lady Connie. Like Anita. Calls me Uncle Dolph!" He threw a doubtful look at Felix. "Like Roworth. Like Hoskins," he added in a burst of inspiration as the corporal returned with a full decanter.

"There's a good chap," said Hoskins soothingly, patting the marquis's shoulder as he passed.

"We like you, too," said Frank. "I don't see why you shouldn't stay."

"Can I? Don't want to hurt you. Don't want to hurt Cousin Fanny. Try not to."

"I'm sure you do. Yes, you are welcome to stay on at the Grange, only don't mention it to any of the others."

"Won't," promised Dolph.

When they repaired to the drawing-room, Lady Yates had already retired, complaining of a sick headache. Lady Vincent, with a terrified glance at Frank and a mutter about early rising, scuttled from the room. Even Lady Elvira appeared as much perturbed as affronted, her usual censorious air diluted by irresolution.

Frank went to join Constantia. "What on earth have you said to them?" he asked in a low voice.

"Oh, I said no more than we agreed

upon." Her eyes sparkled with merriment. "I explained how you are amiable unless crossed, but after all, you are a soldier, an officer used to being obeyed, and you can be quite fierce when opposed."

"Quite fierce?"

"Fanny seemed to think that was insufficient. Ferocious was the word she used. I must say that the bloody exploits she credited you with cannot have left you with much time to aim your guns."

"She had me running amok on the battlefield, did she? No, no, we artillerymen are mild fellows more concerned with ballistics than bayonets."

"Pray do not tell your aunts, or they will change their minds and stay. As it is, they are all prodigious eager to submit to your honeyed decree and leave in the morning."

They were gone long before the duke put in an appearance. Stiff and querulous, he hobbled to the drawing-room, leaning heavily on the arm of one of his footmen. Constantia had taken it upon herself to excuse his family's defection to him. The others played least in sight while she saw him ensconced on a well-cushioned sofa, a glass of the tolerable madeira at his elbow.

Before he had a chance to remark upon the absence of those who ought to have been hovering solicitously about him, she said with what conviction she could muster, "How obliging and considerate your brothers and sisters are, Duke. They have cut short their visit so that you may have peace and quiet to recuperate. Nothing is so detrimental to a swift recovery as the noise and bustle of a house party."

Glaring at her, he jerked upright, then subsided on the cushions with a groan. "Devil take it, I'm black and blue all over and aching in every limb. Those damned spongers may do as they please for the nonce." He made as if to sit up again, but thought better of it. "But where's that oafish son of mine?" he growled. " 'Fore Gad, if he's flown the coop, I'll . . ."

"Captain Ingram has taken Lord Mentham and Anita out in his carriage," said Constantia hastily, glad that Frank had relented and let poor Dolph remain at the Grange. "My brother and Fanny have driven over to Heathcote. I stayed to make sure everything possible is done for your comfort."

Oxshott briefly recovered his manners. "Much obliged, ma'am, I'm sure. So Roworth and my niece are gone to Heathcote? They're looking to wed soon, I daresay."

"As soon as the house is habitable, which will not be long now. They need new furnishings, but the roof is finished, the broken windows mended, the painting and paperhanging begun, and a few servants hired."

"Ha!" A look of such malevolence passed across the duke's features that a cold trickle of fear ran down Constantia's spine. But she must have imagined it. His peculiar kind of forced affability was to the fore as he said civilly, "Be so good as to have Mentham sent to me at once when he returns."

"Certainly, Duke."

Oxshott reconciled to the departure of the rest of his family, her mission was accomplished. She made an excuse to leave him and went up to see if the transfer of her belongings to her old chamber was completed. All trace of the occupancy of Lady Elvira and Lady Yates had been cleared, the window opened wide to dispel a faint smell of medicines. The air coming in had an autumnal chill though the sun was shining.

A shawl about her shoulders, Constantia settled on the window seat to read, but she found herself gazing out of the window, hoping to glimpse the barouche-landau returning. Only because the duke was so anxious for his son's company, she tried to persuade herself.

But it was no use pretending it was not Frank she wanted to see. If only . . . With a sudden shock she realized she had never written to Miriam, her time and attention occupied by the now departed guests. She set down her book and moved swiftly to the little inlaid writing table in the corner.

Two days later, when she went down to breakfast, Thomas presented her with a letter on a silver salver. She reached for it eagerly, though surely it was too soon to expect a response.

"From Vickie!" She tried to hide her disappointment.

"What has she to say?" asked Fanny, cutting up a rasher of bacon for Anita.

Constantia slit the seal, unfolded the paper, and quickly scanned her sister's scrawl. "Poor Vickie! Miss Bannister is unwell so she is constantly under Mama's eye and never does anything right. She is not permitted to write to the Bermans." Constantia kept to herself Lady Westwood's reported opinion that the Squire and his family were unfit acquaintances for the daughter of an earl.

She frowned over a passage marked with blots and heavily scratched out words. "Please tell . . . Pam and Lizzie she misses thim . . . oh no, them, of course, but why has she dotted the e? . . . misses them dreadfully and they is not to forget her. I thought Miss Bannister had drummed more grammar into her than that. And she has run her words together though she left a blank space at the end. She must be sorely tried."

"Poor Vickie!" said Fanny.

"I shall write a note to Lady Berman with her message."

"We haven't seen the Bermans since she left. I suppose they will not call as long as Uncle Oxshott is here. Thank goodness he's rapidly recovering. He'll soon be well enough to go home, if we can only persuade him to remove himself!"

By that afternoon, the duke had recovered enough to insist that Frank take him for an airing in the barouche-landau.

Frank suppressed a sigh. "If you're sure you are fit, Uncle, Hoskins shall tool us about the lanes for a while."

"No need for Hoskins. I want to see your skill with the ribbons, my boy."

"Very well. I daresay the ladies will enjoy a drive."

Oxshott testily declared that he was damned if he'd have the ladies fussing about him. So they went off together, Frank on the box and the duke seated in the back, shouting directions as to the route he wished to take. A blustery, invigorating wind swirled bronze and yellow leaves down from the trees. Frank was sorry Constantia and Fanny were missing the outing, but it was not worth an argument with his uncle.

They were bumping along a rutted lane through a copse when the duke shouted, "Stop!"

"What . . . ?" Frank reined in his pair.

"A poacher!" Oxshott stood up in the back, gesticulating at the trees to their right. "I saw him clear as day. You'd better go after the ruffian or you'll have no game left to call your own. Hanging's too good for the brigands!"

Frank saw nothing but trees swaying in the wind and brambles laden with blackberries, and he did not much care if his poorer tenants helped themselves to his land's bounty. But once again it was easier not to argue with the duke, who was excitedly, if stiffly, descending from the carriage.

Tying the reins to a nearby sapling, Frank started along the nearest path, a rabbit track, to judge by its narrowness. He penetrated some twenty yards into the copse, pushing aside briars and ducking low branches.

"There's no one here, Uncle," he called.

"Go a little farther. The damned miscreant's hiding from you." Oxshott started after him, then stopped and bent over, leaning with one hand against a tree-trunk. "Devil take it, a stone in my shoe."

A shot rang out. The duke screeched, clapped both hands to his buttocks, and fell over.

A crashing in the brush marked the precipitate retreat of the poacher. Frank briefly contemplated pursuit but decided it was more important to go to his howling uncle's aid. He ran back.

Upon his Grace of Oxshott, fortune once more frowned. The duke had been well and truly peppered in the backside.

"Most fortunately it was the lightest gauge of birdshot," said the doctor, closing the chamber door behind him. "Otherwise his grace might well have bled to death. He will be in severe discomfort for a fortnight or so, I fear."

Ingrams and Roworths managed to hold back their groans until the physician had departed. Another fortnight at least, and who could guess how long before he was fit to travel!

CHAPTER 17

"St. Luke's little summer we call it here-abouts," said Mrs Tanner, "though it's a bit early this year."

The second week of October was warm and dry. The duke had been confined to his bed for nearly two weeks of blissful peace. The household ran smoothly and Constantia could not pretend Fanny still needed her support.

Daily she expected another summons from her mother, which she would have no excuse to disregard. Daily she hoped for a letter from Miriam Cohen. The longer she waited, the more sure she became that Miriam was delaying answering her enquiry because there was no remedy for her scar.

And that was another reason why she must leave when Lady Westwood next sent for her. In the meantime, she tried to enjoy Frank's company, the beautiful weather, the changing colours of autumn, without thinking of the future.

Then Miriam's letter came. She took it unopened up to her chamber and sat down in the window seat, turning the folded sheet over and over in her hands before she brought herself to break the seal.

The letter opened with apologies. Constantia had directed her letter to Miriam's father's house in London. It had arrived after the Cohens returned to Nettledene, taking her parents with them, leaving the London house shut up. So the delay was not due to Miriam's reluctance to disappoint her! A tiny seedling of hope sprang up.

A moment later it withered, blighted. Miriam regretted that her attempts to restore badly damaged skin to its original smoothness had never proved successful. If the scar itched or flaked, a lotion composed of . . .

Constantia stared down blindly at the crumpled paper in her fist, the other hand clenched to her breast. In her head throbbed a single word: never, never, never.

"Are you ready, Connie?" called Fanny from outside her door. "The sunshine is so glorious I hate to miss a moment of it."

She had forgotten that she, Fanny, and Dolph were to take Anita down to the bridge, the child's favourite walk. It was no

339

use wallowing in self-pity.

On the second attempt, her voice came out right. "I shall be with you in just a minute." Half-boots, bonnet, pelisse, gloves, anything else? She looked distractedly around the room. The letter lay discarded on the floor by the window. She picked it up, smoothed it flat, and hid it in a drawer. The scar did itch at times.

She did her best to be cheerful as they strolled down the hill, crunching through heaps of yellow elm leaves, but Fanny noticed that something was amiss.

"You are blue-devilled today," she remarked as Anita and Dolph stopped to throw armfuls of leaves at each other.

"The duke will soon emerge from his lair," Constantia said lightly. "Is that not reason enough for blue devils? But you are quite capable of coping with him by now. I shall have to leave soon."

"Oh no, Connie!"

"I cannot defy Mama for ever."

"I suppose not. Oh drat!" said Fanny with a disconsolate sigh. "You will come back before the wedding, to hold my hand?"

"Of course."

In the general gloom caused by Oxshott's return to circulation, Constantia's low spirits aroused no further comment. The duke, still unable to sit on any but the softest of cushions, took to wandering about the house, materializing unexpectedly like a disgruntled ghost. Dolph, who had blossomed, grew more and more silent and unhappy.

One morning, shortly before the hour when the duke usually appeared, Frank met his wretched cousin in the hall and invited him to drive out with him. Frank now drove his carriage about the estate nearly every day. He was thinking of buying a riding horse, for regular exercise had at last restored the strength of his arms and shoulders. If it were not for the sight of himself in the mirror, which he did his best to avoid, he might almost believe the exploding shell at Quatre Bras had never happened.

Dolph eagerly accepted his invitation. "Maybe I can help," he blurted out. "If something happens, I'll try to help. Best if I go too. Won't tell Father?"

"I won't tell. I wonder whether Lady Constantia would care to go with us." He never drove her alone, but his cousin was sufficient chaperon since they would not go beyond the Upfield farms.

"No!" Dolph sounded oddly desperate. There was no understanding the poor fellow. He added with an inspired air, "Busy. Lady Connie's busy today."

"All right, let's go."

As they walked down the passage to the back door, the front door knocker sounded behind them. Frank paused. A moment later Twistlethwaite ran after them.

"Cap'n, sir, 'tis the Earl o' Westwood!" He thrust a visiting card at Frank. "And the Countess o' Westwood, too, the footman says. They're coming in right now, Cap'n! What'll I do?"

The Westwoods! What the devil were they doing at Upfield? He turned back, Dolph trailing after him. "Go and tell Miss Fanny and the Roworths, quickly, man."

When he reached the hall, Lord and Lady Westwood had already entered, their identically inflexible figures silhouetted against the open door. Frank strode forward to greet them, to welcome them to Upfield Grange though he had no very kind memories of his welcome to Westwood.

"Captain Ingram," said the countess before he could utter a word, "is my youngest daughter here?"

"Lady Victoria?" Still more astonished, he shook his head. "No, ma'am. She left weeks ago."

"I beg, nay, I demand that you do not

conceal her from me."

"I assure you, ma'am," Frank said stiffly, "I shouldn't dream of hiding your daughter from you."

"Captain," said Lord Westwood, grim-faced, "you are unused to the conventions of civilized life. I must warn you that, whatever the custom in the army, the penalties for assisting a young girl to abscond from her lawful guardians are severe."

"Sir, I . . ."

"Mama! Papa!" Constantia's arrival, followed by Hoskins, cut short Frank's angry retort. She kissed her mother's cheek and asked somewhat nervously, "What brings you to Upfield Grange?"

Coming in with Fanny, Felix repeated the question.

"Surely that can wait, Felix," Fanny protested, "until your parents have sat down and caught their breath after their journey. Pray come into the drawing-room, Lady Westwood. You will like some refreshment, I daresay. Hoskins, tea and the madeira, if you please."

Lady Westwood regarded her future daughter-in-law with something closely approaching approval.

Once they were settled in the drawing-room, the countess turned to Felix and said abruptly, "Your sister is missing."

"Vickie? Missing?"

"Captain Ingram claims she is not here."

"Nor is she, Mama," said Constantia, incensed. "What do you mean, she is missing?"

"I mean, if she is truly not here, we have no notion where she is." Lady Westwood's rigid back failed her. She leaned back in her chair, though otherwise her coolly aristocratic demeanour altered not a whit. "Victoria's conduct has been utterly unacceptable since she returned to Westwood. Miss Bannister was indisposed after the journey, and then fell ill. By the time she recovered I had come to the realization that she is unfit to supervise Victoria. She was dismissed and . . ."

"Dismissed!" Constantia cried. "Miss Bannister dismissed? But where did she go? What will she do?"

"I did not make it my business to enquire. No doubt she has friends or relatives."

"I wish she had come here," Fanny exclaimed. "She knows I want her for Anita's governess."

"Perhaps she thought you would not want her after she was dismissed." Constantia threw a glance of bitter reproach at her mother. "We must find her."

"I'll have Mackintyre set Taggle to track her down," said Frank, and was rewarded with glowing gratitude in the eyes of Lady Constantia.

"But what of Vickie?" Felix asked.

"Victoria was sent to her grandmother, in Bath."

Frank guessed from Constantia's shudder that her grandmother was not an amiable old lady.

"She was sent by post-chaise," said Lord Westwood, "since I have not yet purchased a new carriage. A maid went with her. After all, it is no more than twenty miles."

"We did not learn for ten days that my mother had previously removed to Cheltenham Spa to try the waters. She never received my letter advising her of Victoria's arrival." Lady Westwood covered her eyes with her hand, looking suddenly old. "We have been unable to discover any trace of her in Bath or its environs."

Constantia hurried to her mother's side and put her arm around her shoulders. "Mama, you are exhausted. Pray come up and rest on my bed." She helped the countess to stand up.

As they moved towards the door, with Fanny following, Lord Westwood said heavily, "We were convinced we should find

345

Victoria here."

Felix shook his head. "We've seen neither hide nor hair of her. Taggle is the man we need."

"Who is this Taggle?" asked the earl.

Frank was about to answer when he noticed Constantia, at the door, had fixed him with an appealing gaze. Leaving Felix to describe the inimitable Taggle to his father, he went after the ladies.

Sure that he had not misread her, he waited in the hall while she and Fanny took Lady Westwood upstairs. Dolph had disappeared and the duke had not yet appeared, thank heaven. Hoskins, Twistlethwaite, and Thomas lingered. Frank sent the Yorkshireman about his business but kept the others by him. Though he didn't immediately reveal to them what was going on, he trusted both. He wasn't sure what Constantia had in mind, and she might need them.

Constantia was shocked by her mother's revelation of weakness. She was less surprised to find that Lady Westwood's chief concern was that her youngest daughter would bring scandal upon the family. However, the countess also seemed genuinely distressed by the possibility that Vickie was in trouble or danger.

346

Where could Vickie be? A faint glimmer of an idea had made Constantia appeal silently to Frank. The glimmer brightened as she rang for Joan and helped Mama to take off her bonnet. Half-forgotten incidents and words, that odd letter . . .

Joan hurried into Constantia's chamber, bringing Lady Westwood's abigail. Leaving the maids to assist her mother, Constantia drew Fanny aside.

"I hate to ask it of you, Fanny, but may I leave you to minister to Mama? I have a notion of Vickie's whereabouts which I ought to discuss with Felix."

"Of course I'll stay with her. Where do you think she is?"

"I had best not say, in case I am mistaken. Pray do not tell Mama, lest it raise her hopes in vain."

Fanny nodded understanding and turned back to the countess. Constantia slipped out. It was true that she did not wish to raise Mama's hopes, but more to the point, she did not wish to be stopped. It was equally true that she ought to discuss her idea with Felix, but then Papa would know. If her guess was right, the fewer people who ever found out, the better.

Dashing into Fanny's chamber, she borrowed a loose-fitting hooded cloak. She would have to go without gloves since her hands were quite different in size and shape from Fanny's.

From the gallery she saw Frank waiting. She knew she could count on him! He came to meet her at the foot of the stairs.

"Captain, I have an idea where Vickie may be. If I tell Felix, Papa will be involved, and I had rather he was not. Will you take me to . . . to Heathcote?" She hated to prevaricate, but her real goal would require explanation and she did not want to waste time. It could wait until they were in the carriage.

"Of course. It's a slim chance she might be hiding there, but worth a try. Hoskins, you'll come with us. Bring my carriage round."

The corporal departed at a run. Constantia would have preferred to go without him, but perhaps Heathcote was still too far for Frank to drive. She turned to her footman.

"Thomas, if Lord Roworth proposes to take any action, tell him to wait until Captain Ingram returns from Heathcote. I must go too, in case we find my sister, but pray do not mention my absence to anyone if you can avoid it."

"I won't utter a word, my lady," said the footman fervently, "not if they was to pull out my tongue with red-hot pincers."

"I trust it will not come to that!" She smiled at him distractedly, then turned to Frank. "I hope Mama will think I am with Felix and Papa, and vice versa."

"Do you really need to come? I daresay I can persuade Lady Vickie to give herself up, if she's there."

"No, no, I must go with you."

"Then we shall go and return as quickly as we can. With luck no one will notice you are gone."

They went out to the front porch to wait for the barouche-landau. It was a windy day, with ragged grey clouds scudding across the sky and leaves whirling to the ground. The saffron-yellow cloak flapped about Constantia's ankles; the hood threatened to blow off, so she tightened the drawstring.

Frank was looking at her with a slight frown.

"I had to borrow Fanny's cloak," she said defensively, "because Mama is in my chamber. I know the colour does not suit me."

"My dear Lady Constantia, the colour was the furthest thing from my mind," he said with a teasing smile. "I was wondering whether you will be warm enough without gloves. We had best put up the carriage hoods."

"Oh no, we must not waste time!" She

frowned at him, suddenly realizing: "You have neither gloves nor overcoat!"

"I don't need an overcoat on a day like today. We old soldiers scarcely feel the cold. As for driving gloves, Hoskins will find me a pair in the coach-house."

Constantia had assumed Hoskins would drive and Frank would join her in the back. How was she to explain her theory with both men on the box? Yet having abandoned decorum to beg him to take her to Heathcote she was reluctant to implore him to sit with her, since he chose not to.

While she hesitated, the barouche-landau came around the corner and stopped before them. Frank handed her in and quickly mounted to the box.

"Spring 'em," he told Hoskins, donning the shabby hat and grubby, well-worn gloves the corporal handed him.

Frank's pair were no fifteen-mile-an-hour bits of blood, but they were willing. The carriage sped down the drive.

Constantia sat tensely on the forward-facing seat, her hands clenched in her lap. She could not cry aloud against the wind what she suspected her feckless sister had done. Vickie might after all have taken shelter at Heathcote, persuading the small staff to hide her. If they went there first, she could explain her suspicions privately to Frank and on the way back . . .

But no, that would waste so much time. The more she reflected on Vickie's letter, the more certain she was that she had guessed right: the words scratched out with "Pam and Lizzie" written in above in tiny letters; "him" changed to "them"; "they" squeezed in as if the t and y were added later, and followed by carelessly unchanged "is" instead of "are". What that passage had originally said was "Please tell Sir George I miss him dreadfully and he is not to forget me."

Vickie spending day after day at Netherfield with Anita while Upfield Grange was set in order; Vickie with her constant "Sir George says . . ."; Vickie refusing to leave without bidding Sir George goodbye, and adding Lady Berman, Pam, and Lizzie as an afterthought; at the picnic, Vickie dragging Sir George off to explore the house — Constantia had thought she was tactfully removing him from Oxshott's company but her sister was not noted for tact; Vickie joining Sir George on the box on the way home from Netherfield, the day before she left for Westwood; the signs had all been there.

Constantia blamed herself for blindness. She had been too taken up with her own feelings for Frank to notice what her little sister was about. If she was right, Mama and Papa must never find out.

The barouche-landau was rapidly approaching the drive to Netherfield. "Turn here!" Constantia called. Frank glanced back, his hand cupping his ear, his face questioning. She flung herself onto the front seat. "Turn left here, to Netherfield!"

"Turn left," Frank repeated to Hoskins.

The carriage swung left as Constantia moved back to her original seat. Something cracked like a branch snapping. The vehicle tilted. She grabbed for a handhold but the door swung open as she touched it and she pitched out.

Landing on her shoulder, she cried out as a dreadful pain stabbed her through and through. The world faded.

CHAPTER 18

Above her, Frank's face floated in a haze.

"Constantia, my love! I can't feel any lumps on her head."

"It's her shoulder, Captain. Look, there's blood on her cloak, there where it's bin tore."

"Oh my God!" Frank fumbled with the drawstrings of the cloak. Constantia felt him push aside the heavy cloth. Her feeble murmur of protest as he ruthlessly ripped open her gown was drowned by his repeated cry, "Oh my God!"

"Look, Captain, her la'ship must've landed on this flint. Sharp as a knife it is."

"Never mind that, Hoskins. Help me lift her to bind this gash. It's not deep but it won't stop bleeding. No, first take off my neckcloth, this handkerchief is too small."

"Here, Captain."

Her head swam again as gentle hands raised her and bound her shoulder.

"Constantia! She's still not coming round."

"Shock, I reckon. Don't fret, sir, it don't look too bad. Mostly bruised, and that's a nasty scrape."

"It must have hurt like the very devil to make her fall into a swoon."

"Likely she wrenched it, too."

With a huge effort, Constantia opened her eyes and brought Frank's worried face into focus. "Not a swoon," she said faintly. "I just feel a trifle peculiar."

His eyes brightened in relief. "I beg your pardon," he said with a grin, "not a swoon, of course."

"I shall be perfectly all right in a minute." She tried to sit up.

He pressed her back, one hand on her uninjured shoulder. "Lie still, Lady Constantia," he commanded. "You're hurt and you've had a shock."

There was something soft beneath her head. She realized he was in his shirtsleeves, white against the fleeting grey clouds. Hatless, too. How handsome he was with his crisp, dark hair ruffled by the wind, his dark eyes concerned, intent upon her. She loved him. She could not help herself.

Had she dreamed of hearing him call her his love?

That was when the full horror of what had happened burst upon her. She closed her eyes, despairing. He had called her his love — before he ripped open her bodice and saw her scar. Now she was Lady Constantia again.

"Hoskins, I must carry her to Netherfield," Frank said urgently. "I'll have to ride bareback on one of the horses and take her before me. You'd better try to move this wreck out of the way with the other horse. They are not injured are they?"

The men's voices moved away from Constantia and she heard the jingle of the harness. Then Hoskins lifted her up onto the horse in front of Frank. The pain of the movement made her dizzy again. Though she had intended to sit upright, she slumped against his chest with a moan. His arm went around her waist, holding her steady.

He had no saddle, no stirrups, only a makeshift bridle for reins, yet she felt quite safe as he set the horse in motion. He was her valiant hero on a charger. It was too much to expect that every hero should fall in love with every rescued damsel.

His friendship would have to be enough for her.

By the time Frank reached Netherfield's

front door with his precious burden, they had been seen from the house and the entire family was waiting — the entire family plus Lady Victoria. How the devil had Constantia guessed?

It was not the moment to ask. Amid a babble of questions, Sir George lifted Constantia down. Frank watched jealously as he carried her into the house, followed by Lady Berman and the girls. Sliding down from the horse's back he tied the bridle to a post and went after them.

Sir George came to meet him. Crimson-faced, he said gruffly, "I daresay you're wondering . . ."

"Not I. Lady Victoria is none of my responsibility, thank goodness. Where is Lady Constantia?"

The young baronet ushered him into the parlour. Constantia was reclining on a sofa, the ladies crowded about her.

To Frank's relief, the colour was already returning to her cheeks. She waved away vinaigrette and cordial, and gratefully but adamantly refused to let Lady Berman examine her shoulder.

"I must hurry home," she said, "that is, back to Upfield Grange. Vickie, Mama and Papa have come looking for you. Mama is sorely distressed. We shall . . ."

"Is Oxshott still there?" Sir George demanded.

"I'm afraid so," said Frank.

"She shan't be forced to marry that old villain!"

"But there is no question of Vickie marrying the duke," Constantia exclaimed. "Vickie, what on earth have you been telling the Bermans?"

With everyone staring at her, Lady Victoria flushed to the roots of her hair. "I only said I was afraid Mama might try to make me marry him," she maintained, her lips quivering. "And she might, Connie. She said the sooner I am off her hands, the better. If it wasn't Oxshott it could be some other horrid old widower, so it wasn't a lie."

Roaring with laughter, Sir George enveloped her in a bear hug. "Never mind, love, I'll take you off her ladyship's hands, soon as ever I can."

"George!" Lady Berman called him to order.

Looking sheepish, he let Vickie go. "Come on," he urged her, "we'll take your sister and the captain back to Upfield Grange and beard the lions together."

Frank wanted Constantia to rest, but she insisted she was much recovered and would be perfectly comfortable in the Bermans' wagon. Lady Berman put her arm in a sling, which obviously eased her discomfort considerably, so Frank gave in. Sir George lent him a neckcloth and went to harness the Suffolk Punches while the girls collected cushions.

Constantia was able to walk out, leaning on Frank's arm. Though he'd rather have travelled in the back with her, he joined Sir George on the box so that a subdued Vickie could exchange confidences with her sister. They set out for Upfield Grange.

At the end of the Netherfield drive, the barouche-landau with its splintered wheel had been hauled aside just far enough to allow the wagon to pass. Of Hoskins and the second horse there was no sign, so Frank assumed they had gone home. He himself was in no hurry to reach the Grange. The one certain result he foresaw from the Westwoods' arrival was that they would take Constantia away with them.

It was for the best, of course, yet he still dreaded the moment of her departure, the blank hole it would leave in his life.

Sir George distracted him with his own problems. He wanted to know how Frank thought the Westwoods would respond to his suit, how best to approach them. Frank was unable to offer much reassurance or advice, but he did encourage the baronet to stick to his guns. If he had been in the same position he'd have gone through hell or high water to win Constantia.

The wagon turned into Upfield's drive. Between the elms, nearly bare by now, Frank saw Felix's phaeton standing at the door, his high-bred team tossing their heads as leaves swirled about their hooves.

"I'm afraid your absence has been discovered, Lady Constantia," he called over his shoulder.

"It does not matter so much since we found Vickie."

"Don't forget, Connie," her sister cried, "you have promised to support us."

Frank didn't hear her answer. As the wagon drew up alongside the phaeton, Felix's groom stared. Leaving the man to keep an eye on the placid Suffolks as well as his own restive charges, Sir George and Frank helped Constantia and Vickie down. Vickie clutching Constantia's good arm, they proceeded into the hall.

They were met by an agitated crowd: Lord and Lady Westwood, Felix and Fanny, and the duke and Dolph. For a few minutes all was a chaos of questions and explanations.

As he put in his word about the accident to his carriage, Frank saw the duke draw

Dolph aside and berate him with quiet ferocity, heaven alone knew what for. Poor Dolph was white and frightened. Frank moved towards them to rescue his cousin. He wished Lady Victoria and Sir George well, but nothing he could say was going to affect Lord and Lady Westwood's opinions.

As he reached his uncle's side, the hub-bub died, giving way to Lady Westwood's cold, incisive voice. Only the fact that she was upbraiding her daughter in public suggested a certain degree of discomposure.

Oxshott turned to Frank with a strained smile. "Mighty fortunate Lady Constantia was not badly hurt. Your man was driving? Turn him off, my boy, turn him off without a character. You can't have clumsy rogues like that endangering the ladies."

"The accident wasn't Hoskins's fault. The wheel just collapsed. I should have had everything checked more carefully."

Behind him, Frank heard Constantia's soft voice joining Vickie's, Sir George's, and the Westwoods' in argument. He wanted to listen, but the duke started inveighing against swindlers who sold unsound goods to unsuspecting gentlemen.

At that moment, Hoskins rushed into the hall. He dashed up to Frank, skidded to a halt, saluted, and announced in his best parade-ground tones, "Captain, sir, that there carriage wheel was meddled with. Half sawn through it was." He rounded on Dolph, who cowered away. "And this here blue-blooded cousin o' yourn's what done it!"

Frank stared at him, stunned. In the sudden silence, the rising wind howled about the house and somewhere a door slammed. "Dolph?"

"I got witnesses, Captain, seen his lordship sneaking about where he got no business to be, poking round your carriage, and another what's seen a saw in his chamber."

Dolph burst into tears. "I did it," he wailed. "He made me."

"Imbecile!" roared the duke. He glared round at the startled faces turned to him. "You can't believe a word he says. He may be my own son and heir but he belongs in Bedlam."

"No, Father, don't send me to Bedlam!" Dolph entreated. "Told you, didn't want to do it. Didn't want to hurt Cousin Frank. Didn't want to hurt Cousin Fanny. Didn't want to hurt Lady Connie."

"Dolt, it's your fault Lady Constantia was hurt," Oxshott snarled at him.

"No, it is not his fault." Constantia swept

forward to Dolph's side. "If you threatened him with Bedlam, of course he did what you told him."

Fanny joined them, laying a soothing hand on Dolph's arm. "You shan't go to Bedlam," she said firmly. The two of them took him to sit on one of the settles by the fire.

Lord Westwood took a hand, his equanimity shaken. "You are responsible for the injury to my daughter, Oxshott? I can hardly trust my ears!"

"Naturally I'm sorry Lady Constantia was hurt," the duke blustered, self-righteously. "Mentham bungled it, as he bungles everything he attempts. It's those upstart Ingrams I'm trying to rid myself of, as you would yourself, Westwood, in my position. Nobodies, marching in and taking my property! I thought I'd have to dispose of the child, too, but she ain't their legal heir yet, as I took pains to find out, mind you. Don't want to hurt innocent bystanders if it can be avoided."

"Good Gad," the earl snapped, "it is you who belong in Bedlam! I'll see you brought to justice if it takes every last ounce of influence I possess."

That was when Frank began to laugh. He simply could not help it, as everything came together in his mind. It was his turn to be stared at as if he were an escaped bedlam-ite.

"Lord Westwood," he gasped at last, "you needn't fear my uncle will go unpunished. He's already suffered. He brought his own punishment upon himself."

"What the deuce do you mean?" Felix demanded.

"Think! Just think back over his grace's visit. Who was standing beneath the gargoyle minutes before it crashed? I was."

"And it destroyed Oxshott's carriage." Felix began to grin.

"Who rises early and goes downstairs before anyone else is about? Fanny does."

Felix's grin vanished. "The stairs where Oxshott slipped on an inexplicable mess of tallow," he said grimly. "If it had been on a higher step, and he had not fallen asleep in the drawing room . . ."

"Precisely." Frank continued his litany. "Who was directed into the copse where an invisible poacher let loose a shot? Again, I was."

"And who was peppered? Oxshott!"

His face livid, the duke charged at Dolph. "You did it on purpose!" he howled, raising his fist.

Even as Frank moved between them, he realized that Constantia was gone. Was she worse hurt than he had supposed? His heart skipped a beat but he said calmly, "Don't touch Dolph, Uncle."

The duke stepped back, spitting venom. "I'll get you yet!"

"I think not, sir. You have too many witnesses now ever to try to harm any of us again. Lord Westwood?"

"If any harm comes to you, or your sister, or the child, his grace shall be pursued by the full vigour of the law. You have my word on that, Captain Ingram."

"Felix?"

"Need you ask?"

"Sir George?"

"Count me in."

"After all, Captain," said Lady Victoria unwisely, "Sir George will soon be practically your brother-in-law."

As Vickie's misdeeds superseded the duke's at the centre of attention, Frank made his escape and went in search of Constantia.

He hurried to her chamber and tapped on the door. When there was no response, he opened it and glanced in. If she was in pain, no considerations of propriety were going to stop him going to her aid.

She was huddled on the low window seat, a picture of misery. Though she had changed her torn gown for a soft blue wrapping dress, her golden ringlets were disordered, her eyes were red, and she sniffled as tears rolled down her cheeks.

Frank recalled a time when he had called her an angel. She was no angel, just a mortal like himself, and very dear.

A vagrant gust slammed the chamber door. Constantia looked up, startled. Frank was striding across the room towards her, the sound of his footsteps drowned by the wind's moan. Hastily she wiped away the foolish tears with the back of her hand.

He stood frowning down at her. "Is the pain very bad? I shall send for the doctor."

"No, truly, it is no more than a dull ache."

"Then what's wrong? What's troubling you? If it's Oxshott's malevolence, you need not fear. His teeth are drawn."

She shook her head helplessly. Despite her efforts, a sob escaped her and the tears flowed once more.

He dropped to his knees and gathered her into his arms, cradling her head on his shoulder, stroking her hair. "What is it? Tell me! Constantia, you must know I'd do anything in the world to make you happy."

"But you saw my scar," she whispered into his borrowed cravat.

She felt his sudden taut stillness. "Scar?

You're afraid that gash will cause a scar? If it does it will be very small," he said in a strange voice.

"No, not that. The scar I already have, the long, ugly one. You must have seen it."

"All I saw was a bleeding cut, a nasty graze, and a red swelling that I daresay will soon turn all colours of the rainbow."

"Don't laugh at me! Look!" She pulled out of his arms and struggled to open the clasp of her girdle. "Help me!"

"You look!"

He tore off his neckcloth and flung out of his coat and waistcoat, uncovering the buttons down the front of his shirt. Constantia reached forward and began to undo them with shaky fingers. As she came to the third, she glanced up. He was staring down at her with a peculiar expression on his face, desperate yearning — and fear.

For a moment their gazes locked, then she went on to the next button. He fumbled with the clasp on her dress, snapped it open, gently drew the gown down over her shoulders as she reached the last button of his shirt.

His chest was a map of pain, a network of chalk-white lines and plum-red blotches, ridged and hollowed. "Oh Frank, how dreadfully they hurt you!" she cried, and ran her fingertips across the worst of the terrible record of war.

And then he was crying, his tears damping her chemise as his lips traced the puckered slash from shoulder to breast. She held his head in both hands, not the romantic hero of her imaginings but a tortured man she loved so very much.

He pulled her close and his mouth descended on hers. A tingling flame ignited, flared, blazed through her.

The door opened with a crash.

"Connie, Mama says I am compromised and must marry Sir George, as though that were not exactly what I . . ." Vickie stopped short, her hand to her mouth as she took in the scene before her. "Gracious heavens, if I am compromised after spending two weeks in Sir George's house with his mother and sisters, then you are utterly ruined, Connie! You will simply have to marry Captain Ingram. Oh, famous! Mama will be rid of all of us, at last. Let's have a triple wedding."

Frank's eyes held a tender smile as they met Constantia's. "That sounds like a splendid notion," he said.